THE
STRING

THE STRING

CALEB BREAKEY

Revell

a division of Baker Publishing Group
Grand Rapids, Michigan

© 2019 by Caleb Breakey

Published by Revell
a division of Baker Publishing Group
PO Box 6287, Grand Rapids, MI 49516-6287
www.revellbooks.com

Printed in the United States of America

Library of Congress Cataloging-in-Publication Data
Names: Breakey, Caleb Jennings, 1986- author.
Title: The string / Caleb Breakey.
Description: Grand Rapids, MI : Revell, [2019]
Identifiers: LCCN 2019002624 | ISBN 9780800735074 (pbk.)
Subjects: | GSAFD: Suspense fiction.
Classification: LCC PS3602.R425 S75 2019 | DDC 813/.6—dc23
LC record available at https://lccn.loc.gov/2019002624

ISBN 978-0-8007-3629-3 (casebound)

19 20 21 22 23 24 25   7 6 5 4 3 2 1

For Brittney, my love and treasure.

1

The branding iron pulsated reddish orange in the corner fireplace.

It was time.

The conductor applied the last bit of cakey white paste to his face and pulled his hood over his eyes. He took a seat in front of a tripod-mounted camera in the center of his basement and pressed Play. The woman on the other end of the private feed was probably picking up static this very minute. He held his breath.

An icon appeared to show that his audience of one had tuned in.

"Hello, Janet," he whispered into the lens. Behind him, firelight cast waves of mango glow onto a crate in which lay Janet's treasure—her companion, her confidant.

The pup yawned.

"Hold a moment, Ruby is stirring."

The conductor walked to the crate, unlocked its door, and tousled the dog's ears. Soft as a lamb's, they were. The Labrador casually scanned the unfamiliar lair, still disoriented from the muscle relaxants he'd snuck into her food dish. She looked into his eyes with such trust, such innocence.

The conductor hooked a retractable leash onto her pink collar and led the delirious pup directly in front of the camera. "Don't mind her clumsiness. This little jewel has been tripping nirvana for hours. She was a very hungry girl."

How was Janet doing so far? Tearing up? Feisty little thing was probably cursing him out.

"This is a one-way feed, Janet—wouldn't want emotion getting the best of us, given your relationship with lovely Ruby." The conductor sat and crossed his legs. "Life and death—we think of these as destinations, but they're not . . . they're *not*. They're choices. And you have a choice to make. For you. For your sister. And for your stupid dog."

The conductor tossed the leash over a support beam and caught it on its way back down. Then he yanked.

Ruby yelped at the pressure and stood on her back legs, whimpering but able to breathe, her putrid dog breath permeating the air.

"Good girl. You were choking but you altered your position." The conductor gazed into the camera, letting his eyes linger. "What a concept."

Still gripping the leash, he walked toward the fireplace and raised his arm to its limit. Ruby was suspended in the air for a moment before the conductor dropped her back to one foot.

He pulled the branding iron out of hissing coals and gazed at its glow. "Animal branding used to be so unassuming. No tattoos, earmarking, RFID tagging. Just stick it in the fire and press it to the flesh." He turned back to the tripod. "But I wouldn't last twenty minutes enforcing an iron's will onto livestock. I'm tired just hoisting Ruby." He leaned forward. "So the simple way to do this is the eyeballs."

He let Janet digest his words as he knelt next to Ruby, gripping the iron in one hand while stroking her ears with the other. "You're one of a kind, Ruby, that blend of serene trust and innocent joy. I wonder if Mama Janet will make sure you stay that way."

The conductor looked at the camera, tilted his head, and flatly said, "Call 555-3203."

Moments later, his burner phone rang and he answered. "Hello, Janet—"

Tear-filled obscenities shot from Janet's mouth like a cannon, quickly chased by a detailed torture regimen she promised to inflict upon him should he so much as look at Ruby again.

A fireball, this one.

But then she melted into spasmodic weeping. They always did.

"As I was saying," the conductor said, "it's time for your next assignment."

2

closed my eyes and pictured the moment when SWAT training would be over and I'd be stepping out of my 4Runner at Steph's house. Neither she nor the girls would come running. We'd only been dating five months, after all. But in this vision, they did come running, and I couldn't suppress how that image made me feel.

A hand cupped the back of my head. "That's the spirit, Haasy—grin like a fool. You got this," said Cody Caulkins, who was never short on confidence. "Just know that if you fail, I get Stephanie."

"She'd crush you."

Cody dropped his head. "I know."

The whistle blew.

Weighted with a twenty-five-pound vest, I started pumping out chin-ups, muscles tensing, eyes fixed on the evergreens surrounding the SWAT training field. Three were required. I racked up twenty-three then sprinted to the sandbag thrust.

I pictured the first day Steph had invited me to meet Isabella and Tilly over spaghetti and plastic teacups. It had only been a few months ago, but something special had happened that day. "Don't leave," Isabella, the older of the girls, had said after I'd risen to leave. "You must eat dessert." Her smile had nestled in my heart. Steph and her girls were as close to angels as I'd ever met. I couldn't think of anything better than to be a permanent part of their lives.

"Sixty-five," I said, throwing the bag and hustling toward the gauntlet.

"Two minutes, twelve seconds," SWAT team leader Jeff Karns said as I sprinted across the finish line.

I crouched and concentrated on my breathing, heart slamming against my chest. Salt stung my eyes, but I could still see well enough to notice Mitchell, Dominguez, Adams, and Mathis avoiding eye contact. Competence earned respect. It was as simple and as hard as that. If you could listen to direction, hear some criticism, and make changes to do better the next time, respect slowly built. But outside of Cody, I had a long way to go with my peers.

Cody walked over to me, looking like he was already doing the math in his head. "You just netted 118 and took top spot away from you-know-who, Haasy." He raised his hands and turned in a slow circle, making eye contact with the other SWAT members. "What'd I say? I said Haas was a Greek god. Did I not say he was a Greek god?"

I'd learned long ago that Cody was going to be Cody no matter what I said—no matter what anybody said—so I just rolled with it.

"How'd you do?" I said.

"If there's a slower version of a Greek god, I'm him."

"How'd *we* do?"

Cody squinted and pursed his lips. "Breachers took first, assaulters second, and the gas guys got third. So . . . gas guys

pay plates, we cover drinks and tip, and breachers eat themselves out of their top spot—for free." He shook his head.
"Next month, assaulters wine and dine like royalty. Book it."

"This the most big-boy thing you two do?" said Mike
Mitchell, a SWAT member from the Trenton Police Department. None of the city guys respected non-city SWAT, especially Mitchell. I didn't blame them, not after the way I'd been
recruited to SWAT.

Cody hit my shoulder, a winsome grin spreading across his
face. "Hear that, Haas? Rhino Butt thinks you're making him
look like wrinkles and ear hair to our commanding officers."

I loved Cody for wearing his heart on his sleeve, even liked
his quick wit. But to me, words were like money: save them,
invest them, spend them, in that order. Cody spent his words
like a slot junkie in Vegas.

Mitchell stepped into Cody's space. "You don't get it. You
put in all this energy out here, but the rest of us, the real men,
put it into the work. You didn't earn this. You're tour guides."

They stared at each other.

"Touch each other and you're both suspended, you know
that," I said.

Mitchell suddenly lost interest in Cody, instead turning to
me. "But not for you, right? How's that flesh wound from
your little operation, anyway? You should call CBS, CNN,
and FOX—make sure they do a follow-up."

I declined to respond.

Cody leaned close to Mitchell's ear. "Where were you again
while Haasy was heroing it up? Oh right, ogling those scared,
underage dorm girls."

Mitchell kept his eyes on me but spoke to Cody. "If your
results were as big as your mouth, Caulkins, you might have

actually done better for yourself than that sorry badge you tote around. Unlike Haas here, who needed to be in the right place and right time—as a *university cop*—to even be considered for SWAT."

I bent down and tightened my laces. I had no idea silence could be so loud.

Cody shook his head. "Say that in a nice dark alley with Haas sometime, see how it goes. Big strong guy like you—I'm sure you'd do fine."

"Hey!" Jeff Karns yelled. "Move it."

The entire team jogged to the weight room, torpedoing the turf with spit.

Thirty minutes into lifting, perspiration forced us to ditch our drenched shirts. I'd need a nose plug to keep working out alongside Cody.

"Haas is getting yoked!" Karns yelled from across the room, gawking at me.

I let a smile nudge my lips. That may have been the first compliment I'd heard since the incident. Praise came sparsely to me, a university cop, and Cody, the county sheriff's detective. We were SWAT outsiders, recruited only for our knowledge of Trenton University and the county's back roads. Every other officer on SWAT worked at the Trenton Police Department, watching each other's backs on a daily basis. But Cody and me? At best, we'd skipped in line; at worst, we didn't belong.

"Tell me if this sounds misogynistic to you, because I don't want it to," I had said sincerely to Stephanie three months earlier. "I think I understand what women face breaking into traditionally male careers."

Steph laughed so hard that she accidently woke Isabella and

Tilly. "That's the cutest thing I've ever heard you say," she'd said through a snort.

A buzzer sounded. Workouts were over and target practice commenced.

We peppered targets for forty-five minutes. Each punctured bull's-eye reminded me that I fervidly wanted to stop evil at a job that may never face it.

I collected my riddled sheet and studied it, paper crinkling in my hands. Kill shot, kill shot, flesh wound, kill shot, flesh, kill shot. I had work to do.

"Not bad," Mitchell hollered over to me. "Think those dorm girls who saved your sorry butt could do better?"

A few SWAT guys laughed. Cody shot Mitchell a glare.

"Wrap it up," Karns said.

Cody and I and the rest of SWAT headed back to the station, took off our vests, then sat for a presentation focused on floor science, in which a professor taught how eyesight and flinch responses work, such as how fast a human can turn around and squeeze off three rounds as opposed to just firing from the hip.

Mitchell craned his neck toward Clint Hopkins, another SWAT member from the Trenton Police Department. "Makes you wonder how many rounds you can get off while high."

This time I tensed up. Mitchell had been in rare form all day.

I turned to look him in the eyes, wanting so badly to drop him and make him feel what I was capable of, but my anger quickly transformed to alarm. A fist was blurring past my eyes and connected directly with Mitchell's forehead, producing a hearty smack.

I caught Cody on his follow-through and immediately shoved him against the wall.

Adams, Dominguez, and Mathis shouted and closed in around us, ready to break things up.

Hopkins and a few other SWAT members picked up Mitchell, who got to his feet and rubbed his mouth. "Feel good, Caulkins?" Mitchell spit some blood. "Enjoy vacation."

Karns burst into the commotion like a wrecking ball of profanity and popping veins. He told Mitchell and Cody to get lost and demanded everyone present to email him reports.

Training was officially over.

I followed Cody as he headed for his vehicle. He'd get suspended for that punch. "Hey, Muhammad Ali," I said.

He turned around. "Was that like a butterfly or a bee?"

"Feel good?"

"Better than you can imagine."

I asked a question I knew the answer to. "Why?"

Cody flicked his hand a couple of times, releasing some of the throbbing he had to be feeling. "You'd already done it in your head, so I figured I'd provide the visual. More exciting, you know?"

"I had it under control. You didn't have to—"

"Yeah, I did." His voice had lost that normal Cody charm. "When your friend gets knocked down, you help him up—or punch the guy who started it."

"Not if it means a suspension."

"I'm tired of seeing Mitchell and the rest of these clowns push you around. You're better than all of them, and you *know* it. We're in the business of justice, Haas. You're not practicing it."

There was much I wanted to say but knew I couldn't go that route, so I practiced silence and let his words sink in.

I nodded. "Thanks. Really."

Cody switched the conversation's direction. "How's university treating you?"

"Let's just say I liked today," I said. "Definitely beats the monotony of patrol."

"You mean, 'Beats slapping students with urinating-in-public citations'?"

"Pretty much."

"What does Steph think of SWAT?"

"She likes that I'm better trained, and she's excited for what it might lead to."

"Lead to? You applying?"

I could only wish that were true. But it would be a move I'd ultimately regret. Climbing the ladder always led to the rest of your life—friends, family, home—spiraling into chaos. Easy as a bachelor; torture as a man in love.

Sure, it was nice entertaining Stephanie's encouragement about career advancement. But that's all it was—entertaining. I even had to be careful with *that* because the temptation was so great.

We stopped at our vehicles: me by my university police–issued 4Runner, and Cody by his Camaro. A few of our colleagues' cars whooshed out of the parking lot.

I leaned against my door. "Next thing circled on my calendar is grilling for students off my tailgate. I like that." I nodded at the training facility and chose my words carefully. "But this training isn't helping me at the university."

Cody popped his trunk and grabbed two water bottles from the back. He handed one to me. "I get it." His breath poofed in front of him a little in the cold evening. "You want some whack job to go on a gun rage, huh?" He winked.

"I don't envy danger. But people are doing jacked-up stuff

every day, and I can't do a thing about it." It felt good to vent
to Cody, even if he had no clue what I was really saying—what
had actually happened with my career. "I feel like I'm trained
to slay Goliaths at a job where bad guys are three feet tall."

Cody spit some of his water. "Well, next time I'm wrestling
a heroin addict with needles sticking out of his arms, I'll give
you a shout, David."

I smiled, we tapped fists, then drove our separate ways.

I just wasn't as needed at Trenton University as I would be
elsewhere. But I couldn't take a job away from Steph and the
girls, not without them coming with me—and I couldn't be
sure she was ready for that, for marriage.

The M-word wasn't optional with Steph but essential. She
wasn't afraid of commitment and didn't need to keep her options open. I liked that about her.

But marriage would be complicated for Steph because the
first man she'd made vows to, Declan, turned out to be nothing short of a high-functioning sociopath. After marrying right
out of high school, getting Steph pregnant, and creating a rich
lifestyle for her and the girls, he'd cheated on her. Not with one
woman but with a different woman every week—a tapestry of
lies and manipulation so ugly that the portrait would hang itself.

Declan had tried to take everything in the divorce, but
thankfully the judge saw through his smoke. So the house—
and much more importantly, the girls—went to Stephanie.
He'd tried inching his way back into their lives after that, creating a new life only a few hours away in Seattle and stopping
by to surprise the kids on holidays, but I'd helped Steph put
an end to those visits and get the court orders needed that
would keep Declan where he belonged: out of their lives for
as many days of the year as possible.

Steph had risen to the challenge of single parenting, found Jesus at a warehouse church where the pastors wore jeans, and somehow kept up her jovial personality through the pain.

I dialed her number.

"Hey, Robo," she answered. "How'd Call of Duty go?"

I smiled. "The controller ran out of battery, so I'm calling you."

"Well, I have two very excited girls over here who can't stop talking about some fort they plan to build with you?"

Whoops, I'd forgotten about that promise. "It's going to be a castle with a moat to keep that stray cat out, if I'm remembering right."

"Poor Puddles," she said.

"Can I bring anything other than the veggies?"

Steph scoffed. "Ugh, yeah. Chocolate. And soda. There also happens to be a girl here who may or may not wear a pink bow every day of her life and *hasn't* stopped talking about the flowers you brought her last week, so, just saying. Points to be had."

"Noted. And what about Tilly?"

"I wasn't going to say anything, but now that you ask—no more lollipops for her. I'm done slathering her hair with peanut butter and coconut oil all because she insists on sleeping with sticky candy."

"I'll make the switch to Starbursts." I grinned. "And would the lady of the house care for wine?"

"Mr. Haas, are you trying to romance me?"

"It's kind of my thing."

"Then wine you shall bring."

"Only if you quit leaving your doors unlocked."

"Old habits die hard," she said in her cute tail-between-the-legs voice.

"I kinda like you," I said.

"I kinda like you too."

We hung up and I felt a familiar swirl deep in my chest.

I wanted to be there for Steph and the girls. What that might mean for my long-term career, I wasn't ready to think about. Not yet. Steph needed stability. The pain she'd faced was more than any person should carry. I wasn't about to add to it.

Right now I needed to find contentment in university work and just be a rock for her. Tomorrow I would barbecue for new students at the orientation fair, and that was just fine.

Others could protect the world from evil for now.

3

Stars flickered above as Officer Mike Mitchell pulled into the wide, gravelly driveway. He loved Friday nights because it meant playing poker and making money. Both were guaranteed after he and his TPD colleagues wrapped up for the night and headed over to Officer Clint Hopkins's pad.

Hopkins had a family, but he'd always kept one foot in the bachelor life, starting with an enormous shop where he did bodywork on cars and trucks. He'd collected pinball and slot machines, a jukebox, air hockey tables, pool tables, dartboards.

As magical as this part of the man cave was, it merely served as the appetizer for what brought Mitchell and his colleagues here weekly. The real banquet sat four steps up to another level of the pad, which was surrounded by flat screens, an industrial-sized vent for their cigar smoke, and a fully stocked minibar that glistened under black lights.

Mitchell noticed the lack of noise and figured none of the boys had surpassed three drinks yet—two if it were Adams. They were probably sitting around the big, felted poker table puffing cigars as they waited for him. But had someone muted the TVs? There were almost no sounds as he walked in. All he could hear was a tapping sound on a counter, like a poker chip doubling as a fidget toy.

"Why isn't the game on, bunch of fair-weather amateurs," Mitchell muttered, stepping onto the landing.

He paused, taking in the scene, and wanted to reach for his weapon but realized it was too late.

A man wearing a fancy hat and the colorless makeup of a clown stood before him. Dark circles around his eyes and mouth sprouted tiny black threads that spread all over his plaster-white skin. He was clutching two pistols equipped with silencers. One was aimed at Mitchell while the other dangled loosely in the intruder's hand, tap-tap-tapping ever so gently against the poker table.

"It's about time," the stranger said in an octave somewhere between a tenor and a soprano. "Been trying to convince your friends I'm a worthy opponent—I can play, raise, bluff. But they all tell me the same thing. 'Mitchell's the best. You've got to play Mitchell. He's the real player.'" The clown shook his head and grinned. "So, Mitchell, glad you're here. Take a seat." He aimed his loose gun at the middle of the table, where all of Mitchell's colleagues' weapons rested. "Leave your manhood there."

Mitchell made eye contact in rapid succession with his fellow officers, each of whom was highly trained in combat. Not a hint that anyone had a plan. Quite the opposite. Their enlarged pupils and ashen skin were telltale signs—they were in shock. How had they given up their firearms? And where was Mathis?

He set his gun on the table with the others. That's when he

noticed the feet sprawled from behind the poker table, a pool of red still growing. He jutted his chin forward for a clearer view, trembling. "What did you do?" he whispered.

"What did I do?" The clown scoffed. "Why'd you show up late to game night, Mitch? All the juiciest stories cascade like vomit the first five minutes of the party, everyone knows this. Come, take a look."

Mitchell stepped closer, not once taking his eyes off the psycho until he had a clear view of Mathis. Three bullets had pierced his friend's chest, his eyes still wide with disbelief.

"Today just wasn't his Lady Luck," the clown said.

Mitchell clenched his shaking hands into fists. "Who are you?"

But the clown continued like he hadn't heard him. "Who would have thought that marriage could save *anyone*." He hunched his shoulders. "But here we are, your colleague kissing the afterlife all because he didn't have someone to go home to tonight. I can be merciful like that, see?" The clown pointed at Mitchell. "Yet here's the twist, Mitch. Those three bullets, they're from Larry's, Curly's, and Moe's chambers." He glanced at Hopkins, Adams, and Dominguez. "And the fourth"—the clown snatched up Mitchell's gun—"is from yours." He fired point blank into Mathis's forehead.

Mitchell's stomach lurched. He pressed his lips together and looked away along with his colleagues.

What had they done to deserve this? What was this lunatic's game? What was he going to do to the rest of them?

The clown shoved the gun into the back of his pants, then picked up a duffle bag on the floor beside him. "Poker's a wonderful game—Texas Hold'em, a national treasure. But the alpha competitiveness of five hotheaded colleagues, always flinging around their egos, well, it was bound to blow amid all the high-stakes bidding, bluffing, and booze. How four of Trenton's finest could kill a friend in cold blood over a few hundred bucks will keep the regional papers busy for weeks, hungry to eat up you white, balding, power-hungry, and crooked cops."

A frame job. This clown was devising a plot to put them all behind bars. "You're sick."

The clown looked at Mitchell with sympathy. "No, Mitch." He glanced at the corpse. "Not I, but you." He began placing items into his bag, a clattering assortment of their guns, liquor bottles, glasses, chips, cigars. "All the evidence points to locking you away. The other juicy parts, like your affairs"—he pointed at Mitchell and Hopkins—"those are just bonus details to make sure conjugal visits are out of the question."

Mitchell couldn't keep up with the horrific thoughts racing through his mind. His career would be gone; his wife and kids, gone; freedom, gone. All because of a whack job in a Halloween costume? "What do you want?"

"You catch on fast, you officer, SWAT team, professional, you. One moment you're ready to unwind and let all that stress melt away. Then the next you're making a deal with the devil, yes? That is the power of the will." The clown waved his hands slowly, as if casting a different future. "Shame your friend was having such horrible thoughts, journaling his hatred for himself and his addictions. It would appear Mathis could no longer take the darkness, so he decided to leave this note and nothing else." He held up a typed letter. "The only problem, it seems, is where did he go to end it? Where did he go so that no one would ever find him?"

The clown flipped the duffle bag over his head and onto his

shoulder. "Follow me, gentlemen—and grab Mr. Mathis. He'll be my guest of honor until our business is finished."

"What business?" Mitchell asked.

The clown peered over his shoulder coldly, barely making eye contact. "Call it the string."

4

"You know you're ruining my life, right?" the shirtless student said, running his hands through thick dark hair.

I hated doing this in front of such a large audience, many of them freshmen and their parents, but the university didn't tolerate drinking in public, and university police needed to be extra vigilant on days like today. The opening round of the NCAA Division I men's basketball tournament was no small event. The country would be watching. Thankfully, most of the folks hanging around the shirtless student and me were conversing through shouting and couldn't hear a peep over the band's attempt at music.

I pulled up the student's identification card on my phone, then cross-referenced it with the rap sheet app used by the Trenton Police Department.

David P. Kilpatrick: six foot one, 150 pounds, an organ donor—never an offender.

"What's your major?" I said.

That seemed to calm him a bit. "Double major. But med student."

I raised my brows.

"What?" he said.

"A bit unprofessional for your aspirations, wouldn't you say?"

David simply looked at his feet. His only clothes were light blue jeans rolled halfway to his knees and forest green boxers, of which five inches showed. "You're driving me away from this town," he said, shaking his head.

I didn't owe David a response, especially one steeped in guilt, but silence created a deeper rift between university police and students, a gap I'd worked hard to fill with big smiles and barbecues. "Dude, you should know better. You can't be drinking in public. And what's with the Jim-Bob fashion and no shirt—they say it might snow tonight."

Tears filled David's eyes. He rubbed his face. "I was just enjoying the sun. My parents . . ." He started sobbing.

I scrunched my brows. I knew what manipulation felt like, and this wasn't it. David was grieving. I put my hand on his shoulder. "What about your parents?"

He didn't respond.

"Listen, I'm citing you at the minimum. Mistakes happen and a line on your file won't dictate your future."

David looked up, but not at me. Something over my shoulder had snatched his attention.

I turned my head.

"This isn't who I am," David blurted out, shaking his head. "These aren't the choices I make."

I stared at him. Could feel the load of shame weighing him down.

He broke eye contact and shoved his hands in his pockets.

"You gonna be okay?" I said.

David glanced past me again.

"What's so distracting?"

He backed up a couple of steps, shrugged, and walked away.

Heavy. The word throbbed in her mind.

Heavy like being smothered with a wool blanket, breath getting hotter and hotter. Heavy like stones in place of high heels and chains in place of hair.

Jaw clenched, Janet Blevins approached the officer's vehicle, which was parked along the edge of the new-student orientation fair. Every brick her heels touched, each person she brushed shoulders with—even the air she breathed—felt like invisible cement seeping into her body and hardening in her bones.

Somewhere in the boisterous assembly, a man with a sick intent stood watching her this very moment. But nobody knew her danger. No one could *ever* know, if she wanted to keep her sister safe. And even that was probably a bald-faced lie to ensure Janet's compliance with the conductor's bidding.

But it was working.

She glanced at the many faces in the crowd, none of whom seemed to know she existed. How could so much happiness be present in her nightmare? Couldn't they see she needed help?

Maybe if she just looked at someone with her eyes shifted just so, they'd understand the chaos inside of her. They'd see that her every move was in direct opposition to her own will and was, in fact, controlled by another's.

Janet closed her eyes. Her only hope was to outlast the

conductor, completing each task until he stopped demanding
and released everyone from the string. She needed to stay
strong and finish the assignment. He'd said she was almost
finished. She could only hope he was telling the truth, and that
his endgame was money or something else material instead of
straight terrorism, straight evil for the sake of a game.

Janet looked at the package in her hands and felt her stomach churn.

A group of students had chosen to chat right next to the
officer's vehicle. She grabbed her cell and faked a text as a
tangy waft of barbecue filled her nose. Glancing up, she saw a
cooler full of ice and soda sticking out from behind the 4Run-
ner. Now she understood. This vehicle belonged to the officer
who grilled for students on orientation day. Haas, she believed
his name was. She'd seen a photo in the student newspaper
several months ago of him barbecuing and connecting with
students, remembered admiring that.

And now she was going to wreck his life.

Janet circled the vehicle in one big loop, passing mobs
of students, parents, and volunteers, positioning herself so
that only one of four nearby students would have a clear
view of her as she approached the tailgate. Thankfully, the
lone student who'd be able to identify her kept smiling at
his phone.

She leaned around the side of the tailgate, spotted Officer
Haas's university-issued cap lying there, and slipped the package under it. Every part of her was screaming to look at the
student one last time to know if he'd be able to identify her.
But the deed was done. What happened from this point on
would materialize no matter what. What she needed was to
walk away as fast as possible.

"Hey, Miss Blevins!"

Jimmy from janitorial. So sweet but so loud.

"Good to see you, Jimmy," Janet said, keeping her voice low.

Jimmy stretched his arms wide and nodded continuously with that infectious grin, eyes squinted. He'd started about a year ago through a local agency that placed adults with special needs into various places of work.

"New students are the best, Miss Blevins. The best! Have you tried Mr. Haas's 'tish kebab? It's the best. The best! Want to get one?"

Janet put one hand on Jimmy's shoulder, perhaps too quickly. He looked at her hand, still smiling but confused. Her heart hurt. She couldn't push him away like this. She'd worked so hard to befriend him and get him to open up. "Oh, there's nothing I'd rather do than get a kebab with you, Jimmy. But I'm supposed to call someone in a minute. Paper football tomorrow?"

His grin returned. "I'll be practicing and getting really good for when the games start."

She tucked her chin. "Super Bowl or bust."

"Super Bowl or bust!"

Janet made her way to the fountain, not once looking back at the students. With Jimmy's voice, she could only imagine how many glances she'd received. But it was out of her hands. She'd finished the assignment—hopefully her last.

Heart racing, she pulled out her phone.

I did it. Leave my sister alone.

She released the breath she didn't know she'd been holding. Lucy was safe. For now.

She snuck one last glimpse of Haas in his last few moments of peace and normalcy. "I'm sorry," she whispered.

———

Standing on the sky bridge connecting the gymnasium and amphitheater, the conductor slipped on his noise-canceling headphones and tapped Play on his phone. Waves of binaural beats flowed into his ears and down to his cheekbones. Gentle numbing vibrated through his core and wrapped around his very heart, pumping it full of electrical current. He slid his hand into his pocket, brushing the detonator.

The conductor's gaze panned to two people in the crowd already playing vital roles in his string. The phone in his pocket buzzed.

I did it. Leave my sister alone.

Speak of the devil. He tapped a reply.

She looks more stunning than ever, doesn't need the wig.

P.S. You're glowing today.

The conductor watched as Janet received the texts and stared at her phone. She glanced at the fair's various attractions, looking like the poster child of spontaneous combustion. Then her shoulders relaxed, likely not wanting to give him the satisfaction. Smart girl.

Janet had covertly dropped the package in the back of the police 4Runner that belonged to the newest knot in the string, the only one who truly intrigued him.

Markus Haas.

Hands suddenly reached around and covered the conductor's eyes. He switched off his headphones and turned around to find Rosetta.

"Liking the view?" she asked. "You can see everything from up here—so colorful."

He smiled.

"I want shish kebabs and soda." She placed her hands on her hips and squinted as if thinking hard. "Why are you all grumps?"

He shrugged. "Not enough sleep."

"So we'll get you a coffee." She put both hands on his shoulders and leaned back to look through the sky bridge's glass roof. "And I will require this for the big game tonight." She swiped the bill off his head and placed it over her dark curls.

The conductor snatched it back.

Rosetta giggled. "Whoa, someone's touchy."

Head down, he positioned the cap just so. "I prefer the cap."

Rosetta shrugged. "Whatever you say, Captain Longface." She laughed and tugged his sleeve. "Let's go scope out where ESPN is setting up so I can get on camera."

Rosetta. Sweet and without a clue.

Taking her by the arm, the conductor stole one last glance out the sky bridge windows and spotted Haas sliding into his 4Runner, package in hand.

The conductor slid his hand into his pocket.

The first surprise would be in Haas's grasp soon.

The second had been under his tailgate all day.

I walked to my 4Runner and exchanged my pen and pad of paper for my steel spatula.

The students I'd left upon spotting David were still clustered near my tailgate. I banged the flipper against the grill. "All right, my friends, I apologize for the delay. Give me a couple minutes."

I clicked on the burner and cocked my head. A gift-wrapped box about the size of a hardcover book sat under my hat. Had that been there the whole day? I grabbed the shiny package, walked around to the cab, and climbed in, leaving the door open to stretch my legs. I unwrapped the box to find a computer tablet and a fancy note touched with perfume. The calligraphy read, *To the man I love.*

Adrenaline burst in my mind and my mouth opened slightly. I wanted to say something but my breath refused. Had Steph really written "love"? I'd refrained from saying the word yet in our relationship, knowing how much the sentiment meant to her and how betrayed she'd been by it in the past.

I grinned, and a small laugh sneaked out as I realized how much the word meant to *me* now. Steph loved me.

I had been patient these past few months, giving her and the girls space. They'd gone through so much heartache. That she was the one stepping out on a limb felt strange. What had made her take this leap? And why now—like this? I looked around, but there was no sign of her.

Tiny pinpricks flowed through me as I activated the tablet. I didn't even know Steph owned a tablet. A simple black screen with a Play icon appeared. I tapped it and a slideshow started.

Syrupy music filled the 4Runner as images populated the tablet from offbeat angles most likely recorded on Stephanie's phone: Steph dancing and laughing with Isabella in the kitchen, Tilly tapping away on the lens as if playing a game, the three of them squished together taking selfies in bed.

Next came a video of Steph and the girls outside playing in the sprinkler. The angle was odd, though, as if someone was filming them from across the street in the overgrowth.

Then came a shot of Steph doing dishes in front of the kitchen window, a pensive look on her face.

Another of Steph in nothing but a towel in her bathroom, tapping away at one last text before getting in the shower.

My stomach twisted. Steph didn't do this. Who was filming the girls?

The screen went dark. I reached for my phone to call Steph, but the tablet came to life again.

I saw a dark room, brightened only by the flickering light of old-fashioned lanterns. Glimmers of antique bookshelves and a single stool flickered in and out of focus. A blurred object came into view, and a man sat down in front of the camera.

A fancy dark hat overshadowed his face, which resembled a scarred-up Marilyn Manson. Black-and-white makeup caked his skin so thickly that not one inch of his flesh was visible. His eyes were deeply set under a large, dark hood.

"Sorry about that," the white-faced demon said, his voice surprisingly high. "I have a flair for the theatrical. The girls are lovely, they really are. But you know that. You know everything there is to know about them, you protective stallion."

I closed the 4Runner's door, probably too hard, and furrowed my eyebrows.

The man who sounded like a woman smiled and leaned back, folding his hands, which were just as white and made up as his face. "I'm going to make this short, because editing these videos can be a real shard of glass to the eyeballs. You are now a member of the string, Markus." Unnerving anticipation filled the man's eyes. "What is the string, you wonder? Think of the string as one long sheet of music, with notes of all shapes and sizes, tones, and pitches. You're a note. And judging from what I see—shaved head, muscular, someone who pushes tractor tires just for exercise—I'd say you're of the bass variety." He pointed at the camera. "But don't pass judgment against the tenors of the world just because you swing lower than the rest of us."

My face contorted. Who in the world was this lunatic, how did he know my routine, and why had he filmed the girls?

"I . . ." The man tilted his chin up like a waiter at a five-star restaurant. "I am your conductor. And that's what you will call me."

I grabbed my cell. Wasn't going to put up with this any longer.

"Now before you do something stupid like call the chief or your girl, Steph, you should know that doing so will hurt someone very close to you. Yes, very close." He laughed.

I put my phone down. Was this guy serious?

"See, isn't it spectacular? I lift my baton and the string goes up. I dip it, the string goes low."

"Who are you?" I muttered, taking a quick peek out the windshield. Nothing unusual. Same scene. Same loud music.

The conductor sat upright. "It all comes down to rules. 'Rules rule the world,' Daddy used to say, that sick old man. So here are the rules of the string." He held up a finger. "Rule one: Each person gets a positive and negative reason to play their part. Your positive is simple. I know how badly you want out of this bottom-rung position. Trenton University Police, TUP—really? You were meant for better acronyms than TUP. I will make that happen, and you'll be smiling the way you do grilling for students." He winked. "Yes, this might be recorded, but I can see you. I can *always* see you."

I looked at the rearview mirror, then out both side windows. Just students, their family members, a couple of early-bird basketball fans, and some faculty. This "conductor" could be any one of them. Or completely bluffing. I put one hand on my leg. Focused on my breathing. What could I do? What *should* I do?

"So, the negative. *Don't* do what I say, and something horrible is going to happen to you. That wouldn't be fair to your lady, Steph, or those two chickpeas, now would it? No, they've already grieved enough."

How'd he know so much about their lives? Stephanie needed to know and to protect the girls.

The conductor got up from his chair and disappeared. Five seconds later, he returned holding a male ventriloquist doll. "My mother gave me this doll years ago. The thing haunted me from the corner of my bedroom. Don't know why I never moved it off its chair. That's what I call it: 'it.' I thought if I ever named it, then it would come alive and stab me while I slept." He sat the doll on his lap and smiled, as if ready to tell it a story. "But today, I'm finally deciding to name it: Markus. It's a solid name. But see, now that I've named the doll, I don't dare fall asleep." The conductor stared at the camera, eyes narrowed. "And I *don't* sleep, Markus." He glanced at the doll. "So if you come for me, I'll be waiting under the sheets with a sharp surprise. I know I come across as all cozy-bear, but Haasy—to borrow your cute nickname—don't test me." He leaned forward and whispered, "I do terrible things." He tossed the doll away.

I clenched my fists. I was going to crush his skull.

"So that's rule one. Rule two: dictator decision," the conductor said. "But I'm not the dictator. You are. You have the power to destroy not only your own life but the lives of every knot in the string. Reminds me of my first solo. I played and sang with all my heart, see, and brought down the house in beautiful fashion. Everyone succeeded because I succeeded." The conductor rubbed his temples. "Oh, but if I had frozen . . . if I had failed . . . if I had so much as kissed off one note, every last person on stage would have suffered. We'd have turned beauty into a mockery." The conductor dipped his fingertips toward the camera. "You are in the spotlight, Markus, standing in heaven's pinprick, and I've given you your cue. All around you stand your fellow musicians, wondering if you'll finish the night with mastery or doom them to despair." He held his hands out as if weighing options on a scale. "Do you follow the baton the way they have? Or walk off stage to their pain and destruction? What are you going to do, Markus?"

Stick a Taser down his throat, that's what I was going to do. How long was he going to go on for? I eyed my phone a third time. My brain said this was just a twisted, elaborate prank. But it was too elaborate. Too direct.

"If you don't play your part," the conductor said, tilting his head down and his eyes up, "you're going to do far worse things to far more people—and they're all going to know you did it to them. And when a knot breaks the string, knots get broken."

A student approached the driver's side window, asking if more shish kebabs were on the way. I put a finger to my ear, acting as if I were talking via Bluetooth and couldn't get away. The student gave me a thumbs-up and walked away. I looked back at the tablet.

"Now, finally, rule number three: your duty. The action you must take. It's my favorite part. Care to guess why? It's that moment your will, which has been your protector, friend, and warrior for your whole life, finally drops its guard, then waves mine through. You're going to—"

I clicked the tablet's power button and tossed it into the back. Called Stephanie.

The phone rang three times and then was picked up.

"Big mistake," the conductor answered.

Just then, something outside of the 4Runner exploded and my head slammed against something hard.

Day turned to night, though I never remembered closing my eyes.

5

The thunderous burst silenced the crowd and band.

Janet, who'd just stepped onto the sky bridge to observe the conductor's sick game discreetly, turned toward the 4Runner. Flames engulfed its posterior and licked air off the tailgate. Had the conductor really used her to plant a bomb? The package she had dropped weighed little more than a pound. Could bombs be that light?

She pressed one hand to her mouth. Where were the students who'd been there mingling?

She ran down the stairs into the gymnasium lobby, stumbling and nearly twisting her ankle at the bottom. Janet cursed, pulled off her heels, pushed through the swinging glass doors, and ran barefoot over red bricks toward the smoke.

Students and parents were still crouching in defensive postures. A few dazed faculty members blurted out confusing instructions.

Janet sprinted past them. She strained to see if bodies awaited her near the 4Runner. Only one other person beat her to the blaze, a student wielding a camera close to his face, taking pictures of the chaos—baffling idiot.

The four students who'd been standing near the tailgate must've wandered away before the blast because she didn't see them, thank the Lord. But one body lay on the far side of the vehicle, blocked from view except his legs. Oh no, those red socks. "Jimmy."

She pointed at the driver's side door and darted toward her friend from janitorial. "Someone help Officer Haas right now."

Jimmy's eyes were wide open, looking directly at the sky. He lay perfectly still except for his quivering lips and stilted breaths. Janet dropped to her knees and slid her hands between his head and the bricks. The hiss of a fire extinguisher filled her ears as someone doused the 4Runner. She inhaled some of the powdery fumes and coughed them away. "It's okay, Jimmy, it's okay now, you're okay."

No blood or breaks that she could see. She leaned down and kissed his forehead. Jimmy's eyes finally moved from the sky to Janet, and he cried.

A lump formed in her throat, but she wanted him to feel safe, feel normal. "Looks like we're both tougher than we thought, huh? You taking a snooze on bricks and me running so fast my heels blew right off my feet."

He still wasn't quite hearing her yet. She glanced up for a quick breath. The first person who came into view was the student snapping photos, a *Trenton Telegraph* badge flopping around his neck. Normally she'd assume he was an overeager journalism student, trying to get the scoop for the school paper. But Janet recognized something else in him, urgency in his movements, fear in his eyes.

Tall and slim with curly brown hair, dressed sharp for student standards, the man met Janet's gaze. He lowered his camera and stared at her for two uncomfortably long moments.

Then he turned and fled the scene.

"Here he comes," a male voice said. "Markus, it's Sidney Scott with the fire department. You took a steering wheel to the forehead, might have a concussion."

I opened my eyes. Four bright lights shone down on me from a low ceiling. The fireman was crouched beside me. I slid my hands to my sides, gripped aluminum poles. I was on a gurney in an ambulance that wasn't moving.

"From the looks of things, your grill decided it'd had a good life and wanted to go out in style," the fireman said. "Students and faculty are fine, a little shaken up. But the back of your 4Runner—hate to tell ya this—looks like a skid mark." He held up a cracked tablet. "And I doubt this is going to be the same."

I sat up. Stephanie, the girls.

The conductor. The *string*.

"Slowly, bud. Soon as Matt and Tim hop in, we're off to get you checked out."

I eyed the medical hardware attached to my finger. "You've got my vitals, I'm fine."

"We do, but it'd be best for a doc to look at you. Concussions can be tricky."

I had taken enough blows to my head while kickboxing to know the difference between a headache and a concussion. *I think.*

"I'm fine." I grabbed the tablet and swung my legs to the side.

"Can't make you come with us, you know that, so I won't

pester. But take care of yourself and forget about cooking ke-babs." The fireman smirked. "Your last batch bombed—sorry, sorry." He chuckled, patted his shirt pockets, then reached into the right one and pulled out a piece of paper. "Oh, and I've got a note for you from a young man. Didn't tell me his name, but he was very helpful."

I unfolded the note.

I know what's happening. Don't trust your cell or any phone. Go to the game tonight and let me find you.

Another member of the string under surveillance? Or a sick trick like the gift-wrapped tablet? I shoved the note into my pocket. The conductor could be watching.

A bluff, a twisted prank—none of my conjecture about him had proved true. The conductor had done exactly what he'd said he'd do.

I recalled dialing Steph. Had the conductor kidnapped her, stolen her cell? Or had he redirected my call somehow? My head ached. I needed to reach Steph and the girls. But how? I couldn't call and risk worse retaliation, especially with the direct warning not to trust phones. Could the conductor really have pulled off such elaborate wiretapping? It didn't matter. I couldn't go against him again until I knew the girls were safe.

Steph didn't check email or her social media accounts but a handful of times per week, and the conductor would surely be tracking those too. With calls ruled out, that left the lone option of borrowing a car and driving straight to her house, about twenty-five minutes away. But the conductor had said he was always watching and had credibly proven it. He'd know where I was headed the moment I got in the car, giving him nearly twenty minutes to do what he willed with the girls even if I floored it.

I shook the fireman's hand and stepped out of the ambulance. The smell of burnt metal wafted about the red-bricked courtyard, scattering most of those who remained from the orientation festivities. A dozen university employees were still mingling around the charred 4Runner, most likely discussing how to fry *me* next for what they would perceive as gross irresponsibility, if they believed the grill blew on its own. Would they bring in a forensic unit to get to the truth of it? Or would the conductor meddle in that too?

Realization then hit me smack in the face. How could I convince the chief that this *wasn't* an accident? Renfroe was probably salivating at the opportunity to rip me a new one.

Didn't matter. Steph and the girls were what mattered.

First priority, vehicle.

The ambulance's strobe lights crossed my face in a repetitive pattern. I squinted at the blackness of what was left of my tailgate, then cursed. Everything was stretched and jumbled in my head. I needed to process.

"You okay?" an unmistakably deep voice said.

I turned to find Doug, the university's boulder-shouldered maintenance chief, along with his friend and the university gardener, Serge. I nodded. "Yeah, fine."

Doug dipped his chin the way he always did when exiting a conversation, and Serge followed suit.

It wasn't five seconds later I heard another voice addressing me. "Heard something was cookin' over the radio, so I came to rescue you, Haasy."

Cody. Could I talk to him? Would the conductor know?

Yes, he'd know. He'd been watching since before the explosion. Why wouldn't he be watching after it?

"Already convinced the spectators that you need space, and if we upgrade that to *mental health* space, I bet we can put off that tasty report you gotta write till tomorrow's second java." Cody swung his arm around me and turned me away from the 4Runner. "Let's get your feet up, brother."

We walked away from the campus hub, past the student marketplace, and found a bench between the humanities and biology buildings, shaded by thick greenery. I couldn't help but glance at every vantage point I myself would be drawn to if tasked with inconspicuous surveillance. The conductor was out here, somewhere.

"Didn't you hear, Waldo's been found. It's just me." Cody sat and tapped the space on the seat next to him. "Dare I ask what happened? I knew you wanted more action, but this . . . Wow, Haas, you stoop low, you and your atomic kebabs." He stared at me, eyebrows playfully raised.

I let a few moments pass in silence—probably a mistake. As much as my instincts were telling me to keep Cody out of the hell I'd just entered, at least until I'd had time to think through the ramifications, I couldn't hide the trauma I was feeling.

Cody switched into his other self, the one that made him such a great sheriff's detective. "What's wrong?"

My cell buzzed in my pocket and I reached for it.

You hung up before my addendum.

Speak of the string and loud-mouthed Cody is finished.

I held up my index finger to Cody as the texts kept pinging.

You got a warning shot, and you only get one.

Stay on campus until you hear from me.

I looked up. "Things aren't good with Steph."

Cody's face relaxed, but then his brows furrowed. "Nah, you guys? What, you leave the toilet seat up at movie night?"

"I just . . . I don't know where she's at right now."

"'Bout applying? Taking it to the next level? What?"

"It's complicated."

"'I love you, love your kids, want the best for us, let's talk about a future together'?" Cody said, leaning back and shaking his head. "How complicated we talkin'? Listen, if you guys can't make it, no one in this world will, not really—especially me. I *need* you to make it. Got it? That her texting?"

I nodded. I had to make sure she was safe, but it couldn't be me checking in on her. "Listen, I need a favor."

"Done."

"Can you deliver flowers to her . . . now?"

"*That's,*" Cody said, drawing out the word, "not what I expected."

"I'd do it myself, but I'm trapped here." With each second that passed without telling him the truth, I felt as though someone were heaping a pound of bricks onto my shoulders.

"Chief's wrath?"

"Something like that," I said. But I knew Chief Renfroe was preoccupied with calls about the explosion and security prep for the basketball game, and even more engrossed with placing dozens of bets on bizarre and improbable NCAA outcomes that would crush him under more debt. Any other day, the chief would jump all over an opportunity to reprimand me. But a defective grill would be the last thing on his mind amid prime-time gambling. That bought me time to compose myself before the conductor texted me whatever twisted instruction he was scheming.

"Consider those flowers Stevie Wondered: signed, sealed, and delivered," Cody said. "By the time I'm done talking you up—"

"She hates your cockiness."

Cody pursed his lips. "Right."

I exhaled.

"It's going to be fine." Cody eased back into his more serious self. "You're meant for each other. Doesn't take a detective to tell you that."

I forced a smile. "If she's not home, give me a call, okay?"

"You got it. Let me give you a lift to HQ."

We walked to Cody's squad car and drove the primary road that connected one end of campus to the other. Outside the window, I glimpsed students packing up chairs, tables, and stereo equipment from the festivities. The transition from orientation to NCAA prep that evening was in full swing.

I felt as though I were having a conversation with Cody without even making eye contact with him: *Why can't I clue you in on my intentions? Why can't you read me?* It was exactly how I felt every time I tried to pray.

Cody dropped me off at the HQ parking lot. "I want you to be honest with me, Haas," he said, leaning out the car's window.

My chest tightened as I turned back to meet my friend's eyes.

"If I deliver these and save your guys' relationship," Cody said, "will she kiss me?" And with that, he honked twice and drove off.

Cody had no idea about my situation's gravity, I knew that. If he did, all his jokes and bravado would've shrunk to a pea while the real Cody, the one I'd grown to understand and admire throughout SWAT basic, would've sprung into action. I could only hope that the steady stream of mixed messages about to hit Cody would trigger his internal alarm.

I walked to headquarters' back entrance and swiped my card. I wanted zero human contact, needed room to think.

I made my way through the hallway to my desk, which sat amid an open workspace that bordered Chief Renfroe's office. The paneled lights above hummed a low murmur. Everyone else either had taken up positions for the incoming NCAA crowd or was on patrol. I reclined in my chair in what felt like slow motion and found myself staring at nothing on my desk. In the reflection of my black computer monitor, fear stared back.

I felt powerless.

Unable to protect the woman and girls I loved.

Trapped in a quiet office filled with nothing but my thoughts and a large clock on the wall, whose hands mercilessly ticked forward until Cody reached Steph's house and dialed me out of either confusion or horrifying confirmation.

What had just happened? Was I really being held hostage by a theatrical white-faced demon on the other end of my phone—in the middle of the university police department? That's exactly what was happening. The conductor had told me to stay, and I was staying.

But I wasn't powerless. I could find and stop this man. I just needed to ensure Steph and the girls weren't in danger first.

Much as I tried, I didn't consider myself a praying man, but I had prayed earlier for the call redirect scenario—and now I prayed that the mysterious demon hadn't made actual contact with the girls.

How had a psychopath like this ended up at Trenton University? My own words echoed through my mind like terrible karma: *I'm trained to slay Goliaths at a job where bad guys are three feet tall.* This conductor was looking like a ten-foot giant, and I didn't have a single stone to fight back.

I shook my head. What was possible in this moment? How could I gain an advantage? The conductor was scheming a horrible plot, one of which I now was a part. But that didn't mean I'd blindly play a part in it. I needed to study it, *break* it.

"OODA," I muttered, closing my eyes to engage my checklist: observe, orient, decide, act.

Observe.

What had I seen? It had all started with that gift-wrapped package. The conductor could've placed it there himself but probably wouldn't have risked being videoed by one of the parents, students, or ESPN crew shooting B-roll throughout the day. Someone had placed the tablet for him, another "knot" most likely, as the conductor called them. If I wanted to find who had dragged me into this sick game, there was a clear path to doing so—but it would take weeks of interviewing and combing through footage. Not an option.

The tablet itself might offer a clue via an IP address, but it wouldn't even turn on, and the entire IT department was undoubtedly frantic about making sure ESPN's live broadcast ran smoothly without any errors from the Trenton University side of the tech crew.

Besides, I believed the note the fireman had handed to me

was in fact another member of the string trying to connect with me—perhaps the very person who had planted the tablet, maybe someone scared or ashamed, in need of reinforcements to challenge the conductor's string. I would likely find out for sure sometime between tip-off and buzzer tonight.

Following the note was a risk, but ignoring it was the greater risk. I needed information if I were to outfox the conductor, and what better way to gain that information than from someone who'd been trapped in the string longer than me?

The basketball game would be packed, noisy, and a great place to meet someone without being noticed. The time and place made sense if the conductor were monitoring.

What else?

The conductor knew far too much about Steph, the girls, and my relationship with them. He was meticulous in his preparation and dug into not only his targets' fears but also their hopes. How had he known, for instance, that I wasn't satisfied in my work? Was that an amateur guess—or a surgical uncovering of my life? Just how much did he know about my past?

What was the so-called conductor's obsession with music? There had to be a clue in there about his motivation, where he'd come from, who he was.

And the bigger question: What *did* the conductor want? If the string was a web of thread, then it wasn't a leap to assume he was tying pieces together to trap and devour . . . *something*. The question was what, and I didn't have a clue.

Orient.

The conductor was prepared—but was he a mass murderer? If I stood up to him a second time, would he really destroy his "symphony"? Or would he fire another warning shot across the bow? I couldn't take that chance. Not without Steph, Isabella, and Tilly safely by my side. What if everything about the string were true? I couldn't risk breaking it at the expense of those trapped within it.

Decide.

The conductor could be a poser who'd collapse under pushback. But if he was unafraid to act . . . I couldn't take that risk. Until I knew more, I would approach him, his crude bombs, and his theatrical makeup as an extension of a deeply troubled soul. I didn't see any other choice.

But would that mean going along with whatever the conductor asked? What if my actions put others in danger? I bared my teeth. Hated every passing moment of my new reality.

My phone buzzed.

Almost time to act, naughty knot.

Excited?

6

Alec McCullers inserted the digital card into its port and began uploading the photos to his desktop. His computer's fan kicked into high gear, its whir filling the *Trenton Telegraph* office. He stared at the blue progress bar and found himself once again sinking into the unfathomable fact that he was living out the most significant story he'd ever report on.

But he wasn't reporting.

He was a character in the plot.

Desks ran along the walls of the *Trenton Telegraph*'s newsroom, and four spacers in the middle of the room created four more workstations for reporters and editors. Every other reporter and editor had gone home or was at the game, covering the big NCAA matchup that evening. But the newsroom seemed so trite now. News stories were just things happening. Sports were just teams playing. Features were just people talking.

Alec had the lone office in the newsroom, little more than a closet but still adorned with an "Editor in Chief" plaque on the door. The fact that there *was* a door to close was the real perk. He could shut out the newsroom while designing tomorrow's edition of the *Telegraph*, for instance, a big deal considering that if other reporters or an advisor caught a glimpse of it, he'd get grilled with a hundred questions and pried for details he couldn't divulge, like, "Where are the A1 stories? Why haven't you laid them out yet? What are you going to do? The deadline is 1:00 a.m."

Alec had already decided that, should anyone ask, he'd simply tell them that the front page would be an all-NCAA basketball spread, ridiculous as that would be considering that Trenton hadn't even qualified for the tournament.

The truth was, he didn't know what story was going to lead. All Alec knew was that the conductor had told him to wait for the story and layout to arrive in his inbox. His hands were tied.

Nobody knew the conductor existed. There'd be no reinforcements coming. If Alec truly wanted to escape the conductor's wrath, either he'd have to play along—which felt like serving as an accomplice to some forthcoming tragedy—or he could do what he did best: talk to people, find the facts, and somehow produce positive change. But he hadn't been sure what that might look like.

Until the conductor had given him the assignment to photograph Trenton University police officer Markus Haas.

Haas had been a local hero around Trenton ever since he'd saved those girls from that horrific basement, and he was a member of SWAT now to boot. If there was anybody who could escape the string and put the conductor behind bars, he hoped it'd be Haas. Haas provided a path of resistance to the conductor. He had a reputation as the officer you liked even if he were citing you. He was real with students, never tried to shame them, and genuinely pushed them to be better human beings. From everything Alec had read about Haas, it seemed the officer knew who he was and what he stood for—not the type to cower in fear. So if the conductor pressed hard against him, Haas would push back.

Right?

No matter the plan, Alec knew the first thing he could do was try to warn Haas about the text he'd received from the conductor earlier that day:

> Tomorrow's the big day, Alec—we're going to
> kill Markus Haas.

Janet understood a couple of things about twenty-something males. First, they were like every other human: self-preservation was of utmost importance. If this student journalist—Alec McCullers, editor in chief of the *Trenton Telegraph*, according to staff listings—was indeed caught in the string, he'd be scared, secretive, and wanting to come out the other end without anyone knowing he'd served as an accomplice in the conductor's schemes.

She knocked and entered the newsroom. This was a binary situation, 1 or 0. Either Alec was a part of the string and she'd make him confess it, or he wasn't and she could grab one of the papers and leave.

Bright overhead lights filled the space with a warm glow, and a refrigerator in a mini kitchen nook hummed. The place reeked of Doritos and gum. No one was at any of the desks along the rim of the main room.

"Hello?" she said.

A chair squeaked and a door around the corner creaked open. The young man she'd seen taking photos earlier peeked out, holding a coffee mug. He definitely recognized her from before. "May I help you?" He took a sip but was clearly attempting to hide his trembling mouth.

Janet wasn't going to deal with any pleasantries. "Feeling tightly wound? Like someone's dangling you on the end of their string?"

Alec choked on his coffee. Half of the java fell back onto him while the other half splattered on the floor. He yelped in pain and his eyes morphed into hellfire. "What's wrong with you?"

"He's got you, I know it."

Alec strung several obscenities together and ended with, "Why not just ask?"

"Sorry." She wiped down his collared shirt with the back of her hand. "I needed to know and there isn't an easy way of asking."

"Well, you know now. What do you want? You're going to get us killed." He glanced out the newsroom's third-story windows overlooking campus. "Get in here."

They stepped into his postage stamp office and shut the door.

Janet crossed her arms. "This necessary?"

Alec's eyes grew large. "He's *crazy*. We're three stories up with maybe two vantage points that can even see into this office, and it feels like he's crawling up my back. Are we talking about the same person?"

"You're right." Janet sat in the chair she'd wheeled in. "He's everywhere. I've experienced that truth firsthand, unfortunately. But I don't think he tracked me here. I've been as stealthy as possible."

Alec pushed aside his chair and sat on the floor with his

back to the wall. He rested his arms on his knees and looked as though he hadn't breathed in a month.

She needed to remember that this kid had likely been through hell too. "I'm sorry. I know the power games he plays. I saw you snapping photos and my gut screamed, because you looked just like the face I've stared at in the mirror every day since that white-faced psychopath told me he'd kill my sister if I didn't do what he said. You're the first I've found that I wasn't assigned to. Thought if I tracked you down . . ." She put her hands to her head, trying to find and say the right words. "Maybe we could do something to stop him."

Alec looked up, but his eyes were absent. "I reached out to another too."

"Who?"

"The guy you almost killed."

"You talked with Haas?"

"Not really. I slipped the fire department guys a note to give to him. I'm shooting the game tonight, so I told him to come—that I'd find him. I gotta warn him. Conductor says he's going to kill him."

"And?"

"And what?"

"A bomb exploded in his truck—you think he won't know he's being targeted? What's your plan after you meet him?"

Alec squinted. "A psycho is making me take blackmail photos, publish God only knows what, and creeping on my phone while I'm trying to pass classes. I've barely had time to think. This cop is a local hero and knows how to shoot guns. I figured he could take it from there."

"He's more than a university cop, he's part of the city's SWAT team."

"I know."

"Then you know he can vouch for what's going on and get actual law enforcement involved." She said it more to clarify her own thinking than to inform Alec.

Concern filled Alec's eyes.

"What?"

He showed her the conductor's text. "What am I supposed to do with that? The conductor went from 'photograph this' to 'we're killing someone' as if there was no great leap between those two things."

Janet pursed her lips. "We have to warn him. Tonight. Then get him to contact law enforcement, something higher up."

Alec suddenly looked uneasy. "I know. We have to. And I'm not saying we shouldn't." He leaned toward Janet. "But if we screw up, then it'll be a nightmare. Everybody's nightmare. If Haas contacts the FBI, CIA, whatever—what if they investigate? The conductor will do terrible things to us all and get away with it. He's not going to sit around when he knows someone's looking for him. But if we come up with a plan that keeps things *contained*, well . . . maybe he won't see it coming. Maybe we can stop him."

"So you *do* have a plan. Or at least the reasoning for one."

"I guess so."

She jutted her chin. "Then I'm in, at least until we contact Haas. If he has a way of getting authorities involved quietly, that's what we do. Otherwise . . ." She stood. "I'm going to that game and will find Haas. He'll be expecting *someone* to approach him, and better me than you. You have to wear your badge and take photos. I can blend in with the crowd, wear the colors, play the fangirl—whatever." It wasn't the most convincing argument, but she trusted herself far more than a student she'd just met to contact Haas.

He flicked one of his wrists. "What do I do then? How can I help?"

"Look for the conductor, strange things, people who could be members of the string, I don't know. He's been planning for this game. He'll be there. So get your photos—but not of the game. Look for him and others in his string. I spotted you easily enough."

Alec's face scrunched. "ESPN is here tonight, so there's more access points to place cameras. I might be able to get 360 shots—live, even."

"Video of every face in the building? Do it. All we need is a face, a build, anything to go off of. The moment we identify him, he loses power." She smiled angrily. "And he'll *hate* that."

"And after you confront Haas—you thought this through?" Alec said.

"Of course I haven't. I wasn't sure what was going to happen five minutes ago. But hopefully I can do more of what we're doing now."

"Which is?"

"Strangling the conductor with his own precious string."

7

Boy band lyrics belted from her five-year-old daughter—
something about love, a leap, and "horsies from the sky,"
though Stephanie highly questioned the validity of that last
line—and she found herself amused. She rubbed another dish
dry and peeked into the living area as Alexa played on.

Isabella raised her teacup and crescendoed at the apex of
the song.

Not an hour went by without ten different forms of passive
entertainment in the Banks home.

Stephanie grinned and scooped a spoonful of yogurt and
chia seeds into her mouth. "All right, missy." She turned to
Tilly, who was entertaining herself in her high chair in the
middle of the kitchen. Stephanie picked her up and gave her
a good sniff. "No poopies to interrupt Mama's workout? High
five, kid."

She hauled Tilly into the living room and set her in the
playpen. Isabella saw what was up and immediately engaged

her protest face. "Do you have to do Jillian today? I'm having tea."

"Bella, you're not having tea," Stephanie said, rolling out her yoga mat. "You're experiencing some sort of mosh pit in which tea is the new lighter." She turned on the television and navigated to the on-demand workout. "And yes, Mama has to do Jillian shreds every day if she wants to fit into her date-night dresses."

Isabella's eyes widened. "Is tonight date night with Mr. Markus?"

Stephanie dipped her chin and smiled. "No, Miss Crush Much, yesterday was date night, but Mama doesn't want to scare Mr. Markus away by having too many date nights—because she really likes your tea-party friend."

"Me too," Bella said.

About twenty minutes into her workout, right about the time sweat declared war on her deodorant, she felt the need to call Markus. She hadn't heard from him today, which felt . . . odd? It was no big deal, but she'd just grown used to the daily text or quick call. She liked that about Markus. He was invested without being pushy, good to her and her kids, thoughtful, and . . . yes, sexy.

He wanted more commitment in their relationship, she knew that. But she couldn't give that to him, not yet. Not after her failed marriage and the monster her husband had turned out to be, and her new faith. She didn't know if she could trust a man again.

Stephanie sighed. She wanted to at least hear his voice today, that's all. No biggie. Grabbing a towel, she wiped the sweat from the back of her neck and looked around until she spotted her phone on the table.

Just as she was reaching for it, the doorbell rang. Stephanie groaned. Maybe that was the universe's way of saying, *Don't pursue him if you're not ready yourself.*

"I'll get it!" Isabella shouted from the downstairs bathroom. Tilly started to fuss.

"No you won't, I can smell you swinging your feet in there." Stephanie covered her mouth. Hopefully the door person had just dropped a package and scrammed. She grabbed Tilly and headed for the door.

Upon opening it, Stephanie leaned back in surprise, Tilly tucked close to her neck. "Cody?"

"Hey, Steph." His hands were linked behind his back.

She tilted her head at him. Had she just heard solemnness in his voice? This was not the posture and cadence of Cody Caulkins.

"Mind if I come in?"

Now she wondered if he was okay and if she should text Markus. "Of course, come in. Alexa, play John Mayer."

"Playing *Requiem* by Mozart," the device responded.

"She never hears me right," Steph said.

They sat in the living room and Stephanie turned on a couple of lamps.

Isabella poked her head in from the kitchen, chin tucked close to her collarbone.

"Come here, Oh Curious One. It's Mr. Markus's best friend, Sir Cody."

"Sir?" Cody whispered in response, the tension easing from his face.

"Of course, Sir Cody—we treat our law enforcement with the utmost respect around here. Isn't that right, Bella?"

Isabella blushed a smile and sat on the couch next to Stephanie. *My goodness, this one was smitten with boys with badges.*

Wait. There were roses on the coffee table. Where'd they come from? "Hey, did you bring me my favorite flowers?" Stephanie picked them up, gave them a long whiff, then scrunched her brows at Cody. "Is everything okay?"

"Does he like you?" Isabella butted in.

"Quiet now," Stephanie said.

"Oh yes, everything's fine." Cody chuckled and turned to Isabella. "And I do like your mama—just not the same way Mr. Markus does." He grabbed one of the roses and handed it to the little girl. "These actually come from *him*, not me."

"Does Mr. Markus love Mama?"

The question hit Stephanie right in the stomach. She knew she was falling for Markus, but hearing those words still broadsided her.

"He does love her," Cody said, cranking up his solemnness again.

"Okay," Stephanie said, shooting to her feet. "We have poopy alert. Excuse me a second." She repositioned Tilly in her arms and headed toward the bathroom. "Whoo-wee, we've got a winner."

Stephanie shut the door and locked it. "Sorry, Tilly," she whispered, setting the toddler on the bath mat. "You smell fine, but something out there *doesn't*." She reached into her back pocket—she seriously needed to text Markus and find out what was going on.

She clamped her eyes shut. She'd left her phone in the living room.

Well, might as well roll with it. "Good girl, Tilly," she said loudly. Stephanie shrugged as if to tell Tilly sorry. "Clean as a whistle."

She opened the door to find Isabella forcing a teacup into

Cody's hands. She walked to the playpen and set down Tilly. "Isabella, would you please twirl the animals above Sissy?"

Bella responded with a look most girls would serve up had they been forced to end a tea party that was just getting started.

"No pouty lip, missy." She whisked her hand at the air. "Tut, tut—right now."

Isabella's shoulders and lower lip drooped, but she obeyed.

Stephanie turned back to Cody, who was now standing, and mentally cracked her knuckles.

"I'm sorry, it wasn't my place to say that," Cody said, still quiet.

"Cody, would you cut the crap for a minute? I can't even look at you, you're so funeral processional right now."

This remark seemed to kick in some of the normal Cody. "Sorry, Steph, I just didn't realize how bad I am at this."

"There." Stephanie spread out both arms. "What's *this*? Why are you here and why are there roses on my coffee table?"

He stared at her, trying to talk but not quite able to do so.

"Out with it."

He breathed deeply. Smiled in frustration. "I know about what's going on with you and Haas."

Stephanie flinched. "Going on?"

"Yeah, you know. Fighting, arguing, things not going well—I don't know, Haasy wasn't specific. He just told me to deliver flowers, and I thought I'd give it a personal touch by reminding you how great you are together or *something*, but then I found out that I suck at doing that exact thing and . . . that's about it. Apparently."

Stephanie grinned and shook her head. "I don't know *what* you are talking about, but now I have so many questions." She patted the couch. "Sit, sit, normal Cody."

They both sat.

"What gave you the idea that we're not doing well?" Stephanie's curiosity meter was about to pop out of her chest.

"Haasy."

She pursed her lips. Wasn't buying it. "As in, he was having a hard day and you assumed it had something to do with *us*?"

"No. I mean he just told me that you two are on the rocks."

She involuntarily recoiled and found herself staring at the floor, searching her mind for anything she could have said or done to make Markus feel that way. "Nothing," she said absently. "Nothing's wrong. I can be insensitive at times, but I wouldn't have been able to sleep last night if we weren't okay. What did he say?"

"You weren't just texting him like an hour ago?"

"No."

Now Cody looked pensive and focused, suddenly deep in thought. Up until today she'd seen only one Cody: brash, arrogant, and always talkative about himself, his car, or his most recent fling. Then she'd been introduced to a shy and awkward Cody only minutes ago. And now here was a third Cody—the one Markus frequently mentioned in defense of his friend, but one Stephanie had never seen. This was the county sheriff's detective. And his serious expression nearly made him unrecognizable.

"Look," Stephanie said, rising to her feet, "I'm going to call him right now."

Cody's eyes locked on her, and in all that same seriousness he said, "That's nice of you, Stephanie. Please do grab me some tea."

Stephanie stared at him, dumbfounded.

Cody jutted his chin toward the kitchen. "Please, tea."

Whoever had planted the explosive was tying Haas's hands somehow. What better way to do that than with his love for Steph and the girls? And in response, what better way for Haas to help Steph and the girls—Cody eyed the flowers—than to send Cody to them immediately?

Haas's line started ringing. Cody should have known something was wrong. He *had* picked up that much. But Haas was good. He'd rolled with their conversation seamlessly, even though now it was so clear to Cody. What had he said again?

Things aren't good with Steph.

I don't know where she's at right now.

It's complicated.

If she's not home, give me a call.

Haas had handed him everything he'd needed to make these decisions right now. Cody wouldn't let him down.

"Cody," Haas said, voice laced with worry.

"Hey there, my brother, I got your message," Cody said, upbeat and confident. "Your flowers have done been delivered, and Steph and the girls, bless their hearts, are making me tea right now as I rest my heels on the coffee table. Thinking I'll even stay for dinner. When you coming back?"

"Soon as I can," Markus breathed. Relief was evident in his voice.

His friend wanted to ask more, Cody could tell that much, but was holding back in case someone was listening. He stood and walked toward the living room window. Peered outside. "That's good, Haasy, because I'm feeling like Texas sheet cake tonight. And I *will* eat all of it if you're not back by dessert." Would be nice to get a distress confirmation from Haas, something more concrete than just his tone of voice. "Not every day you're the victim of shish kebabs gone bad." Cody let out a chuckle for good measure. "Renfroe is gonna come down hard. You, uh—do you think you're in deep you-know-what?" There, he'd given him the question. This was it.

Behind him, Alexa came to life without anyone having given her a command. "Playing 'Every Breath You Take' by The Police."

Cody turned toward the white cylinder as music played softly. Red dots popped up all over the living room, entering through various windows. For a moment, they remained perfectly still, at least half a dozen of them.

"Stay calm," he whispered.

Stephanie's expression twisted in shock and horror as she tucked Isabella and Tilly into a tight ball.

Mother of mercy, what has Haas gotten himself into?

The red dots suddenly organized themselves, swaying and jumping in sync like musical notes accompanying the song.

Haas said something on the other end of the line, but Cody found himself unable to understand, his focus jumbled as the singer crooned about stalking every step he took.

A shiver ran up his spine as the first chorus finished on what felt like a promise.

"I'll be watching you."

8

SATURDAY, 5:55 P.M.

When Cody hung up on him, a text notification popped up.

> Good friend, that Cody.

> Clever, sending him to check on your squeeze.

> A violation of my rules, no?

My heart raced. The conductor was watching Steph and the girls, and he'd somehow put the fear of God into Cody. I had heard it in my friend's final words before he'd hung up, and I found myself pleading before God again. For Steph, for the girls, and for Cody.

I stared at my phone, thinking through how I should respond.

The conductor was texting again.

> You're a curious one, Haas—never took you for the guy to put others in danger.

67

How you'll make things interesting.

Go to the game. That's all.

The game? That's where the mystery note had told me to go. Coincidence—or coordinated trap? It seemed like the perfect lure: go to the game to get information; go to the game to get your assignment.

I slid my phone into my pocket, clutching it too hard. I needed to be smart and strategic in my responses. Spilling emotion rarely gave an advantage.

I hustled to the armory and chose the Glock 9mm. Then I loaded the inside of my jacket with extra clips and rustled up the rest of my gear: flashlight, Taser, pepper spray, baton, boot knife.

The door leading from headquarters to the department's garage closed behind me. I found the lone available patrol car not already in use for the game. The mounted AR-15 was ready and loaded. I drove out of the garage and turned toward the gymnasium.

Dusk had fallen. Red light shone from hundreds of brake lights easing toward the parking lot, which had already overflowed into the shuttle parking lots.

I crawled over the curb and onto the red bricks, making my way between buildings and toward the gymnasium. The pace wasn't any faster than walking, as hordes of fans carrying foam fingers, team towels, and most likely a hidden alcoholic beverage or two marched toward the NCAA showdown. I flipped my lights on, strobes swirling, but that only persuaded a handful of fans to give more space to my car. They were caught up in basketball frenzy, smiling the way one does when they've left every care in the world at home. A dressed-up madman triggering a bomb under their feet was the last thought on their minds.

Heads turned toward me one by one, and it occurred to me that any one of these seemingly harmless spectators could be *him*. Or controlled by him.

I found myself studying the multitude of faces. That guy looked apprehensive, didn't he? What about the woman who'd glanced back at my squad car multiple times? Was she drawn to the strobe, in need of help, or just worried that a car was making its way through a sea of people? Anyone here could have planted that explosive in my 4Runner. Anyone here could have scouted Steph's place weeks in advance in preparation for what had scared Cody to his core. Anyone. I could practically feel a transformation in my eyes as paranoia crawled over my vision.

I was responsible for the safety of every one of these faces, yet one of them might be a danger to everyone.

Long before I'd ever considered wearing a university badge, this was why I had chosen my career path. It wasn't just about keeping people safe. It was about keeping people *free*—unhinged from anyone who'd try to enforce their will on them. In this case, the people of Trenton University.

My people.

I parked and worked my way through the crowd. Light shone down on us from the newly renovated face of the gymnasium. The all-glass entrance featured high-performance LED lights that served as a beacon for basketball enthusiasts trudging their way toward the first tip-off of the NCAA's shootout.

My badge would get me in, but I couldn't just supersede

security. So I picked a ticketing line. No reason to rush through and risk drawing more attention to myself. He was already watching.

A female attendant inside the ticketing booth, bundled up and no older than twenty, leaned out the window and greeted fans, regardless of their team affiliation, with an unusual joy and brightness—not just the ones closest to the booth, but those eight or nine deep. "Hello, sir, how are you? You look like the captain on that movie where the boat sinks." Then to another person, "Hello, ma'am, how's your evening?" And she still somehow managed to take tickets and stamp hands.

This was the person I needed to see right now. For every psychopath hell-bent on ruining lives, there were thousands more like this girl, giving smiles and genuine warmth.

"And you, sir—love the bipartisan look," she hollered to me.

I glanced down at my uniform, forgetting I was one of the few not wearing a team's color. I nodded at the girl.

When I reached the window, she looked at me from head to toe, then toe to head. "You are *rocking* that uniform—I need one for Halloween. But with a gorilla head, you know? Like the movie!" She tilted her head as if transported to a Marilyn Monroe photo shoot. "I think I'll look ravishing with a beard."

I allowed a small grin.

"Careful, Rosetta here likes older guys," the ticketing person opposite her said.

Rosetta gripped the windowsill and stretched her leg out to kick the guy. "Zip it, we're professionals."

I held up my badge.

"Perks, huh?" she said, waving me through and handing me a flyer.

Actually, no. Chief had purposefully kept me off duty this evening. Renfroe would never admit such—he'd said he'd drawn names out of a hat for those interested in a courtside view of the tournament—but I knew better. Renfroe didn't like me, trite as that sounded. He'd hired me, but only I knew the real reason why.

After I had butted up against unwritten rules and established norms within the department, most of which favored a run-out-the-clock mentality, the chief had become distant and hard. The latest example happened to be the NCAA game, for which the chief waited until tickets had sold out before informing the department who'd be on tournament duty. This ensured that no one in the department could attend the tourney if they'd waited for but didn't receive the assignment.

I wish I'd handled things better as a rookie in the department. Nobody liked the ambitious greenhorn with rigid opinions on policies that had been shaped over decades.

I continued into the lobby. Had someone led me here to help, or was it all just part of the conductor's game? Trophies were displayed prominently, and vendors were buzzing with pregame sales of T-shirts, memorabilia, and all kinds of salt and sugar. Normally I'd enjoy experiencing something new and exciting like the NCAA tournament kickoff game. But right now, all the smiles, fandom, and squeaking of basketball shoes in one overly crowded room looked and sounded violent.

Nobody knew. Except *him*. And he could be any person here.

What was I supposed to do? I didn't have a ticket to sit in the grandstands, and I technically wasn't on duty, so there was no official assignment for me. The moment other officers spotted me—both university and city—they'd think I'd gone behind the chief's back and used my uniform to get a free courtside ticket.

My pocket buzzed. I pulled out my phone and stared at it.

Got your bracket filled out?

Go to the press box.

Convince Chief to put away his gambling long enough to be honored at center court.

Was a big night for him before you came along—now it's gotten bigger.

What did that mean? Why did the conductor want the chief at center court? How would this even be possible with the game set to start in twenty minutes? I glanced at the flyer handed to me at the ticketing gate. A basic itinerary revealed only one item yet to occur before tip-off: "Special Presentation." Something was already planned. But what?

Every fiber of my being rejected the idea of doing *anything* for the conductor. But my decisions now would determine whether or not something terrible happened to Steph, Cody, and the girls. I had to operate with that assumption. I couldn't live with myself if anything happened to them.

Clock's ticking, Markus.

You haven't so much as moved a muscle.

I jerked my head up and surveyed the lobby, searching for any anomaly in the colorful crowd. How close was he? Manning a booth, standing in line, waving a foam hand, trying to find his seat? Or did he simply have eyes on me electronically?

I walked briskly through one of the double doors leading into the gymnasium, where I assumed I'd find the entrance to the press box. *Where are you? What do you have planned?*

Energy buzzed as concession workers pleaded their case for overpriced peanuts and cotton candy. Players were running through pregame warm-ups, knocking down jump shots and executing layups. The speakers blasted the Chicago Bulls' electrifying theme song, which years ago had made Michael Jordan seem untouchable.

I spotted a Trenton police officer and quickly turned away. It was Mike Mitchell. I wondered where his buddy Clint Hopkins was. The two brownnosers usually traveled together.

"Haas?"

I turned around. It was Hopkins.

"Didn't know you'd made the cut for tonight," he said. Why wasn't he glaring at me? Why weren't his words dipped in sarcasm and topped with malicious intent? He'd spoken as though he were almost relieved to see me.

I didn't have time to find out right now. "One of the lucky ones, I guess. Excuse me." I walked away and headed toward the aisle leading up to the press box.

"Haas," Hopkins called out.

I turned back.

"I'm not going to say anything."

His sudden shift in charity felt about as natural as taking a snow sled to California's Death Valley. Either this was an olive branch extended because Hopkins was enjoying getting to cover the game, or it was a tough guy's cry for help as a member of the string.

I gave him a nod and continued toward the press box.

University Police Chief Jack Renfroe sprawled his notes in front of him like clues from an evidence box. Two twenty-ounce bottles of cola, a jar of peanuts, four fun-sized candy bars, and three separate vending machine bags of chips stood guard over it all, ready to quench any distracting tinge of hunger or thirst. You could always find an edge in the numbers, and he expected to find those edges even in the final minutes before tip-off.

The ESPN crew had relegated him to this booth, which was more or less known as the storage closet of the press box, with countless boxes stacked in the corner and a trash can filled with a potpourri of rubbish and foul, molding pizza. But he wasn't going to let that ruin his night.

He put on his headphones to tune in to the live podcast about to start, "NCAA Gunslingers Pro." He reached for his radio absently and muttered into the receiver, "Everybody excited?"

One by one, his chosen officers responded:

"Oh yeah."

"Great view, Boss."

"Thanks for the 'work.'"

They sounded more relaxed with him than usual. And why shouldn't they? This was an assignment of a lifetime.

"Remember, whoever guesses the winner and final score accompanies me to the big Celestial show tomorrow. Was harder to get tickets to that than tonight."

A smattering of responses returned as Renfroe reached for his minibar-sized bottle of Jack. He poured the rest of it into his cola and realized he'd need something else to eat. There were only fifteen minutes left until tip-off.

He stood and opened the door into the spacious standing area of the press box, then locked it behind him. He furrowed his brow at the sight of the officer walking toward him. Markus Haas, whom he'd purposely left off duty tonight. That overzealous rookie had actually used his uniform to get into the game? If this wasn't leverage against him, Renfroe didn't know what was.

"Haas," he said with a friendly question underneath.

"Chief, listen, we need to talk."

They both stopped at the midpoint of the press box. Everyone else was much closer to the viewing area, distracted by the pregame host, who'd just started announcing the evening's agenda from midcourt.

Renfroe didn't like taking commands, especially not from an insubordinate. "I've got a national event I need to protect, Haas, and quite frankly, *I* need to talk—not *we*. What are you doing here, in uniform, when you're off duty? Disappointing use of the badge."

"I know how this looks, but there's a reason I'm here. Can you talk a minute—in private?"

Renfroe checked his watch and shook his head. "No, I can't. I'm not done with my pregame checklist and tip-off is in less than fifteen now. We'll talk tomorrow—about a lot more than freeloading the tournament. You exploded a grill and put students in danger on a day when the university is trying to *impress* parents? Haas, you couldn't have picked a worse time to demand anything." He adjusted his cap. "Tomorrow." He started past Haas, but the junior officer put his hand out, blocking the path to the exit. Renfroe could feel his face burn. "Haas, what part of—"

A freckle-faced press box attendant wearing a red staff shirt interrupted them. "Sorry to interrupt, but they're trying to get, well . . ." He pointed down toward midcourt.

Renfroe tuned in to what was being announced over the loudspeakers.

"*Aaaaand*—we got him, folks. So as the honorary chief and other special guests make their way to midcourt for this surprise honor, I'll step aside so that your homegrown Celestial Orchestra, which started its ascent right here in Trenton nearly twenty years ago, can get this tournament started with a *baaaaaaaaang*!"

I'll be darned.

Renfroe knew the globally famous group had touched down locally earlier this week and would be performing on campus the next night—an extremely spendy event that he'd scored tickets to, thanks to Anita Postma and Franklin Iseman. But playing at the NCAA opening game? Impressive.

Renfroe looked back to his press box suite. Could he get back up here in time? He needed to try. That was a big spotlight to miss down there.

"Kid," he said to Freckles, "I have to get down to the court, but I lost a bet and need to make good on some promises." He pulled out his wallet and produced two twenty-dollar bills. "Go to concessions and grab as much of that garbage as you can in as much variety, got it? Just leave it by the box suite at the end there."

The kid nodded and turned straight for the press box exit.

Renfroe noted that Haas was still standing there. "And you—go home."

But the young officer stepped directly in front of him. "Sir, I don't have time to explain, but you can't go down there."

Renfroe cursed loud enough to draw glances from others settling in for the pregame entertainment. He grabbed his radio. "Mitchell, Hopkins—get up here."

"Look, the explosion wasn't an accident. It's part of a game that someone's playing on campus, possibly deadly—and it's being played tonight, right now at midcourt."

Being a fiercely loyal man, Renfroe never forgot those who'd attacked him. "Out of my way, Haas." He pushed the officer aside. "I want it all in a report before I'm at my desk tomorrow—and these details better be in there, because right now it sounds like grasping at straws."

The press box door swung open and in walked Officers Mitchell and Hopkins. "Officer Haas needs to cool off immediately." Renfroe held up his radio. "Be advised that Officer Haas is not to enter this building for the rest of the evening." He clicked off. "That reminds me. Medic said you have a concussion"—Renfroe undid Haas's badge from his uniform—"rendering you unable to do your job until docs check you out." He stepped back and held out his hands. "Weapons."

"Chief, you're making—"

Renfroe gripped Haas's arm and leaned in so close that their noses almost touched. "Weapons," he growled, struggling not to make a scene.

Haas handed over his Glock and Taser.

Renfroe scowled. "Get out of here."

For the first time, Haas shut up as his colleagues—one of them appearing amused, the other concerned—escorted him out.

Renfroe shook his head. He adjusted his collar, took a deep breath, and started toward midcourt.

Alec McCullers found himself leaning forward with anticipation in his seat despite having run to the restroom mere minutes ago to puke from sheer anxiety. He'd dreamed of attending a Celestial Orchestra performance for years, but it had always felt out of reach both financially and geographically. Now he had a media pass for front-row viewing, but he couldn't take in a single moment of joy.

The conductor was here. The *string* was here.

He couldn't be sure of it. He just felt it.

Alec raised his camera. He already had an idea of the shot he wanted for the sports section of the *Telegraph*'s next-day edition, but you could never bet on capturing it, so contingencies were key. Besides, the more he kept his face in his camera, the less the conductor—who surely had eyes at the game—would suspect his real motive tonight.

To help break the string.

The Celestial Orchestra's presence, which hadn't been announced, was worth the hiked ticket price to the game alone. Alec had grown up listening to their music and had never stopped. It was the kind of music that made you feel like you were a part of something transcendent.

The fact that musical prominence had descended upon the university while Alec was being threatened and controlled by a man who called himself the conductor was not lost on him. But what connection could there be between his favorite musical group, which stood for all that was right in this world, and a psychopathic maniac?

The orchestra marched down separate aisles in the stadium, all of them in sync. They flowed into formation, half on the right, half on the left. One of the group's runners unfurled a giant purple carpet down the center aisle, leading toward three purple circles at the front. The orchestra suddenly burst into a rendition of the *Star Wars* throne room theme song. All their heads turned in, awaiting the guests of honor.

"Would our revered patrons—the ones who all those years ago paved the way for us on our day of destiny—please make your way to the carpet: University Police Chief Jackson Renfroe, Vice President for Business and Financial Affairs Franklin Iseman, and Vice President for Academic and Student Life Anita Postma. We have in store for you something . . ." The announcer paused, letting silence stir the crowd. "Breathtaking."

The three trickled down toward the court, the most noticeable one being Renfroe, who was impossible to miss in his uniform and throwback police cap. His cheeks were flushed and his eyes smiled as he led the way through the orchestra tunnel, which remained in perfect sync.

"Please take your stand on the carpets, for tonight your feet shall trod only on rugs of royalty!"

They each took up their position on the trio of circles.

Alec kept clicking the trigger on his camera as fast as he could.

"Now, ladies and gentlemen, we ask that you take your seats for the next few moments, as things are about to get *dark*."

Suddenly, the gymnasium went black, save for three spotlights focused on the honored guests.

Out of the corner of his eye, Alec saw cameras hovering through the air. A fourth light shone, brightening the large televisions high above. The base of the televisions detached and floated downward to reveal a man standing behind a music stand, his hands behind his back. The platform slid to just above the hoop in front of the honored guests, all of whom were now grinning ear to ear.

Alec felt as though his inner fanboy might pop out of his eyeballs. *Wow, this is actually happening.*

The orchestra's brainchild and champion needed no introduction—his presence alone spoke volumes. Ivan Mikolaev,
the man of humble and tragic beginnings, moved his hands
with the intensity of a cheetah and the grace of a dove. He
motioned for the orchestra to continue without his lead. His
smile widened as proud and big as one could achieve without
showing a single tooth. Arms swung wide, he looked down at
the three before him, as if to say, "Look at those who honor
you; behold those who thank you."

The crowd erupted in applause and whistling elation.

A text came in, and Alec lifted his eyes from his camera.

Yes, Mr. Camera, wait for it.

Alec scanned the crowd, his gut clenching. How many had
their phones out, texting at this exact moment? So many taking
selfies or smiling down at their phones.

Ivan motioned for the guests to behold the thunderclaps
of praise being heaped upon them from every direction. One
by one, the faces of the honored three lit with a wonder that
could only be achieved when the recipients hadn't thought
they'd done anything worthy of such praise.

Chief Renfroe removed his cap and raised it to the right,
to the left. He turned back to the two rows of the orchestra
behind him and nodded at them as well.

Hands softly gripped Alec's shoulders out of the blackness
behind him. Alec flinched and tried to turn his head, but the
person stopped him.

"I saw what happened in the courtyard, who you met at
the *Telegraph*—what your plan is with the cop," a male voice
whispered. "The conductor already sent a text for a rule bro-

ken, said someone's gonna pay. Maybe *you*." The stranger's grip tightened. "Play Russian roulette with my family again, I'll make sure it's not the clown who kills you."

With that, the whisperer released Alec.

It took him several moments before he worked up the courage to look back. He rubbed his throbbing neck while Ivan continued his speech.

"These three before you opened the doors to something this world has never seen, all by way of stepping into a risk on an ambitious performer"—his booming voice sputtered and weakened—"and this otherworldly ensemble of talent before you."

Ivan grabbed his chest and bent slightly at the knees.

Something wasn't right.

Something was happening to him.

9

Pleading my case to coworkers who I knew despised me didn't seem like a helpful course of action as Mitchell and Hopkins escorted me out of the gymnasium. People being escorted out of anywhere always pleaded their case—and they always sounded like fools.

But Hopkins had given me reason to think that he may be caught in the string. I needed to lean into that now. If the conductor proved to be half as dangerous as he seemed, then tens of thousands of people were at risk.

We stepped out of the gymnasium's side entrance into the biting cold.

"This is weird even for you, Haas." A gust of wind tousled Mitchell's hair. "But I'd be lying if I said I wasn't enjoying it."

He shoved me and I stumbled forward onto the red bricks. My fists clenched involuntarily.

I wanted to shout. To *scream*. To burst back into the gymnasium and stop the chief from walking into a deadly trap—not only for Renfroe but perhaps for every person in attendance.

"Let's go," Mitchell said to Hopkins. "Chief's midcourt and it's gonna be awful."

"Sorry, Haas," Hopkins said.

They both turned back inside.

"Hey!" My mind was spinning as I tried to communicate the danger they were in.

Mitchell and Hopkins both glanced back at me. I focused on Hopkins. "Keep your eyes open—it's not safe. You know that, don't you?"

Hopkins stared back at me, eyebrows scrunched, pensive.

Mitchell smacked Hopkins's chest with the back of his hand. "You bet it's not safe—not with them dorm girls milling about. They'll swipe your gun right off your belt, isn't that right, Haas?"

Again with the references to that night that changed everything for me.

I stepped directly into Mitchell's space. "Let me tell you something." I looked at his left cheek, right cheek, forehead, refusing to make eye contact. I wanted him to know I was looking past whatever facade he'd barricaded himself behind. "Fear loves to hide—hates to be known. But it's got a weakness, a stench to it." I leaned closer. "You *reek* of it."

Mitchell pushed me and lunged toward me, fist cocked, but it was half-hearted. Hopkins, who now looked as though he were experiencing an awful dream, grabbed Mitchell from behind.

They were showing their hand.

"Those people are in danger." I pointed at the gymnasium. "You get that? Let's do something about it."

Hopkins looked to Mitchell.

Mitchell scoffed. "Neither of us know what you're talking

about, Haas, just like you don't know what you're talking about. If you're smart, you'll go home. You're drunk." Mitchell put a hand on Hopkins's back and herded him through the gymnasium side door. "You've done enough already," he whispered over his shoulder.

The door locked with a loud *click*. On the other side, Mitchell rebuked Hopkins, but his words were too muffled to make out.

The conductor had gotten to them. I was sure of it. They were a part of it. And they were not going to go against the white-faced demon, fearing only God knew what.

I had always believed that, like passengers aboard a sinking ship staring at the life buoy, people paralyzed by fear like Hopkins and Mitchell would be the first to leap and take hold of freedom if given the choice at the right moment. But that wasn't happening here.

If I was right, then what had Mitchell meant by "you've done enough"? What did he know that I didn't? Had the conductor done something terrible because of my choices?

I needed to move.

Going back in the way I'd come wasn't an option, not with my colleagues on the lookout. But there were other entrances for vendors and shipments around the side of the building. Would anyone be there to let me through?

I rounded the building. The first door I came upon was closed. But water was pooled on the ground right outside as if a concessions worker had dumped it moments ago. I rattled the handle. Should I wait for someone to open the door or search for another way in?

Standing like a wall around the gymnasium were dozens of rhododendrons, and under each sat several softball-sized stones. If I didn't find a way inside on my first pass around the building, I could bust an office window.

The athletic director and coaches each had an office toward the back of the building. I could snatch a hat and one of the T-shirts in the athletic department, blend in, then search for the threat. I glanced at the time on my phone.

The game might last two hours, and I had about thirty or forty thousand suspects. Or half of that if the conductor were indeed male. But his high voice made me wonder if he were a girl trying to throw me off.

I continued along the side of the gymnasium—

"Hey," a voice said from behind me.

I turned to find a woman holding the door I'd tried opening. She looked to be a decade older than me, early forties, with stylish hair and wearing glasses under one of the team's hats. Pure business but decked out in basketball gear. She gazed at me as if she knew me.

Why wasn't her face registering?

She waved me to hurry inside. I stepped in and the door closed behind me.

We were standing in a hallway that served as a loading dock to the lobby. Boxes, crates, and chairs lined the walls, all of which emitted a musty smell.

"Thanks," I said. "I know you?"

"No need for pleasantries." The woman crossed her arms. "I know what's happening. I've been hiding in this garb"—she ran her hands down the sides of her jersey—"and followed you out. I'm Janet Blevins."

"Are we safe?"

"No idea, but I blended in then slipped away. What's done is done—we have to talk."

"The note—that was you."

She drew in a breath. "No, not me. But I know who left it for you and I took his place in finding you. First I need to tell you that I'm the one who dropped that package in your truck today."

"The tablet?"

"That's what it was? I thought I'd dropped off a bomb. Thank God. I'm sorry for looping you into his sick game. I had no choice."

Her directness surprised me. "No one's at fault but him."

She closed her eyes for a moment, appearing thankful for the response.

"I understand how dangerous and awkward this is." I glanced down the corridor. "Let's start with questions."

My abruptness seemed to awaken a lion in her. "Shoot," she said.

"How long has he been threatening you?"

"Four weeks."

"What are you doing for him?"

"I'm head of IT on campus. I've helped him spy on whomever he wants. He has eyes and ears everywhere because of me. Emails, texts, calls, purchases, secrets—he's been watching for a long time, much longer than when he pulled me in." She reached into her handbag and withdrew her cell. "Don't use one of these—he can hear and see it all."

"Is there an alternative?"

"I haven't been able to find one, not without him knowing. Nearly cost me my Ruby."

I squinted.

"My Labrador," she added.

"Were you followed to the game?"

"No clue. Any number of them could be tailing me . . . or you."

I nodded. "What's he holding against you?"

"My sister has cancer." Emotion crawled up her throat, but Janet composed herself. "He's threatened to *visit* her wing of the hospital. And not only that. He poisoned one of her nurses. I can't prove it, but he did—I went against him like I am now . . . and he did it." Her eyes seemed to be making a plea for trust. She wanted to know in this moment if she'd stuck her neck out to the right person.

"Understood." I peeked around her to see if anyone was lurking down the hallway. "I'm going to help you stop him and keep your sister safe. You're doing the right thing."

She nodded. "I believe that. But I've still got a question: Why did you get booted from the game by your own colleagues?"

How many eyes had I drawn while being escorted out? "He's holding people close to me and sent me here to get the chief to midcourt. I couldn't go with it. I think he's a target. And my two colleagues—they're a part of it, I'm sure of it, but *not* of our shared intention. At least not yet."

Images of Stephanie, Cody, and the girls cowering in a basement flashed in my mind, their eyes laced with fear as the conductor approached. I shook my head.

"Family?"

"Close enough." I checked my phone. No messages from the conductor yet.

Janet frowned and spoke softly. "What are their names?"

The fact that she wanted their names threw me off a bit. "Isabella and Tilly, five and two—daughters of my . . . other. Stephanie."

"It's not the end." The bite in her tone had returned. "I've butted against him. Twice, actually." Her lips quivered, showing bared teeth. "But he didn't hurt my sister after he said he would. He went for the nurse instead, then Ruby. His string means too much to him. If he needs you for it, he'll hit you where it hurts, but not always where it hurts most."

That raised a question: How badly did the conductor need me for his plot? Janet had a valuable skill set for his agenda. She could hack this and that and spy from behind a screen. But what did I offer that he couldn't replace? He may not be as lenient with me.

The monster had given us both an initial free pass. But Janet's second offense almost cost her a pup that, while not her own flesh and blood, still meant the world to her. For my second offense, he'd gone straight for Steph and the girls—and I had no way of knowing whether or not Cody could keep them safe.

What would he do next, knowing I'd tried to warn the chief and was now conspiring with Janet?

I shook my head. Needed to focus on the action, the steps to take to stop the conductor. Anything else—giving in to him or fleeing town with the girls—was an illusion of a solution. The only way to win was to put an end to the string.

We needed to move fast.

I reached into my jacket pocket and withdrew the charred tablet. "Can you track whoever programmed this? It's the only lead I've got."

Janet's eyes went big. "Let me see."

My shoulders softened as I handed it to her. It wasn't me versus the conductor anymore. It was *us*. Janet was smart and may have already found a chink in the conductor's armor. Her skill set complemented my own. Together we'd stop him faster than either one of us could on our own.

"Who's the other?" I asked.

"Earlier today, one of the paper's photographers was taking shots of your truck after it happened. He looked so scared. I knew the look and confronted him. Alec McCullers. He's a part of it, the first I've found who I wasn't assigned to—here tonight, on our side now."

Janet's gumption was an incredible asset. She wasn't a woman in distress. She was a wolf looking for others to join her pack.

"But Alec told me something about you, something the conductor texted him. I trust I can tell you, and that you'll keep your wits about you."

I nodded.

"The conductor said he was going to kill you tomorrow and that Alec was going to help him."

My brows furrowed. Was this the retaliation, killing me? That would bring attention to the university and stir up an investigation. Unless what he had planned was set to go down soon.

"You're providing info to him. Where is he? How do you reach him?"

"If I knew he'd be dead already," she said, practically seething. She tapped her bag. "Just my cell."

The gymnasium erupted into continuous applause, too loud and boisterous for lineup introductions. Whatever was going on was exhilarating the crowd.

I blocked out the noise. "The conductor: any idea of age, ethnicity, height, weight?"

"High-pitched, pathetic tone. Maybe Caucasian but I'm not

sure. Height?" Her eyes looked as if they could cut through steel. "Small. A weak, tiny man. That's how I picture him. In reality, I have no idea." She looked at her heels, then back up at me. "But he's intelligent. I don't know if he's figured out that we're talking yet or that we're finding each other, but it's only a matter of time. We need to find him first. And frankly, that's why I came to you." She held up the tablet. "Maybe you already delivered."

It was a start. But only a start.

Observe.

I tried to focus on any strategic advantage we might have now that we were two instead of one—or three, depending on the student journalist. Janet offered technical help, I had the punch. But neither of us knew what the conductor looked like or how to find him.

Even so, no mastermind was perfect. He had to slip up somewhere, with someone.

"Well? What's the plan?"

I held up one finger. "OODA."

"Whoda?"

Before I could explain myself, an ear-piercing scream split the air, followed by a collective gasp from the fans.

Both of us turned toward the horrible echo ricocheting down the corridor.

"I have to go," I said. "It's him."

"Wait." I could tell she was searching for the right words. "I'll take the tablet to my office, second floor in the communications building. Where can I find you if I get something?" Her eyes popped open a little bigger. "Wait, give me your phone."

I did as she asked and she maneuvered some things around on it. "There. I can track your phone now."

I looked down at it skeptically. "Just like that?"

"I'm good."

From somewhere outside the stadium, the on-site ambulance's siren shrieked.

"Go, go," Janet said before sneaking out the door she'd used to let me in.

I took off and pushed open the door at the end of the hall, which spilled into the lobby. No other officers in sight, but the on-call paramedics were rushing toward the gymnasium. I followed them in.

Everyone in the grandstands was standing, most covering their mouths. But there wasn't mass hysteria, and nobody was sprinting toward the exits.

What had happened?

I followed their gazes to the court, where Renfroe sat, surrounded by a couple of high-level university officials—Franklin Iseman and Anita Postma, if I was remembering their names right. They were asking the chief questions.

One of the paramedics joined the three, shining a light into Renfroe's eyes. Behind the chief crouched a larger cluster of people, and that's where the rest of the medics were rushing.

The bunch broke open just enough for me to see Ivan Mikolaev, and my mind immediately did a double take. This was the popular leader of the Celestial Orchestra.

No, not leader. Conductor.

Alarms were blasting in my mind. Ivan, the famous conductor, in town at the same time a psychopath was parading himself around as the conductor?

Ivan was lying with his cheek pressed to the three-point line, motionless. Had he been shot? I couldn't spot any blood.

Above Ivan floated a platform. He must've fallen and landed directly on the chief.

I felt a buzz in my pocket.

I jogged back into the lobby. Brought the phone up from my side as I pushed through the exit into the bitter cold outside.

Naughty, naughty knot, Markus.

Franklin Iseman recognized an opportunity from a mile away. He also recognized that there were some people in this world you didn't mess with. But he'd never experienced these two absolutes battling for his attention at the same time and in equal measure.

Until now.

The opportunity: leverage the string for a truckload of money. The person not to mess with: the conductor—that much had been clear long before tonight. But after the circus that had just gone down in the gymnasium, Iseman was beginning to think that the conductor was even more disturbed than he'd imagined.

He glanced at the text he'd received after Ivan had fallen on the chief.

You feared that the opera had reached its end. But this was merely the prelude.

Down goes Ivan, down goes Chief. What could it mean, what could it mean?

And what of the flanks, Mr. Iseman and Miss Postma? What's to happen to them?

Iseman folded his arms, looked at the door in front of him, back to his phone, then to the door again.

It was the office of Anita Postma. She was arguably the most powerful person at the university—even more so than the president, due to her deep pockets, relational equity, and political connections.

She was also a crow of a woman who'd earned many promotions at Iseman's expense. She certainly didn't need all her money. And really, a generous proportion of that wealth should've been his. He'd done better work, fought harder for his status, and was far better liked than her.

Iseman withdrew the envelope he'd forged from his pocket. He'd done an incredible job, if he did say so himself: the font, the mahogany coloring, the sickly obscure and verbose tone.

He tapped the envelope into his left hand. Paydays like this didn't present themselves except once a lifetime, and only to those smart enough to see them. The conductor's latest text, which Postma had almost certainly received as well, was perfectly vague enough for Iseman to use to his advantage. Postma would be shaken up once again, vulnerable, willing to do whatever the conductor asked just to stay alive.

Like give the conductor money.

He unlocked Postma's office door. He'd seen her return to her seat at the basketball game and knew he had enough time to pop in and out without anyone ever knowing. "Hello?" he said, peeking into the office.

No one responded. He stepped inside and closed the door.

After listening a moment to make sure no one was in the space's private bathroom, Iseman walked past the secretary's area and through a doorway to Postma's desk. Everything about the décor was rich—the pelmet, the console, the davenport, the sconces and hassock. But the place smelled of her spoiled-rotten cat, the only attractive thing others probably found in Postma.

He deposited the letter on her keyboard, a note with a not-so-subtle request and directions to transfer a great deal of money so that "the conductor" could execute the rest of his plan.

But Iseman's stomach still churned. He imagined word getting back to the conductor that someone was impersonating him. Would he suspect Iseman? Maybe.

But what were the odds that Postma would cry foul? A lot of things would have to break against Iseman for something terrible to happen.

Eyeing the envelope, he allowed a grin and exited Postma's office.

That's when he noticed the pet camera in the corner, green light dimly glowing.

Chief Renfroe closed the door to his press box, waving off media members and staff asking if he was all right. The paramedics had wanted to whisk him off to the hospital to check him out, but that was par for the course for first responders. He was fine—unlike Ivan, who had fainted and fallen nearly fifteen feet onto Renfroe's shoulder, which now burned like fire.

But he wasn't going to let a little pain ruin the perfect weekend.

Renfroe hobbled toward his chair. He didn't feel good, especially his stomach. But that couldn't be related to his shoulder pain. His belly was simply in knots over all that had occurred in less than an hour: dealing with that insubordinate Haas, being pulled onto the court for the spectacular honor, then experiencing a freak accident in which one of the most recognized people in music had skydived on top of him. That reminded Renfroe—he needed to check YouTube soon, because he was about to become the world's most recognized chief. How about that?

Ivan had given the crowd the thumbs-up while being wheeled out of the gymnasium on a gurney, but Renfroe had his doubts. He'd heard an awful crack even though he'd helped break the man's fall.

After a peek over his shoulder to make sure he'd locked the door, Renfroe sat and reached into the bag of crinkled cheddar chips. A sharp pain poked at his abdomen, so he loosened his belt buckle.

Finally. It was here. Four quarters of NCAA basketball to soak in and win a boatload of earnings from.

He moved his hands over the notes on his desk like a DJ, lightly tapping them to reposition them just so. A burning belch escaped him without warning, and he winced. Just experiencing pre–junk food backlash, a little too excited for tip-off, that's all.

He twisted off the cap of a soda, which was now warmer than he liked, but this was hunker-down time. The medics had gone, the court was clear, and the players were lined up on the sideline as the national anthem started to play.

As he bumped his mouse to awaken his laptop, a strange webpage filled Renfroe's screen. He cursed. "Pop-ups." But he paused before closing the browser.

It was the URL to an archived article from the *Trenton Telegraph*, dated twenty years earlier. He recognized this edition. It was the grainy black-and-white photo accompanying the article that captured his attention. The photo was of Ivan Mikolaev during the Celestial Orchestra's first performance all those years ago, a day Renfroe had tried to forget.

His stomach lurched again, but he held it down and turned toward the door. No one was around. Who had come in here—with a key, apparently—and brought this up on his computer?

He'd blocked out the memory of that night so well for so many years. He'd even come to the game tonight knowing the orchestra would be here and hadn't really felt much of anything, as basketball and betting helped press down the terrible memories buried deep inside of him.

Renfroe's cell pinged. He didn't recognize the number.

> Chief, Chief, Chief—here we are again, me and you. Waited a long time for this, you know?

He frowned and put on his glasses to see the screen. The mystery number was texting more.

> Hadn't planned on your coming-in party until tomorrow, but someone needed to pay and you just fit the bill—what with you having so little to live for.

> Welcome to the string.

Who in the world was sending these texts?

A violent coughing fit attacked Renfroe. What felt like a thousand needles poked him from inside his gut.

He groaned and slid from his chair to the floor. He needed to call 911. His vision was dimming, and his arms suddenly felt heavy.

Something in the room moved. Noise from the boxes in the corner.

Now footsteps.

Coming his way.

The lights of his eyes were turning off. All Renfroe could see were sneakers planted right next to his head and gloved hands reaching down to lay a tablet on his chest.

A toolbox thudded onto the ground beside him.

10

Snow began to fall as I stood there staring at my phone, waiting for whatever retribution was to come. But no other texts were coming in. Did the conductor know I'd met with Janet? How was he going to retaliate, knowing that I'd tried to tip off the chief? Or was Ivan's fall in the gym the retaliation, *a* conductor putting down *the* conductor?

I shook my head. Had to get to the girls.

I hustled back to the squad car and couldn't believe what I was seeing: a boot on the front tire. Even in the icy weather, anger warmed my face. The chief had sent his lackeys to lock down my car. I'd have to take an Uber or . . . *something*.

"Hey," someone whispered.

A young man who had been in the shadows stepped into pale light. He was sharply dressed and showing me a *Trenton Telegraph* media badge hanging from his neck. This was Alec McCullers, the journalist Janet had confronted and recruited. He motioned for me to get into the car.

I opened the door and sat in the driver's seat. Unlocked the passenger door. Alec slid inside and closed us in silence.

This time I spared the pleasantries. "What's he have on you—since when?" I said.

Alec raised his brows and demonstrated solid eye contact. "All right, honesty. Nice to know Janet found you. I saw you peek into the gymnasium during the chaos." He took a deep breath. "I've been ambitious in my freelance pieces. Witnessed a bystander get killed reporting on an underground racing ring." He glanced at the dashboard, then back to me. "I ditched with the rest of them, destroyed evidence."

Involuntary manslaughter. That was no small thing to hold over someone's head, let alone an ambitious student with his whole life ahead of him.

"At first he left me notes, just messing with my mind—telling me he was watching me, that he knew what I'd done, to wait for further instructions." Alec rubbed his forehead. "Then he sent me a link to a live feed, and I've been doing chores for him ever since. It's been weeks." He nodded back toward the gymnasium. "Someone made me in there. Another member of the string trying to cover his butt, I think. Warned me about meeting with Janet—and you. Threatened, actually. So the second the commotion happened, I slipped out and hid out here where I could see your car, figured you'd have to walk this way. I take it Janet found you and told you about me. Did she tell you—"

"You're going to kill me tomorrow," I interjected.

He nodded. "The conductor has been using me to study you—digging up newspaper archives, video footage from news crews. He's got you well documented, but today . . ." Alec waved a hand as if he didn't have a clue in the world. "Texted me that we were going to kill you. *We*—he and I. Why'd he escalate to that?"

I shook my head. "I don't know why he wants anything." I rehashed the incident with sending Cody to check in on Steph and the girls, then my encounter with the chief. "Killing me would only make sense if it were done at the same time he finishes whatever he's got planned."

"So something big happens tomorrow?"

I checked the mirrors of the parked car as I thought on it. Looked down at my phone. "Could anyone have seen you waiting for me?"

Alec shifted his body, looking pained as if his limbs had all fallen asleep. "Everyone was in the gym. I don't know. It's impossible for him to watch all of us all the time. But I can't be sure. You got a plan? I want to help. I'm great with cameras and fact finding. All we need is a lead, a description, anything. Just tell me how I can help you."

How could I utilize his talents without putting him in greater danger? "Janet is trying to locate him using a tablet. How would *you* locate him?"

This question seemed to throw Alec off, if only a little. "I'd find other members of the string. The more I'd find, the more I'd learn, and the closer I'd be to ending this."

I showed Alec the last "naughty knot" text. "He hasn't been in touch since. I've got to go. Steph, Cody, the girls—he's got them. I heard it in Cody's voice."

Alec lit up. "Can you get the boot off?"

"No."

"Then I'll take you. But we have to get to my car behind the comm building."

"It won't be safe. You okay with that—the conductor finding out you helped me?"

Alec lifted his car keys in front of his face, letting them dangle.

"If he hasn't found me out yet, it's only a matter of time. Janet's doing what she can; I might as well do damage while I can."

A small amount of hope lifted in me. He was a good kid.

I reached behind me and unlatched the AR-15.

Just in case anyone was watching, I stepped outside and started fiddling with the boot, leaving the door open behind me. All the main vantage points could only see the front of the car, so Alec could sneak out my door and stay low, using the car as cover until he reached the university courtyard. From there, he could head toward the back of the buildings that ran parallel with the evergreen-filled hills on the west side of campus.

I waited a few minutes, then walked in shadows through the campus, which had transformed from mobs into an eerie emptiness. Ahead and to the right sat the comm building, where Janet was hopefully finding a way to track the conductor.

It would take twenty-five minutes to get to Steph's house in the country, and that was with clear roads without snow on them.

I skirted around to the back of the communications building. Alec stepped out from behind a truck and clicked a key fob. The lights of a Honda Civic blinked twice, and we both hustled over to it.

Then I cocked my head.

On the sidewalk, about thirty feet away, lay a pair of shoes dotted with white snowflakes. Women's shoes.

"Those . . ." Alec said. "Those are Janet's."

SEVEN MINUTES EARLIER

Janet opened her office window—it was about to get hot.

She placed the mangled tablet on her desk, opened her

laptop, and fired up her desktop, then hooked up the attachments she'd need to get the tablet to talk to her about the conductor. She ran program after program, snippets of code flashing before her as all her processing power went to work. The conductor was hidden in this puzzle—the digital trail told all. But what would she do if she found him?

Giving the conductor's location or last known whereabouts to Markus Haas seemed like the right thing to do. But a part of her wanted to scope out the conductor for herself. Wait for him to step into a glorious new morning, and then stick a knife so deeply inside him that he would think he'd swallowed it whole.

Her computer's fans kicked into high gear as she tapped her fingernails on the desk repeatedly. A thought kept nagging at her: Had the conductor learned of the tablet handoff and surmised what she was doing?

Janet pulled a drawer open and grabbed a few items to try to relax. She walked to her sitting corner, turned on the lamp, and opened her book to the bookmark, which was a hot pink fidget spinner. Holding the spinner between two fingers, she felt as though her world was right again, even though it wasn't. She gave it an aggressive spin and closed her eyes, the whir filling the office.

Something broke her thoughts—a sound, a *creak*. She looked up. Her computers and fidget spinner continued to whir.

As she stared at her office door, the thought of the conductor approaching her sank deep into her stomach. What if she wasn't on the hunt but about to become the prey? She couldn't think like this, not now. All she'd heard was a creak. She was on a mission and couldn't let fear win.

But she couldn't keep her eyes off the door handle. She wished the door had one of those tiny windows so she could see what lay on the other side.

Janet brushed a finger against the fidget spinner and it sputtered to a halt. She wanted to leap toward the door and lock it, but she also wanted to listen.

Nothing but silence.

Nothing but silence.

She exhaled.

Creak.

It could be the aged building yawning, it could be a branch outside her window stretching, but her door was getting locked *now*.

Janet stood as quietly as possible. She slipped off her heels and slid one foot forward, barely lifting it off the hardwood. She did the same with her other foot. Her heart thumped in her chest and pulsed in her ears. What felt like a bamboo shoot grew in her gut, wiggling this way and that, creating violent tremors with every turn.

The closer she got to the handle, the more aware she became of every sensory fiber in her being: the fleshy parts of her lips, the pressure of her glasses at the bridge of her nose, even the air filling the grooves of her fingerprints.

She gripped the door's dead bolt and slowly turned—

A body slammed into the door.

The dead bolt, only half engaged, rattled.

Janet shrieked and fully engaged the bolt. Hustled to her desk, heart thrashing in her chest. Her face went numb.

Only a minute left before her programs finished running. But the door was the only way out. She was trapped. Unless . . .

She looked out the window. *Unless* she could make the leap from her second-floor office to the portico directly diagonal to her window.

"*Jannnnnet*," a high-pitched voice said. "What am I ever going to do with you, sneaky woman?"

It was him. Here. Outside her office.

Something slipped under the door, a miniature tube no wider than a pencil. Its black head curved into Janet's office like a snake. A valve twisted and a white, steam-like substance began emanating from just under her office door.

"When I'm in my kitchen, chopping vegetables, searing meat, caramelizing onions, I don't move without pace or rhyme," the conductor said. "I glide from station to station to the mastery of Beethoven, Bach, or Mozart, depending on my mood."

The white gas was growing into a cloud. Janet closed her eyes, breaths coming fast, too fast. She needed to slow down, steady herself. She opened her eyes, snatched up the tablet, and tucked it into her pants, body shaking, eyes tingling. She couldn't make the jump from her window. But he'd kill her if she stayed. Lucy too.

"The food was merely the activity, see. What whet my appetite was the overtaking, the closing of my eyes as each note danced up my vertebrae, cleansing me of stress and worry. And the very best part, Janet? The part I looked forward to most?" He took a long drag of air. "The deep breath that followed."

Janet leaned over and gripped the windowsill, fingers burning from the pressure.

"The gas isn't harmful, you know—I vape it every night

before I sleep. Or, better phrased, I sleep after every time I vape it. It's fantastically relaxing."

Her office had turned completely white, but she could now breathe fresh air. The conductor started doing something to the door again, working to get it open. Janet leaned out to take a deep breath. She couldn't make that jump to the portico, she knew that. She'd fall and incapacitate herself, crush her ankles or break her knees. But she had to do something.

She took off her heels and tossed them out the window to see just how far she was about to fall. How much longer could she hold her breath inside?

Behind her, masked in the white cloud, her office door burst open.

Janet slipped to the left of the window, toward her desk area, lungs burning from lack of oxygen. She extended her shaking hands in search of the one item hard enough to deliver a massive blow. She couldn't see the conductor, but she could hear his steps. He must have been wearing a gas mask because he was walking toward the window in no apparent hurry.

As he peeked outside, no doubt eyeing the high heels on the concrete below and wondering how she'd managed to spring out of sight, she raised the vase in which sat her bonsai plant.

"Clever gir—" he said, just as Janet swung the vase and smashed it into the back of him—his head, neck, or spine, she couldn't tell.

Janet ran into the hallway, pulled the fire alarm, and sprinted down the hall, turning left toward the conference room, then right toward the stairwell. Running barefoot made her feel balanced and grounded, but the tendons and muscles in her feet were already screaming from slapping against the marble floors.

Racing down the stairs and spilling onto the first floor, she pulled out the tablet and tucked it under the last stair at the bottom, just in case he caught up to her. He obviously valued it and she wouldn't give him the satisfaction.

The alarm continued screaming, but no help was in sight. Someone had to be on campus. Even just a student meandering. The fire department would be dispatched to her location, along with a campus officer. But five to ten minutes would be an eternity in this living nightmare. And unless her bonsai blow had done serious damage, the conductor couldn't be far behind—

An almost unnatural pounding of feet smacked the second-floor hallways like a jackhammer in fast-forward.

Janet jerked her head toward the building's exit options. Before her, a hallway ran straight to the quadruple-door exit. But she wasn't fast when she wore her expensive runners, let alone barefoot. He'd see her, catch her, and drag her into some dark corner if she tried that route.

Her opportunity, then, was to the right or left, where propped-open doors led into computer labs C and D. She ducked into D.

The lab, lit only by moonlight and a slight hue from the hallway, was set up in long rows of angled workstations that stretched from the teacher's station at the front all the way to the windows in the back. Under each desk was enough room to hide a person. With university police coming, the conductor would have to take more time than he'd like to check under all of them. He'd be forced to leave.

Janet thought about running to the farthest row of computer stations, but the conductor was smart and, if he looked in here, might check that spot first. She ran to the back of the third to last row, moved the computer chair, crawled under the desk, then rolled the chair back toward her.

Footsteps pounded down the stairs.

A deep breath caught in her throat, and she froze. Her heart pounded like a subwoofer beating in her chest, ears, and behind her eyes.

The conductor had reached the first floor but now was still.

Janet could almost hear his thoughts whir like her computer fans had only moments ago. He knew she couldn't have run the length of the hallway, which could only mean . . .

She prayed he'd choose lab C.

She heard him step into D.

Unlike Janet, the conductor wasn't breathing hard. He remained steady, silent. "This is one of my favorite times of the year, you know? Every spring, regardless of what this unpredictable climate dealt, my grandmother used to take me to see the tulips, a wondrous sight to any child."

She pressed one hand to her stomach and tears blurred her vision. She could vomit this very moment. What would he do to her? How much would it hurt?

Janet pursed her quivering lips and bared her teeth. She needed to get ready to fight, not faint. Which direction was he moving?

"Vibrant colors as far as the eye could see, and that wasn't even the best part. No, the best part was the scent. The tulipa kaufmanniana, greigii, humilis. I had such a nose, enough that it was my sick old man's first compliment. 'You're as girly as those Powerpuffs,' he'd tell me. It's a gift. I can smell *anything*."

Janet closed her eyes, trying to concentrate on her hearing so she could pick up any noise beyond the throbbing of her heart. *Please, someone, just get here.*

"What I loved about you the moment I met you, Janet, was your lovely perfume—your spectacular scent."

Sweat beads formed and slid down her face. She leaned forward an inch to dry it on the chair's seat cushion.

With numbing legs, she kept her hands pressed to the floor like a sprinter ready to jump off the blocks. Her nook under the desk made her feel like she was crouching between two furnaces.

The chair, which only a moment ago had soaked up her sweat, smashed into her face with incredible force.

The back of Janet's head crashed into the desk and blood sprayed from her nose.

The confined space spun.

Her hands trembled.

Watery eyes blurred her vision.

Hands pulled her out from under the desk, rendering her weightless. The next thing she knew, she was being slammed on top of the desk, sending pens and a stapler flying.

She screamed.

Janet tried to kick, but the highways on which her brain signals traveled appeared to have been destroyed. Her body wasn't doing what her mind was telling it to.

But her eyes were working well enough to see the pale demon.

"Janet, Janet, tablet, tablet." The gas mask the conductor had been wearing dangled from his white neck. "Where'd you put it, dear?" His hands groped up her legs and, after failing to find anything, punched into her diaphragm, knocking the wind out of her. Her blouse tore open, but again, he didn't find what he was looking for.

"One word, one location, Janet."

Glass shattered in the distance and the conductor snapped his head to the left. One of the lanes of her brain's highway must have reopened, because Janet thrust her fist up into the lunatic's throat.

He stumbled back.

Janet tried to stand but couldn't. Whatever chest muscles she used every day had suddenly vanished. She gasped for breath but only managed to get tiny bits of air, her entire body limp. Unable to do anything else, she shifted her gaze to the conductor.

He was experiencing his own coughing fit, but looking at her immobilized state with a twisted excitement, as if she were the cover of his favorite magazine.

He walked away—whether smiling or snarling, she couldn't tell.

Fire alarm screaming, Alec and I burst into the communications building through the side entrance.

I swung the AR-15 into shooting position as we passed several classrooms and cut through the commons area. "Janet?"

Out the other side, we spotted the stairs that would take us to her second-floor office and hustled toward them. At the bottom were doors leading into computer labs.

"I hear her," Alec said, turning into computer lab D.

But I didn't follow. I was frozen.

Slowly, I turned to look down the length of the hallway we'd busted through.

At the far end, past the commons area connection and near the building entrance, stood the conductor, wrapped in a pinstripe dress shirt and black raincoat, his face a nightmarish twist of black and white. A Von Boch hat, slightly tilted, shaded his eyes, and around his neck dangled a gas mask. His build looked slight and he stood maybe six feet tall. Two shiny objects were wrapped over his fingers and forearms—some sort of brass knuckles.

"Markus Haas, the brilliant paradox. Unbreakably broken, but not like the rest—no, not like the rest."

I took aim. "What happened at Stephanie's house?"

"A wonderful weapon. But you really should test your artillery before bandying it about in such militant situations. Especially with Cody, Steph, and the chickpeas all just hanging in the balance, yes?"

The conductor had known the squad car I'd drive—he'd emptied the AR-15 of its ammo, hadn't he? I lowered the barrel. "Where are they? What have you done?"

The conductor pulled out his phone and texted something.

My phone buzzed.

"Look at it."

I pulled up my phone so that I could glance at it while keeping the conductor in my line of vision. But I couldn't just glance. There were several photos, each more grotesque than the last—an amateur surgery in which a body had been opened, implanted with a device the size of a skipping rock, and then sewn shut.

"Know who that is? Of course you don't. You're on stage and don't have my vantage."

My face burned and I found myself lifting the AR-15 back up at him, even though it was probably without rounds. "Why all of this? What do you want?"

The conductor continued as if I hadn't spoken a word. "I ordered that little surgery after you sent Cody galloping to the farmhouse. I imagined you'd be the hard one to crack—but it still surprises and *delights* me." He lowered his chin and looked at me the way a starving cannibal might look at his next meal. "How far are you willing to go? What will you sacrifice next? Janet? What about the reporter boy? The possibilities are endless."

He tilted his head and clicked his tongue, mouth stretching into a grin. "My knots, all tangled up like Christmas lights. Hate that, don't you? But the science behind the solution isn't of the rocket variety—it's quite simple." He pulled the mask over his nose and mouth and raised his other hand, fist clenched, then popped it open. "Get new lights."

A tiny canister dropped to the floor and, upon impact, started spraying white smoke with the force of a fire extinguisher. All the lights in the communications building shut off as a loud pop rang in the distance.

I held my breath and broke into a sprint, shifting the AR-15 in my grip to wield it like a baseball bat. Couldn't kill him. Not without knowing if he'd taken Steph and the girls. But I could capture him.

The conductor hadn't looked particularly athletic. I could—

From somewhere in the darkness, what felt like a cinder-block smashed into my face.

The AR-15 slid across the marble floor and I thudded onto

my back, involuntarily sucking in a breath of the white smoke. Almost immediately, my limbs started to tremble and go numb.

My head shook as I tried to fight whatever was taking over my body. But it was too late. The numbing crawled up my neck and touched my brain, shutting it all down.

11

I jolted upright and took in my surroundings. Moving car. Alec driving, Janet passenger. I had been lying down in the back seat, and what felt like shards of cement were scraping against my skull. What had happened?

The conductor had escaped. Knocked me down and gassed me.

How'd I get in the car? Where were we going?

Stephanie. Cody. The girls.

I must have been speaking my thoughts because Janet turned around and shushed me. "You got knocked around, a decent bruise to show for it. We know he has your people"— she looked at Alec—"so we ducked the other university police and got out the back."

I noticed she had the charred tablet on her lap, hooked up to a laptop. I pointed at it, then closed my eyes for a moment. If it could lead us to the conductor, he would have taken it; if it couldn't lead us to him, Janet wouldn't be working on it.

She flicked its screen as if it had caused her nothing but

trouble. "Slid it behind the stairwell before he caught up. But having to use Alec's laptop is making things more complicated."

"Anything?" I rasped.

Janet shook her head. "Time's all I need. If something's on here, I'll find it."

I leaned forward and looked at both of them, back and forth, back and forth. Janet and Alec had done nothing shady or untrustworthy—but I had been out for a while, and the conductor could have messaged them any number of things that would make them turn on me or one another. "What's he texted?"

Snow fell like feathers out the windows. Alec adjusted the rearview mirror as we passed a long stretch of white-laced evergreens on either side of the road. "Group texted Janet and me. Said we'd made mistakes, that the string wasn't happy."

"And?"

Alec stared through the windshield. "That he'd be surprised if we lived through the night."

I pursed my lips, wanting to put a bullet in the conductor.

"Where are your people—Stephanie, the girls?" Janet said. "We're all in whether we like it or not—so let us help you."

Alec nodded.

These two people—practically strangers before today—were willingly driving into danger for me. But not without cost. "Forty-five sixty Aldergrove Lane." I wiped my mouth and reached for my holster instinctively, forgetting that the chief had stripped me of my firearm.

"Here," Janet said, handing me a pistol. "Yours was empty so we drove to my house and picked mine up. Don't have a clue what it is, but it fires and the clerks said it was no peashooter."

I looked at her, eyebrows raised.

"What, a girl can't own a gun?"

I checked the clip and tried to get a feel for it. Looked like the clerks had known what they were talking about. It was a Smith & Wesson M&P 9mm. "There's a long driveway. Drop me off a quarter mile in. I'll foot the rest."

"Forget that, tell us what to do," Janet said. "We're all breaking the string now, and you heard what he wrote—we're in danger whether we help you or not. Don't act like some hero. It's not about you." She turned back to me. "Frankly? We feel safer together."

I looked away from her for a minute, staring at the double lines in the road. She was right. It just didn't *feel* right. They weren't trained like I was. The thought of using civilians to help bring down a terrorist would be absurd in almost any other scenario. But this wasn't any other scenario.

"You know I'm right," Janet said. "This is about stopping the conductor, so . . ." She paused a moment. "We do it together or I do it separately. Nothing changes that fact. End of discussion."

"You thought through what he'll do if we aren't successful?" I said. "You checked on your sister?"

"I called in an anonymous threat on her life. Hoping it beefs up security."

"Alec?"

The student journalist looked pensive. "My secret's needed to come out. I can do jail time; I *can't* sit back and do nothing anymore." He gripped the wheel and glanced over his shoulder. "In other words, I'm good."

I kept my eye on him in the rearview mirror an extra moment, trying to gauge him. "Let me see the text."

Janet and Alec shared a glance.

"Here." Janet held up her phone and I leaned forward to read it.

A couple of teenagers, you two, making bad choices.

I can be forgiving, but not the string. Ruthless, that string.

I'd hoped you'd stick around for the finale, but I doubt you'll survive the night.

The string of texts ended with an emoji: a spool of thread.

We turned onto Aldergrove Lane and zigzagged Steph's elaborate private driveway. Darkness and snow blanketed the headlights and made for an ominous tunnel of blackness through which the road twisted and turned. The normally gravelly path had been covered in white, and the pace at which Alec drove felt unbearably slow.

My stomach roiled as I thought through the scenarios the conductor may have orchestrated for Steph, Cody, and the girls. "Come on, hit it."

"Want me to slide off the road?" Alec said. "This stuff is slick."

I forced my hands to my knees and breathed. Even though the conductor's manipulative game had only started hours ago for me, it suddenly felt as though Mother Nature had decided to join the madness as well, keeping me away from the one place I needed to be.

I looked out the window—

As if in slow motion, I saw the black raincoat, tilted black hat, and a white face staring at me, slowly turning his back and walking away into the obscurity of the wooded terrain.

"Stop!"

Alec hit the brakes and the car skidded forward in tiny spurts as the ABS kicked in. The tires shifted and we slid off the road, Janet bear-hugging her equipment the whole way. She craned her neck toward me, face ashen, shoulders tight.

I opened the door and jumped out, pointing my firearm at where I'd seen him. "I saw him. Get the car turned around. You see *anyone* but me, get out of here."

Alec tapped the gas, but the tires just spun. "I think I can get out. Go." He gripped the steering wheel with trembling hands and glanced into the blackness on either side of the road.

Snow crunching under every step, I ran to where I'd seen the conductor, keeping Alec and Janet in my periphery. The road provided a pale glow, but beyond the tree line—total blackness. I pulled out my flashlight and swung it and the Smith & Wesson left, right. Darkness swallowed the light like a black hole consuming a star. It was as if nightfall had formed a pact with the monster and was concealing him.

But I'd seen him. I knew I had.

I stepped lightly into the blackness, biting my lower lip and scanning the darkness with the pinprick of light from my flashlight. An eerie shiver worked its way through me, leaving me feeling as though the conductor were watching me with all the clarity of high definition. I had zero advantages in this situation. But if he were here, Cody and the girls had to be close.

My mouth twitched at the thought.

I slowed my breathing and eased farther into the dark,

glancing at the ground for prints and back up for a potential ambush. Fresh snow clung to my head and face.

There. A footprint. Two more. Leading deeper into the tree line. But he wasn't this simple. Why was the conductor hoofing around in the woods and not at the house?

I followed the prints for twenty yards before they crossed a different set of footprints. A pit formed in my stomach. At least one other person was roaming out here with the conductor, and I wasn't sure it wasn't the devil himself.

He was trapping me.

Being the seeker put me at a disadvantage. Being outnumbered put my odds of overtaking the conductor at next to zero.

But Cody, Steph, and the girls needed me. There wasn't any backup or time for a plan. I was the plan.

Whatever force had pulled Steph through her darkest days, I wished I could access it in this moment. Because every ounce of desire and determination inside me felt coldly hollow.

I continued following the first set of prints but found myself glancing in the direction of the other prints every few seconds.

A third set of prints crossed over the original prints in the *opposite* direction. I could be in the process of being surrounded.

Then I heard it.

The crunching of snow up ahead, in the direction of the original footprints—someone was there. Running.

I sprinted ahead, waving my flashlight. "Stop!" I shot twice at the air.

Ahead, I heard a rustling of sorts.

Full-on running, I nearly dove into what I thought was a person but turned out to be a tree trunk. My free hand jammed into the bark, but I managed to hold on to the gun. I glanced left, right, searching for tracks. But there were none.

Then a branch cracked above me.

"Someone's coming," Alec said, looking ahead at oncoming headlights. "They're driving kamikaze fast." He tapped the gas, trying to pull back onto the roadway. But the tires were gripping the icy snow about as well as butter grips oil.

If Alec wasn't mistaken, the conductor had deployed a suicide driver—and if they didn't move right now, they were dead.

He swung his head to Janet. "What do I do?"

Janet gripped the laptop and tablet in one hand and the door handle in the other. "Punch it or bail!"

He did the former, this time pressing his foot to the floor. The engine screamed with all the shrill power of a jumbo-sized teapot, whistling bloody murder into the night.

The oncoming vehicle veered off the road, thundering toward them like a derailed train.

What looked like a giant bat, silhouetted against tree branches and moonlight, fell from above and dropped on me like a sandbag.

I collapsed under the weight but rolled and spun on the snow, coming up with a fistful of the bat's jacket and jamming my knee into his bony back, gun pointed at his head.

The attacker's hat fell off as he turned his white face to me. "Please—I'm not him!" cried the man who I thought was the conductor. Though the attire was correct, the deep voice did not belong to the psychopath.

Just then another blur ran past me only a few yards away, dressed in the same garb as the stranger under my knee: black hat, coat, and a face that looked as though it had been coated in baking powder.

I swung my gun toward the mystery runner, but he was already fading into blackness. The conductor was toying with me.

"Where is he?" I twisted my knee into the man's vertebrae.

He cried out. "I don't know, it was an assignment."

"What assignment?"

"Draw you into the woods—away from the house."

In the distance, tires spun like a dragster off the block. Alec and Janet. That wasn't the sound of Alec trying to get the car unstuck. Those tires screamed *desperation*.

I cursed and bolted back toward the road, bursting out of the tree line.

A black Sprinter van was barreling down the driveway, coming from the house. It smashed into Alec's Civic, scaling it like a snowboard up a half-pipe. The momentum hurled the van sideways and its driver's side rocketed across the terrain, scraping against snowy gravel.

I sprinted toward the wreckage, gun trained on the hostile vehicle. But I needed to check on Janet and Alec.

Snow stuck to the mangled Civic's broken glass, creating a black-and-white mosaic impossible to see through.

Oh, God, are they in there? Please tell me you got them out.

My SWAT training kicked in, and reluctantly I turned to the van. Needed to take control of the hostiles. I ran to the front of the sideways van and swung the Smith & Wesson's handle into its windshield. Glass shattered.

If anyone was still breathing in there, I needed to keep them overwhelmed. "Don't move, *don't* move!"

A lone man was sprawled across the cockpit, midforties, Mexican descent. Blood covered his face, but I recognized him. Serge. He was the head gardener at Trenton University. I'd seen him earlier today with Doug.

I crawled through the windshield and checked his pulse. Lowered my head.

Serge's cell was in his pants pocket. I grabbed it and backed out of the van.

"Haas," a voice said.

I turned to see Alec. What felt like invisible strings suddenly lifted the load I was carrying. He was holding his left shoulder but otherwise unharmed, from what I could tell.

"Where's Janet?"

Alec looked back at what had been his car. "Didn't she jump out?"

We both hustled back to his smashed hunk of metal and peered through the spiderweb glass. I turned my weapon to use its handle as a hammer.

"It's fine, I'm fine." The voice had come from the other side of the road.

We both turned to Janet, her laptop and tablet still connected by a cord and in her grasp.

"You okay?" I said.

"See any blood?" She crossed the roadway to meet us and nodded at the van, looking as though she might kill someone. "Driver?"

I shook my head and withdrew the cell phone I'd lifted from the van.

"Give it to me." Janet grabbed it and navigated to the most

recent text. "Conductor sent a message." She read it aloud as
I looked over her shoulder.

> Oh shame, what a shame. Knots being naughty,
> so uncaring. Of you. Of my string. You know
> what this means.

Under that text, a collage of images had been shared: grue-
some pictures of operating instruments cutting human flesh
adjacent to the spine, then suturing it shut. I recognized them
from when the conductor had sent them to my own phone.

There was a gap in time between the text Janet had just read
and the next one on Serge's phone. The conductor had let the
gardener and the rest of the string digest fear.

Janet continued.

> But what kind of conductor lets a few
> incompetent instruments destroy the
> orchestra?

> NEW RULE: mend the string, receive reward.
> Take Janet Blevins and Alec McCullers from the
> stage, and wrath will not only be withheld—but
> riches will be extended.

The next text listed Stephanie's address.

> Save yourself and loved ones—then spend like
> mad.

That explained the fake conductors. But what had it taken
for Serge to kill himself?

The conductor was using the string against the string. Janet,

Alec, and I weren't just up against a lunatic. We were up against the knots who together comprised an ecosystem of survivalism and extortion. Fear was driving normal people mad.

My phone buzzed and I read the text.

I get larger when I eat but shrink smaller when I drink.

I turned to Alec and Janet.

What am I?

Through the downpour of snowflakes, I gazed at Stephanie's house. "Fire."

My legs couldn't be pumping any harder, but the road seemed to stretch farther away from me with every stride. I tried to think, to plan. Action without thought led to failure, and failure now might mean death for Steph, the girls, Cody.

Janet and Alec hadn't liked being told to stay put, but they'd be more of a liability than a help if I were rushing into a combat situation. I needed to focus.

I slowed to a jog then veered off the driveway and into the woods. Needed to avoid being an easy target. My best shot was to approach the house from the back.

When the farmhouse finally came into view, my stomach lurched.

Bullet holes dotted the paint, and most of the windows were shattered. So many shots fired.

Classical music blared from inside. Mozart's *Requiem*.

I ran to the house from an angle so that anyone looking to pick me off through a window wouldn't get a clear line of sight. If even half of the shooters responsible for the bullet holes remained on the premises, then I was outnumbered and outgunned.

It didn't matter. I needed to get to Steph, Cody, and the girls.

I pressed my back to the side of the house, checked my weaponry. Five rounds in the clip and what was left after the chief had confiscated my own gun: a single throwing knife tucked at my ankle, flashlight, and pepper spray.

I listened. No sound other than the music.

The conductor was far more dangerous and organized than I'd thought. How many knots was he orchestrating? Why hadn't he used them to off me yet? Why sic the string on Alec and Janet and not me? A single bullet from the conductor imposters would have been so simple. It didn't make sense.

Easing around the corner to the back of the house, I made it to the door. It stood wide open.

The house looked as though a forklift had done a dozen do-nuts inside. Glass scattered and spread across the dining room and kitchen. Broken dishes. Fallen lamps. Turned-over tables.

Several bottles hung from the ceiling, tied together by string and swaying as if touched moments ago, liquid swooshing inside. Accelerant? If so, the entire house could be engulfed in less than a minute.

Please don't let the girls be inside.

I stepped inside and crouched, flashlight tucked under my gun hand. "Cody, Steph?"

No response. No baby crying. No chattering Isabella. Just the awful music.

Moving forward and keeping low, I approached the living area and a cold sweat broke out.

"Haas," a voice practically sang. "Mr. Markus Haas."

I killed the flashlight.

"You think I don't see you squatting around the corner, oh favored SWAT brute? Your appreciation of my capabilities is . . . underwhelming. I just want to chat." Light suddenly flickered from the living room. "No iron fist or nasty smoke waiting for you around the corner, pinky promise." He whistled. "The things I do for you, Markus. You *fascinate* me, this code you live by. Have I mentioned that? The star of the show, you are. Come in."

If the conductor knew my position, why hadn't he taken his shot? The wall between him and me would split like paper if peppered with bullets. What was his game?

It didn't matter. I had to play it.

I stood and eased into the cathedral-style living area, where I'd played with Isabella and Tilly only a day ago. A candle licked the air from the mantel above the fireplace, illuminating half of the man standing there.

"Thank goodness you're not the curtain man—everyone would leave the show before you swung open the drapes." The conductor, the real one this time, caked with white makeup and hooded in darkness, stood but a few strides from me. Armed or unarmed, I couldn't tell.

I tucked my firearm close, keeping my eyes on all possible areas of ambush. He had a calculated plan. The question was whether or not it had a hole in it. "Where are they?"

"It's no wonder your colleagues hate you like a toneless chorus—so uptight, untrusting. Even I, with a view of self far superior to anything you've dared to dream, know that without trust, people are powerless."

I wasn't interested in his verbose diatribe. "Why shouldn't I put a bullet in your head?"

"Now *there's* your redeeming quality. Directness. Too bad it comes only when you're desperate." He linked his fingers in front of him, soft and sickly. "Let me tell you what I want. I want you, Markus. To play your part. Your gall amuses me, but I need you on key if you want your precious sweets to live. Otherwise you'll never find them." He flashed a crooked smile. "No one will."

My trigger finger pulsed with hot blood.

"That's it. I like that. The full attention of Markus Haas, the uncompromising cop who's stopped analyzing and succumbed to feeling. Bravo."

I couldn't hold in my emotion any longer. What had gone so wrong for this man that he'd play dress-up and murder without a tinge of guilt? "I swear I'll put you down." My voice shook.

The conductor's half-lit demeanor morphed into pure darkness. His unusual tenor dropped and flatlined.

Didn't like that. A trigger.

He leaned toward me and spread his arms. "I'm your god now." He scoffed. "Until you do what I say, when I say it, and however many times I say it, I will crush your soul. I'll make you want to shove the barrel of that pistol into your own ear canal." He smelled the air as if it were steak dinner. "It's happening already, you feel it? Here I am, all you could want, mere steps away. But you can't. You won't. Feel it? Your soul's caving inward like a doss-house in an earthquake. Your will's under siege, Markus, and you're the one left starving."

What felt like lava was eating through my chest. I tried to see through the darkness that shaded the conductor's face and actually *see* into his eyes, one question repeating in my mind over and over. *Why?*

Why was he doing this?

"Message received, I see." The conductor resumed his high-pitched, arrogant tone. He pressed his fingers together and kissed them. "You're not like the others, begging for mercy, blabbering about family, prostrating yourself before me. In that sense . . ." He looked away, deep in thought. "I understand why a devil exists. God must've found him just too captivating not to keep around."

"Sacrilegious garbage," I said. "Tell me where they are."

"Do the assignment. Do it well and they may not be dead by the time you finish."

I stopped breathing.

The conductor squeezed his hand into a fist. "Power, control." Light from the candle waved across his face. He relaxed. "I want every weapon in your arsenal, *every* one."

I cocked my head. "At headquarters?" Why did he want so many guns? "I don't even have access to the building."

"You should know better than to lie. Get the guns." The conductor laughed. "If he's still alive, you may even get help."

"Cody," I said.

The conductor knocked over the candle, which I now saw was attached to a thread. Bottles started crashing and shattering throughout the house, saturating the air with some sort of chemical.

The moment I turned the flashlight back on, it was no longer needed. Flames burst all over the house.

The conductor was gone.

I dodged pockets of fire and started yelling Cody's name, flames spitting pops and hisses all around me. No one on the main floor, which meant Cody must be in the basement.

Heat burning my face and arms, I reached the door that

would take me below into the level that served as a separate apartment. A splintered door frame met me at the bottom of the basement stairs. Fewer flames, but smoke had already started to plume.

In the far corner sat a barricade of furniture. Cody must have hidden the girls in the windowless closet while he took up the defensive position.

I climbed over the blockade. Cody was lying facedown on the floor. I dropped to my knees and rolled him over. A huge, purpling bruise covered his forehead.

I shook him and yelled his name.

My friend groaned and grasped for a gun that wasn't on his hip anymore. He tried wiggling out of my grip, nostrils flaring.

"Cody, it's me. We have to go."

He sat up on his own, holding his head. I picked him up and dragged him out of the basement, up the stairs.

The house had grown into an inferno, flames devouring the floor, walls, and ceiling while emitting streams of dark smoke. More pops, more hisses.

In one swift motion, I flung Cody over my shoulder and sprinted toward the front door.

Flames licked their way into another bottle of accelerant from somewhere behind us, and the boom of the explosion thrust us forward.

Facedown on Stephanie's front lawn, groaning, Cody and I coughed and hacked out the smoke in our lungs for several minutes.

A helicopter whipped the air from somewhere above, and

water suddenly splashed over the house. I stared at the night sky, unsure of what to think other than this was the conductor's way of subduing the attention a bright glow would cause.

Cody stared at me, solemn. "They gassed us, took them." He tried to stand but fell back onto his side.

"Haas?" Alec called, jogging toward us from the long driveway.

"Is he okay?" Janet said, running alongside him.

Cody grabbed my hand and I helped him stand. They all stared at me. But I wasn't ready to speak.

The conductor had taken the girls. I was going to save them. And I was going to kill him.

Finally, as a second chopper dropped more water on the house, creating an enormous splash and a *whomp*, I told them what had happened and what the conductor had assigned.

"There's one option here," Cody said. "FBI. Right now."

Janet paced and wasn't making eye contact. Alec glanced at his phone and looked as though he wanted to say something but was restraining himself.

"He's got Steph and the girls," I said.

"Exactly." Cody stretched a hand out. "Agencies have the capacity to hunt this guy."

"He has eyes *everywhere*," I said. "He'll know the moment we bring in help. But listen, it's more than that. I know going along with a psychopath isn't the right play. But the conductor has us playing a game—his game. Which involves variances, contingencies, *opportunities*. The moment we bring in help and he feels as though we've taken his control, those opportunities vanish." I locked eyes with Cody. "I'm going to find him, I'm going to stop him. All in or all out right now."

Cody put his hands on his hips, looked at the ground.

Alec held up a finger. "Agencies probably won't be an option." He held up his phone, which was zoomed in on a photo of the *Trenton Telegraph*. "It's from Oscar, who works the press. They're in production of today's edition. I think I know what the conductor meant by me helping to kill you, Markus. This story's about you—both of you."

Cody's brows furrowed.

I reached for Alec's phone. A photo of me filled a sidebar of the paper with the headline, "Local Hero under Investigation amid Sex Ring Allegations: Trenton Sheriff's Detective Also Involved in Probe."

Thoughts raced through my head so fast I couldn't process a single one. The conductor knew something about me that no friend or family knew, and he was leveraging it to discredit me before I even had the chance to reach out to the FBI.

"Aren't you the editor?" Cody said. "Stop it."

"The conductor sent proofs to the printer without me ever seeing them," Alec said, suddenly looking unsure.

"What about you or you then?" Cody said, pointing at Janet and Alec. "*You* go to the FBI. Here." He snatched Alec's phone from my hand and gave it to Janet. "Call. Tell them everything. Get as high up the chain as you can."

Janet's lion within returned as she turned the cell toward Cody and me. "Any of this true?"

"Of course not," Cody said.

"No," I lied.

Janet stared at me, then Cody. "I can find the conductor. If you two can take it from there, that's what we should do."

"You're not hearing me," Cody said.

Janet turned to him. "No, you're not listening. I'm not risking my sister, Markus isn't risking *his* people, and no one here is calling the FBI. He'll know. He'll do something terrible. The cavalry isn't coming. And if they do, our loved ones are dead. Got that? The conductor is working with new rules, and right now those rules are giving us a chance. I'll take that and won't risk changing it."

Cody stepped into my personal space, ignoring Janet. "We can't let him tell us what to do. We need to counteract him."

I stepped closer to him, our noses almost touching. "We *are.*" I kept looking at Cody but spoke to Janet. "How long till you have something?"

She pulled out her laptop. "Today."

Cody took a few steps away, shaking his head.

My brain still racing with implications of just what the conductor knew about me, I led the group into the detached garage, which had been spared from the flames and in which sat Steph's old Jeep. The keys were still in the unlocked vehicle's ignition—of course they were, that beautiful girl.

I fired the engine.

12

White gas was all Stephanie could remember.

A putrid mustiness filled her nostrils. She opened her eyes and blinked several times. Tried to wipe away the blurriness. But she couldn't. Her hands were tied to a chair she was sitting in, and next to her—in chairs on either side facing the opposite direction—sat her daughters, motionless but breathing.

She yelled into a gag that she just realized was in her mouth. What was wrong with them? Why weren't they waking up?

They'd been abducted.

Canisters of gas had been thrown into the basement where Cody had herded her and the girls. But then . . . nothing. She couldn't remember what had happened next or who had brought them here.

Where was Cody? Where was Markus?

Stephanie screamed while shaking her chair, trying to find any loose restraint.

She was in a viewing room of sorts. In front of her, scratched-up glass looked into an adjacent chamber that was set lower than the floor at her feet, the walls streaked with black sludge. Under an auburn glow sat a leather chair fitted with shackles, which was the only object in the eerie interrogation room. And behind the chair, a stairway—from which a man was descending.

His face looked as though it had been dipped in hot white wax. His hood and coat clouded him in blackness. Staring at her silently, he smiled and stepped closer to the glass, pressing one finger to his lips. "Stop screaming, woman—chickpeas are fine."

Stephanie could tell he could hear her but not see her through the two-way mirror, even though his eyes were peering almost directly into hers. She stilled herself, but another glance at her limp children produced another shout that cracked into a whimper. Then uncontrollable sobbing.

"Settle," the white-faced man said. "Got the best pharmacologist around. They'll awake rested and with plenty of questions about their dreams." He took a slight bow. "I'm the conductor, and I have so much to tell you. You think a monster stands before you, but in reality there's a different monster in your life."

He meandered around the chamber room. "I know what you're thinking. I know *who* you're thinking." He tilted his chin up. "But you would be wrong. Your monster is no cheating ex. Your monster's closer than that. They always hide in plain sight. Let me demonstrate."

The one who called himself the conductor whistled, and a man with cropped hair in a gray suit and blue tie descended the stairs into the chamber, shaking.

"Take a seat, Iseman."

The man's pleading eyes glanced at the chair, then back to the conductor.

"Come. Sit and let us tell Miss Stephanie and her chickpeas"— he tapped the window—"a story."

Iseman proceeded to sit.

The conductor strapped him with restraints and stuffed a gag into his mouth.

"Please," Iseman slurred.

The conductor turned to the two-way mirror. "Sitting before you is one of the wealthiest good old boys at Trenton University, Franklin Iseman. Grand opening, he's there. Graduation, he's there. Quote in the paper, yessir. If there's so much as a crowd gathered around a hot dog stand, there stands Franklin. Visible. Likable." He mimicked how a crooked politician might look sipping scotch with the boys. "Shaking hands and kissin' babies!"

Stephanie was so confused. Why did this man raid her home and take her and her daughters? What was this about monsters and the man on the chair?

Iseman's lips were trembling, his face turning nearly as white as the conductor's.

"That's the way it's always been for Franklin: be enough places that people think you're important, then take advantage of skewed perceptions. A fine living he's made off this, yes indeed. But the problem with Franklin is, like fame, money is a *drag.*" The conductor motioned with his hands as though he were climbing a ladder. "He just . . . can't . . . get enough. Making money off the innocent for years."

Iseman protested, but his gag muffled his words.

"Unsurprisingly, he's gone and decided to profit some more." The conductor looked at the ground, then pointed forcibly at the glass. "Let me ask you, Stephanie." He looked up. "What would you do if this man suffocated your daughters?" He turned back to Iseman. "You wouldn't be able to forget it, anger boiling inside, year after year, never a release . . . until you finally *popped* from the pressure." He tapped his head. "That's how a person becomes me, you know—pressure. One day normal, and then the next thing you know, you're lathered in makeup in an abandoned building with one person you want to kill and another you want to save."

The man on the chair closed his eyes. Began to whimper.

Stephanie chewed at her gag, teeth clenched and grinding.

"A bit confusing, coming into this cold," the conductor said. "I hunt monsters, okay? I hunt them and make them suffer." He pressed his fingers together and shoved them against his temple. "Problem is, it takes a monster to do away with them. Get it? Do you get it? I can't see your face, but I hear your thoughts, Stephanie. You're thinking, 'I didn't ask for this; don't hurt my girls; just let us go.' So understand when I say that monsters left roaming will soon roam near you. And you have monsters roaming near you, Steph, *so* many monsters."

The conductor once again approached the window separating him from her and the girls. "So, Miss Stephanie . . ." His playfully evil eyes churned her stomach. He glanced over his shoulder at Iseman. "The only way he's leaving is if you and your girls *don't*. Understand? He'll do what it takes to live. But the choice doesn't belong to him. It belongs to you. So, the monster or the children, Stephanie? I need to know you're capable of making the right decision."

Stephanie couldn't breathe. Her shoulders, arms, fingers all were trembling.

"All you have to say is 'him.' Go ahead. I can hear you. Say the word, be rid of this monster, and you and your girls will be saved from *your* monster." He pressed his ear to the glass. "Say it. Say 'him.'"

Stephanie's mind was locking up. She couldn't let anything happen to her girls, and she couldn't play executioner. She glanced right and left at her daughters. Still motionless, still breathing.

"Isabella and Tilly won't see a thing," he crooned. "Backs turned, still snoozing, sounds like. Last chance, Stephanie."

The conductor's smile faded. He sighed and stepped away from the window. Turned back to Iseman. "My, my, oh lucky day." The conductor loosened the restraints on the man. "Putting you on scholarship at the expense of her own children. Bravo, Mr. Iseman. You, sir, have won the day."

Iseman shook off the restraints, eyes manic and glued to the glass between him and Steph.

She couldn't do this. Couldn't let her daughters die.

The word kept pinging in her mind. *Him. Him.*

HIM.

Come on, you're free. Attack him!

But Iseman did no such thing.

The conductor handed him a key. "Up the stairs, around the corner to the left. Make it gentle but quick."

Sweat dripped down Stephanie's face. Her breath caught in her throat. "No," she whispered.

The conductor linked his fingers behind his back and turned to her again, confident enough to turn his back to Iseman, whom he spoke to over his shoulder. "Once you're done, you're free to go."

Iseman stumbled off the chair, legs shaking, and headed toward the stairs.

The conductor put one hand on the mirror, as if offering condolences to a straggler begging at a door that had been bolted shut. "It wasn't supposed to end this way." He looked down with glazed eyes. "But I suppose . . . once touched by a monster, always a monster."

"Stop it!" Stephanie screamed into the gag. From somewhere outside the observatory room, footsteps padded toward her and the girls. Iseman was coming.

She couldn't let Iseman touch her girls. But with her back to the door, she couldn't even face him once he entered. He could walk up to her and, right between her daughters, choke her from behind without ever making eye contact.

She watched the conductor. He seemed to know exactly where to look to stare directly into her eyes.

The door behind her rattled as Iseman inserted the key. The lock sprang free.

Oh Jesus, Father—help me!

"Please, get me untied," Stephanie said over her shoulder. But the words were a muffled mess.

The door swung open and the man's footsteps crept toward her.

"Your life for ours," she garbled.

She could hear Iseman breathing, but nothing more.

She tried to turn her head to look him in the eyes, but her neck just didn't go that far. "These are my babies, just babies."

Hands gripped her neck.

"HIM!" Stephanie screamed, nearly throwing up.

She pushed off the ground with her legs, ramming the man backward as the chair slammed against the ground. One of her restraints loosened, and she yanked her arm in front of her face, ready to fend off another chokehold.

But Iseman pounced on her, straddling her head between his knees like a vise. He thrust his hands down awkwardly, trying to grip her neck.

Stephanie swung her free hand and connected with his temple, which loosened the grip his knees had on her head. She bit his leg and he cried out.

But it was unlike any cry she'd heard before.

It had started with the sort of bloodcurdling fierceness that Isabella might have shown had she stepped on a rusty nail. But near the cry's apex, it had gone eerily silent, as if pure shock had suppressed the man's vocal cords.

Franklin Iseman, muscles tensing, wheezed and looked at her with questioning eyes. He dropped on top of her but was suddenly thrown off by the conductor.

A knife was stuck in his back.

After setting Stephanie upright on her splintered chair and, upon her request, turning the girls around so as not to see Iseman's bloodied body should they awaken, the conductor untied her gag and paced back and forth. He pressed his right foot on her chair, right between her knees, and leaned forward. "I'm going to ask you some questions and I want you to answer: What do you really know of Markus Haas? What do you *feel* when you're around him?"

Stephanie didn't hesitate. "A great man. Committed to making sure people like you never win."

The conductor smiled. He connected his phone to a device and engaged a projection feature, which appeared like a television on the room's wall. The picture that appeared was the photo the *Trenton Telegraph* had used after Markus had broken up a sex slave operation right under the university's nose.

"That sounds like a fine, fine man. The kind women look for," the conductor said. "Marriage material. But then you've gone that route before." The conductor tapped his phone to his chin. "What was his name?"

Stephanie's eyes darted to the ground. She could feel the conductor staring at her, so she glanced up.

The conductor was extending his open palms to Isabella and Tilly. "The father of these beauts—surely you remember his name."

"Declan," she muttered.

"Just Declan?"

"Declan Ross."

"Ross, that's right. MBA. Sharp as a razor. The kind of man your littles couldn't wait to throw their arms around." He leaned toward Isabella as if inspecting her eyelids.

Stephanie felt as though her skin could rip open at any moment from the violent tremors tearing through her bloodstream. "Leave them alone."

He flicked his wrist. "Just seeing which one has more of Daddy in them—eyes, nose, et cetera."

Tears sprang to her eyes. "Just stop it."

"Six years is a long time to be married to someone you don't know. I would have thought a strong woman like you would have, how should I say this, *adjusted* your dating criteria after Decky."

"What are you talking about?"

The conductor gazed at the image of Markus on the wall. "He's a fascinating one, so dedicated to his craft, top one percent in every category—a mental and physical specimen!"

He folded his arms and leaned back, pursing his lips. "But then . . . why? Why work at the bottom rung, this great man? Why not climb the ranks of elite world protectors? Why remain unrecognized and disrespected amongst colleagues and superiors when the world of law enforcement should be his oyster? Something's held Markus back, something dark and hidden. I am drawn to such darkness, Stephanie."

"If that's what you think, you don't know him at all."

The conductor stepped over Iseman's body toward the projected image of Markus, reaching out to touch the wall. "Eyes of a dark soul trying to show it's capable of light."

She leaned forward. "You manipulative lunatic, hiding behind your mask, you don't know anything."

The conductor spun around and showed a bit of a smile. "Tell me, Miss Stephanie—"

"Don't call me that."

He kicked his foot back onto her chair, between her knees. "You forget so easily," he said, glancing at Isabella and Tilly, "where you are and who I am." He pressed his face down to hers, breathing hot breath onto her cheek.

She looked straight ahead, breathing hard, unwilling to meet his eyes. She needed to shut up, just shut up—her babies were in danger.

He pressed his lips into the corner of hers and pulled at her lower lip.

Her body shook.

"*Miss* Stephanie," he said, an inch from her tearstained cheek. "Your makeup is smearing."

He pulled away from her.

Stephanie choked back a sob.

The conductor clicked to another photo, this one of a house, early twentieth century, remodeled and beautiful—one of the original homes settlers built in Trenton. "Familiar? It's the house in which your boyfriend made his mark, did something heroic, finally got noticed. How your heartbeat must've quickened when you learned *this* about Markus. Hand on your heart, radiant glow on your face, perhaps telling baby Tilly that you may have actually come across a true man, someone you could possibly love?"

He paced, motioning as if he'd stepped out of himself and into Stephanie. "The way he treats the girls, his dedication to being the best he can be." He looked her directly in the eyes and let his jaw hang open. "Those good looks." He winked. "So many boxes checked, it's no wonder you said yes to coffee and a stroll by the bay. He's just too good to be true." He tapped his phone against his head. "Too good . . . to be true."

He clicked the device. A photo flashed on the screen, a picture Stephanie didn't recognize featuring a group of partying people she hadn't seen before, save for one face on the far right of the photo: Eric Ward, the lynchpin behind the sex slave scandal that Markus had uncovered.

"Every graduation at Trenton, Mr. Ward invited the seniors' best and brightest students to his lovely home to throw them a party they'd never forget. It was all well and good until your Haas stumbled upon what transpired in the deep, deep basement of that home. You know the story. Or, you know the story that's been told. See, I've dug deeper into your Haasy. Limited information available, all told—almost suspiciously so—but after what I've found, it makes sense why it was so well hidden."

The conductor's lips curved into a smile. He clicked the projector to reveal more of the photo—a person standing next to

Ward, arm wrapped around his shoulders. "None other than Markus Haas," he said with a deadpan voice. "Loves students, is loved by students, makes sense to attend graduations, yes?" He began flipping through photos, the only sound in the room the clicking from snapshot to snapshot.

The pictures showed Markus arriving at Ward's mansion, not once, not twice, not a dozen or multiple dozens of times. And not just for Ward's graduation bashes. Markus had been to that house hundreds of times, wearing uncharacteristic buttoned shirts and slacks in every photo—his 4Runner pulling into the driveway, him walking to the door, giving a courtesy knock before entering.

Photos snapped from afar showed him dining, laughing, and partying. Women hung off his arms as he drank and guffawed.

Stephanie's brows furrowed. What felt like a life force broke away from her heart and rode a thin breath out of her mouth.

"The dagger to any woman's soul." The conductor clicked to the next set of photos. They showed Markus escaping upstairs, sometimes with one woman, sometimes two. Then leaving the property, always as if nothing had ever happened.

The conductor killed the projector and turned Stephanie's chair so that she could no longer look at him. "You'll have to excuse me. I have a meeting to get to."

Stephanie's heavy breathing filled the room.

The images flashed before her like firecrackers: Women hanging off him. Drinking. Disappearing to some suite upstairs. She bared her teeth.

And cried.

"Here." The conductor tossed a white rag onto her lap.

It was smeared with his black-and-white makeup.

The chirping of crickets filled the night as the conductor stepped into Trenton University's oldest and largest piece of art, which edged the evergreen-rich hilly terrain backing the campus. He appreciated art almost as much as it appreciated him. Whereas paintings, drawings, and sculptures used to be considered a luxury, the first budget cut in tight times, the day was coming when people would see that creators ruled the world and breathed life into the ordinary and mundane.

This circular maze of stone, for instance—he ran his hand along the smooth rock—was on the outskirts of Trenton University, reminding students that structure and chaos coexisted in unending permanence—

Smacking lips snatched his attention.

The conductor maneuvered through the maze on his tiptoes, deeper and deeper to its epicenter. Upon making a turn into the middle of the spherical labyrinth, he found two students locking lips. Their hands were racing all over one another, and they were completely unaware of the godlike power practically standing over them. Young. Naïve. Filling themselves with dopamine.

He slid on his pair of custom-made brass knuckles. What made these knuckles so extraordinary were the long brass fingers that not only ran up his forearms, providing excellent defense in hand-to-hand combat, but also shot forward little spikes upon a simple click of his palm. Not enough for a kill, but enough to make prey feel as though they were being attacked by a mythical deity rather than a mere mortal.

The couple was making enough noise to draw the gazes of creatures of the night. But the conductor was still able to discern another sound that drifted from the outer boundaries of the maze: the rub of shoes against stone.

He slipped out of the lovers' pod and retraced his steps, spotting his appointment a moment before his appointment spotted him.

The conductor raised a finger to his mouth, signaling that they were not alone. "Love is in the air."

The appointment nodded. "You're younger without makeup."

The conductor moved closer to the appointment—but not too close, for they were both crafty and cunning. He wouldn't put it past the appointment to try something foolish, even though the conductor had stacked enough leverage against him to hang an ox.

"So unexpected, yes?" the conductor said. "So exciting. Forget the agenda. You have a much more urgent assignment."

The appointment understood but didn't seem so sure.

"Come, don't tell me it's your first?" The conductor pressed one hand to his chest. "I must admit, body bags rather bore me—I much prefer death of the mind. But you can't experience the latter without a touch of the former, not fully. Make it quick."

"I came to talk, not kill," the appointment said.

"Well, I have a distaste for whispering. So snuff the love-lings."

"You're sick."

"Which makes you . . . ?" The conductor grinned and turned to the side like a matador, waving the appointment past. "Ándale, protégé."

The appointment glared at him and stepped past him. It almost felt like sending an apprentice through their rite of passage. The conductor knew a thing or two about that.

As the appointment slinked around the corner, the conductor could practically feel the pounding of the first-time killer's heartbeat. Speaking of dopamine . . . These kids may have had theirs, but it was nothing compared to what the appointment was experiencing now.

And to think, all it took was a few premeditated actions, leverage, and a dash of misdirection. He'd mastered the art of breaking the will.

The conductor counted off a few seconds, then lightly stepped in the appointment's tracks until he caught up. He pounced on the appointment from behind and pressed his brass knuckles against the appointment's pretty face. The appointment struggled and grunted something inaudible.

The explosive romance in the maze came to an abrupt finish.

"What was that?" the girl said.

"I don't . . ." the boy said.

The conductor laughed as the two lovebirds hopped the maze's walls and ran. He pressed his mouth to the appointment's ear. "This—this is power: taking or giving life at will. Soon you'll get yours." He let go of the appointment, stood, and smacked his lips together. "Now that we have the floor, it's time to talk about the finale."

13

SUNDAY, 4:15 A.M.

We drove to the only safe 24-7 location we could think of to determine our next move: Saint Mary's Hospital.

After deliberation in the cafeteria, we decided that Cody and I would take the Jeep to the university, while Janet and Alec would stay behind to work on the tablet in the public setting—not to mention stay close to Janet's sister.

Janet and Alec would be without a vehicle, but Janet assured me she could convince one of the staff to give them a lift anywhere—no problem. I believed that.

Cody and I turned onto the freeway en route to the Trenton University police headquarters, where we were going to steal an arsenal of weapons for the conductor. You'd think it was the apocalypse with how dark and quiet the road remained.

"You're making the wrong call," Cody said. "We're not dealing with a druggie whose best trick is losing his clothes so our dogs can't smell him. You weren't there, Haas. He had it all rigged, all orchestrated. This guy's been planning for months. And all we've done is helped him make it happen." He shook his head and looked out the window. "This has to stop, Haas. Has to. We don't know what he's planning."

There was so much I wanted to say, so much anger and love right at the edge of my tongue, but I held it in. "I'm trying to think."

"Great. Well, while you think, this sicko is winning. Let's call, Haas. We have to get others involved."

"We will," I said.

"Then let's do it. What's your plan? You really think swiping those guns will save Steph and the girls?"

"Janet's on to something," I said. "We're going to find them."

"The IT chick? She fixes computer viruses for a living— you're trusting *that*?"

I shot him a glare, then gripped the steering wheel. Everything I'd managed to hold back was about to break the dam. "Do you know loss, Cody? Do you know heartache? The kind that wakes you with teeth clenched 'cause it's gnawing through your blood?" I held up my hand. "Have you once shut up long enough to listen and understand what's important? Has anything ever been so important that without it everything else seemed pointless?" My voice lost its edge involuntarily, and suddenly I felt as though I were talking to myself. "If it were to vanish, *you'd* vanish?"

A lone car passed us, heading in the opposite direction.

I forced myself back to Cody. "Do you know how to love a woman from your heart? Have you ever sat on the floor with a child—with anyone other than a bar girl—and felt yourself disappear? Because it's about being there for them, being strong and selfless and available to them? You might love women, but you haven't *loved*. You might want to settle one day, but settling isn't a choice—it's character. You think I don't know I need help? I'm taking a risk with what I foresee as the highest probability of success. Understood? You keep pushing to say this, do that. Know why? Self-preservation. You want what you want because it's what you can live with." I pointed to my chest. "Well, this is *my* self-preservation. Steph and the girls die, *I* die. I'm going to own that. So either shut your mouth or get out of the car."

I kept my eyes on the road but could feel him staring at me.

"That . . ." Cody said. "*That* is what I've been wanting, Haasy. Where have you been?" He turned his palms up and looked as though he were juggling invisible plates. "And when were you planning on teaching me this feelsy wordsmithing? No wonder Steph loves you." He relaxed. "I get it. I'm in. Just tell me that as soon as Steph and the girls are safe—and they will be—we bring in the cavalry."

"I've got a contact."

"Who?"

"Doesn't matter. She'll send the right people."

He leaned back. "All right then. Let's steal some guns—and God help us."

Cody's quick plea reminded me that I'd been conversing with the higher power at a staggering rate since the string had hit the fan. I didn't find these prayers unusual—distress caused people to say all kinds of things. What I found strange was how naturally they'd flowed from my lips for the first time.

We parked on the street closest to university headquarters' outdoor parking garage, which would make for a quick exit if things went according to plan. Staff would be minimal at this hour, with just enough of my colleagues on duty to answer emergencies, provide security escorts from classrooms to cars, and of course handle the inevitable prank calls they'd get from the emergency intercom boxes strategically placed throughout campus.

"What's the plan?" Cody said.

"You."

"I don't even work here."

"Yes, but I'm suspended without a working key card, and not one person in that building is looking to do me a favor." I adjusted myself on my seat, trying to get a better look at the building's surroundings. "But you, well, your reputation precedes you. We just need one of the female dispatchers working."

"Your plan is me flirting my way in?"

"You can't do that?"

He looked the other way and held up a hand. "Oh, I can do it."

"Stop asking questions then."

I told Cody exactly where to go and which doors to open to sneak me inside if he was successful in gaining entrance. "Got it?" I said.

"That door will be swinging open in five minutes flat."

Waiting near the station's back entrance, all I could see in my mind's eye were guns. Rows of guns hanging neatly in HQ's armory along with cases of ammunition. Then, just as clearly as I could see them in my head, they all vanished as if we'd already taken them, already dispersed them—already enabled the bloodlust of a madman.

The conductor wasn't going to let me keep these weapons. It was just a part of his plan—maybe even the reason he tolerated me standing up to him. These guns could be the piece of the puzzle the conductor had earmarked for me, which meant I wouldn't be valuable to him after this task.

But then, he had said I was the star of the show, whatever that meant. He may have more planned for me yet, which could mean both more slack and more terror.

I needed Janet to locate the conductor *now*. I didn't have any time. I didn't have any leverage.

Except for the weapons.

If the conductor wanted them, he'd have a plan in place for Cody and me to hand them off after our heist. What if we *didn't* deliver them? What if we used them to get back Steph and the girls?

I shook my head, which felt as though someone were beating it with a stone. The conductor had already burned down Steph's house. He wouldn't barter over guns.

Movement in the bushes startled me.

"Hey." Cody stepped out from behind one of the bushes lining the station. "Got four minutes, and I need answers." He held up a finger. "One: tell me about Brielle—likes, dislikes, anything useful. Two: got a non-issued police key sitting in your office?"

Cody's silver tongue could wear down Mahatma Gandhi. But when it came to getting the job done, he executed assignments quickly and with maximum results.

With only four minutes, I skipped the why questions and got straight to the answers, rattling off conversations I'd heard Brielle engage in: *Gilmore Girls*, her affinity for slow-motion videos, and an obsession with Shiba Inus.

Cody leaned back and squinted. "What am I supposed to do with that?"

Just as I was about to fire back, he hit my chest with the

back of his hand. "Messing with you." A strange smile worked its way across his face. "I'm set."

I knew that look. "I said charm your way in, not ask her out."

"Want us to keep cover or not? I'll be the perfect gentleman." Cody checked his watch. "Gotta go." He disappeared back into the bushes.

We needed this to work to buy Janet and Alec time to find the conductor's location. I wanted to text her to check in, but the conductor would see anything I wrote, be it cryptic or straightforward, and I didn't want to provoke him any more than I had. There must be a limit to how much he'd tolerate from me, and I had to be close to surpassing it.

What if the tablet yielded nothing? What if the conductor had wanted it back just as a precaution, when really it was already too fried to be helpful? That meant the guns would be my only remaining leverage.

Just once I wanted to be a step ahead of this lunatic.

The back entrance into HQ opened. "Come in, the water's fine," Cody said. He handed a business card to me—Brielle's, with her number written on the back. He winked.

But the combination of numbers didn't string together an actual phone number. It was a coded two-worded message involving a four-letter word followed by a three-letter word, which, translated, could only mean one thing. "Sorry you struck out."

Cody took back the card, read it again, then mumbled something unpleasant as I stepped into the building.

To the left were the officers' cubicles. We ducked inside mine.

"How long do we have?" I said.

"How long does it take Brie to pee?"

"Wait here and let her escort you out. I'll get you back in."

Cody wrinkled his nose. "Your security really this bad?"

I strode to the closet that doubled as a coatrack and cleaning supplies space. Stepped inside and closed the door. I could still see Cody through the lattice. He gave me a curt nod and pressed his lips together.

Heels clicked down the hallway, and Cody made himself look busy looking for a key that didn't exist.

I readied myself to stop the only things that could betray me in this moment: a sneeze or a cough.

"Any luck?" Brielle asked.

"I've looked everywhere and tried Haas's cell three more times—nothing."

"Drawers? Shelves? Sometimes they put their jackets in here." Brielle walked toward the closet.

A rock dropped from my chest to my toes.

"Wait!" Cody said, startling her. His chin pointed toward the floor and his chest caved. "I—I just have to ask you something." He'd certainly grabbed her attention. "Why the fake number?"

She crossed her arms. "Come on." She tilted her head and smirked. "I know all about you, Cody." Her voice took on some bite. "You shouldn't even be back here. Let's go."

Good. Easy out, Cody. Get out of here.

"Hold on, hold on," Cody said. "Just one more question."

I cursed silently. My friend's pride truly knew no bounds.

"And that is?" Brielle said.

"If you'd never heard stories about me, actually got to know me—the real me, no preconceived notions—would you give me a chance?"

She looked him up and down with disdain. "I *do* know the real you. Let's go."

Cody sulked after her into the hallway.

I waited a minute and then stepped out of the closet and rolled my neck and shoulders, trying to get my mobility greased after having stood like a statue. Peeking around the corner, I scooted toward the door Cody had let me through.

Footsteps padded on the pavement outside, I popped the door open, and in stepped Cody. "No comment," he said.

We maneuvered toward the back stairwell. All the doors from here to the armory were windowless, with no way to peek at who might be on the other side.

Upon reaching the bottom of the stairs, we headed straight for the armory. Thankfully, it was accessible by key, which I had.

Remington 12-gauge shotguns and MP5 submachine guns hung from the walls, each capable of devastation. I found myself paralyzed, my mind thrown into an onslaught of memories that had occurred not two miles from here in a different kind of basement, a prison basement, with different kinds of weapons.

The room before me and the room from my past blurred into one. I couldn't believe the anguish those girls had suffered then, and I couldn't believe I was here now helping an evil man accomplish more heinous acts in this world.

Cody put his hand on my shoulder. "Hey. None of these are getting fired. We're going to stop him."

I picked up one of the TUP duffle bags and stacked it full of weapons and ammo. Cody worked on a second duffle.

We made quick work of the entire inventory, then swung the loaded bags over our shoulders. We exited through the door leading into the partially covered carport. We'd have to hop a fence, but that was a lower risk than trying to exit the way we'd entered.

Cody dropped to the other side of the fence first. One after the other, I launched the two bags over to him before scaling the fence myself. We started back toward our vehicle.

I almost did a double take but managed to control myself. "See the F-150 parked along the street?" I said.

Cody didn't show a hint of alarm but scoffed under his breath. "Defrosted windows a big giveaway. Should have known Mitchell would be a willing participant. Can't get a visual on persons in the cab."

"They're in there. Here for these bags."

"Plan?"

I kept walking as if nothing were wrong. "See those stairs?"

"We'll have a big head start on them, but the bags will weigh us down."

"We go on my count, then head for the path leading into the woods. They follow, that's on them. We're the ones with a small armory's artillery."

Cody puffed his chest. "I'm going to beat your SWAT score on this run."

"Good luck." I took a deep breath. "Now."

We broke for the stairs, duffle bags swinging from our backs.

The doors of the F-150 opened and slammed, and voices shouted indiscernibly from behind us. They were in pursuit.

We sprinted past two dorm buildings, past the silhouettes of two students—a boy and a girl—lounging underneath the dorms' joint canopy, smoking something.

"Out, get out!" I shouted.

Bullets thwacked against the cement at our feet, fired from

weapons equipped with silencers. Cody cursed as the bullets ricocheted off the stone walkway.

Out of my periphery, the students scattered.

"Ahead," I said, racing onto the university lawn that would take us into the woods.

With eyes not quite adjusted to the darkness, it felt as though we were running into an abyss. Our feet crunched over the rocky pathway, leaving no mystery to our whereabouts. The trail was slightly illuminated from the moonlight's reflection off white gravel, but barely.

I could hear Cody growling. "Can't outrun them with these."

"I know. Turn."

"The bullets," Cody huffed.

"They didn't sound right."

"But why would they use . . . ?"

We veered off the gravel into a clearing in the middle of the evergreens, which students often used for Frisbee golf. On the other side of the clearing, we could connect with the main road. No dorms, residential houses, nothing—out of harm's way. In fact, the road had deep ditches on the far side. Ditches in which we could barricade ourselves and rain fire on Mitchell and whoever else he'd brought with him.

We hopped in the ditch on the far side of the road.

I unzipped my duffle and pulled out an MP5. "Ammo," I said.

My phone started pinging, but I ignored it—I knew who it was and what he was probably texting.

Cody was already unzipping an ammunitions bag and loading up the guns. "I swear, if they're shooting rubbers at us— biggest mistake of their lives."

A car sped our way from a distance of one hundred yards, its four-way flashers blinking. What did that mean?

"Only if you see a weapon, got it?" I said. "Keep your finger off the trigger. If they're firing rubbers, then the conductor wants me alive. Let's keep it that way."

The car, which had now halved the distance to us, slowed.

Cody cocked his shotgun and pressed into the side of the ditch. I did the same.

"Car isn't crawling slow for a late-night drive," Cody said. "It's looking for us. Who else would know we're here but *him*?"

"Not until there's a weapon," I repeated.

The car pulled close enough for us to tell its make and model. It was a clunky Corolla with a single person inside. Didn't fit the bill of someone the conductor would use to chase us down.

The driver hit the brakes. "Get the other guy and get in, Haas," a voice called.

Who in the world was out at this hour and knew me by name? I glanced back at Cody, then jogged to the driver's side door, MP5 level in front of me, half expecting to find Alec, the only male student I could think of. But it wasn't Alec.

"David?" I said. It was the student I'd written up for drinking in public at the orientation fair.

"Yes," he said. "Would you please lower that?"

I fixed my aim between his eyes, flung open the door, and pulled him out, slamming him against the side. "What are you doing here? How'd you find us?"

He cried out in pain. "What are you—"

"Shut up," I said as I frisked him.

"Back at the dorms—I was with my girlfriend. I know about the string. Just trying to do something right."

"There!" a voice cried from the open field we'd crossed. "The car. Hit the tires!"

The *thipping* and *thwacking* returned, peppering trees and tearing apart bark behind us. I hit the cement and pulled David down with me, then returned fire, spraying left and right to lay down cover for Cody.

The shots they'd just fired were *not* rubber baton rounds.

"Get back in!" I yelled at David.

He shot up and dove into the Corolla. I followed, slamming the door behind me.

Cody rammed against the other side of the car for protection, returned a burst of fire, opened the back door, and crammed himself and the duffle bags inside. "Scums tried to kill us!"

I punched the gas as bullets smacked the side of the car.

After picking up steam and turning a corner, taking us out of our pursuers' line of sight, I shifted to David. "You're a part of it, now start talking."

But all I saw in the student's eyes was pain. David reached across his body, holding his side.

I leaned forward for a look. A baseball-sized crimson stain had blemished his shirt. "Cody, give me your belt."

14

Tires screeched against asphalt as I whipped into the emergency room portico of Saint Mary's Hospital, where I hoped Janet and Alec were still holed up in the cafeteria.

I swung my head around to Cody. "Go find Janet and Alec."

He exited the car, leaving the door open. I helped David out and held him up as a nurse came running out of the double doors.

"I'll get the stretcher," she said, turning around and shouting for more help.

I pulled out my phone and read texts the conductor must have sent after we broke protocol with the guns.

First Janet and Alec, now Cody and Golden Boy Haas. What am I to do?

That's the beauty of the string, Markus. I am to do nothing. The string is about to do everything.

Even the strongest break. The better question
may be: How much can you take?

My mind raced through what had happened on Stephanie's
property. Members of the string had been tasked with distracting me, then Serge had given his life crashing a van into Alec's
car. What had it taken for him to do that?

The conductor had already recruited Mitchell and probably
other officers. Who was he about to unleash on us now—and
with what as leverage?

I shook my head. Hated thinking about it.

A minute later, Cody, Janet, and Alec came bursting through
the ER doors.

"Is he okay?" Janet said, running up to the car just as two
paramedics took David and hoisted him onto a stretcher.

"In the car, Haas," Cody said, holding up a piece of paper
with an address. "She found him." He shook it violently. "She
found him and we're going to kill him."

"What?" I hustled back to the driver's side and plopped
behind the wheel. Cody got in the passenger seat.

Janet followed me and leaned down to look at me. The
duffle bags drew her gaze. "You got them. What happened?"

"We slipped his guys—Trenton badges—but more are coming, Janet, be sure of that. Don't trust anyone. He's leveraging
the string against the string, threatening people with . . . only
God knows what. Cody and I are going after him *now*. If you
hear from him, just—don't let him win." I tossed my head
toward the hospital. "The kid was there at the orientation
fair. Find out how he's involved and assume the conductor
has manipulated him, got it?"

She nodded.

I gripped the steering wheel and exhaled slowly. "The kid may have also just saved our lives. He'll need someone by his side if that's true."

"The address is for the World War II armory owned by campus," Janet said.

I knew the place she spoke of. It was a castle-like structure the university had inherited and now used for storage, chairs mostly. University police took turns checking the building every time spring graduation rolled around when extra seating was needed. If someone knew how to get inside, it would be a perfect place to hide out, film videos . . . take prisoners.

"I don't know if it's right," Janet said.

"It's right."

Alec jogged up next to Janet and opened the back door. "I did a feature on that building—I'm coming with."

I glanced at Janet, then back at Alec. It was better that he stay with her than risk getting in my and Cody's way. "You're more needed here."

"You don't get it." Alec's feverish eyes darted between Cody and me. "Story took me two weeks to write. I know every inch of that place. Imagine World War II indoor target practice, thousands of women volunteers doing aerial surveillance on a chalkboard, a roller rink, school dances, basketball games, and musical theater all mashed together in one blob of a structure—then wrap it all in cobwebs, graffiti, and odd cosmetic demolitions. It's a maze and a house of horrors all in one. If he's there, you'll need me if you want to find him. I even know how to get in the back without a key. I'm coming."

I wasn't going to waste any more time arguing.

I watched in the rearview mirror as Janet walked back into

the hospital while we drove away. I couldn't shake the feeling that the string ran through every floor of that hospital, just waiting for its opportunity to strike.

The conductor, shrouded in darkness, appeared to Janet in a memory from the computer lab, leaning over her, ripping at her clothes.

She tried shaking the thoughts away as she strode to David's room, unsure of what to do or expect until Markus, Cody, or Alec contacted her. *Could* they contact her? She supposed she could track Markus's phone, should she need to find them. But if it reached the point of her searching for them, then wouldn't the conductor and his string have already won?

She'd never had problems standing up to anyone. She'd encountered plenty of twisted cybercriminals throughout her career, but this burrowed into horrific depths she'd never thought possible. True evil. And it was squeezing the lifeblood out of her.

What if the conductor had gotten bored of Markus? Hired someone to walk up behind him—and Cody and Alec, for that matter—and stick a knife in his back? Where would she go if she were the last of the string trying to break it? When would the conductor come for her or her sister—or would he just let the string perform his violence for him?

She wished she could go to Lucy's side this moment, but she was committed to Markus and their plan to stop the conductor. If finding out what David knew and also protecting him was a part of that plan, then she would stay.

Janet tapped on the door to David's room and pushed inside. The hospital room looked like most: fake wooden floors, an enormously clunky bed that looked like it belonged on a spacecraft, a sink, two chairs, and a fake plant.

David stirred and opened his eyes. A tremor seemed to course through his body at the sight of her.

Janet needed to calm him and take the lead. "David, I'm a friend of the men you rescued. Sort of." She checked the time on her phone. "We all met yesterday."

"I need my phone," David said groggily. His breath smelled like one might expect from a disheveled student.

"Why?"

"I need to know if he knows."

Janet stepped to the windowsill where his belongings lay: cell, wallet, clothing. "He—the conductor." It wasn't a question.

"Yes, give me my phone." David was in no mood for chatting.

Janet handed him his phone and he unlocked it. His mouth trembled and his eyes widened. He flexed his fingers around his phone, pressing it to his chest.

Even though his circumstances warranted it, he was a bit of a drama queen. "What's it say?"

He turned his phone toward her. The conductor's text read:

You were such a good boy at first.

Why stop so suddenly, try to break my string?

You know what this means.

"I got this over an hour ago." David's bated breath seemed to pump shivers down his arms and legs. He tossed his sheets to the side and tried to swing his legs over the bed. "I have to get out of here; he'll find me."

"Stop, just stop. We have to outsmart him, not outrun him."
Janet's mind shifted to her sister, who was just a level up from
them in the hospital. The conductor hadn't done anything to
her, either by choice or because his string couldn't penetrate
through hospital security. Either way, it seemed rushing out
of here was ill-advised. "We're in a hospital, not the easiest
place to off someone." She spoke with some bite. "Tell me how
you got looped into this. Markus and Cody are going after the
conductor right now. You're not his biggest problem."

He pushed himself up against his pillows. "Guy gives me a
video out of nowhere, shows me photos of my parents at work,
at home . . ." He choked back tears. "Then a live video—him
walking up to my mom as she was getting home from work,
shaking her hand as if he were new to the neighborhood, and
my mom just smiled and went inside." He took a deep breath.
"The guy walked to a parked car," he said flatly, gaze directed
straight ahead, "opened the trunk, and let the camera linger
there."

Janet kept herself perfectly still. "And?"

David's gaze fell to his lap. "A saw, some shackles . . . and
my dad—just stuffed in there like a box of groceries."

Janet covered her mouth with one hand. She knew she had
to ask him what the conductor had forced him to do, but she
was relieved when he continued without prompting.

"At first he told me to act drunk at orientation to distract
the cop. But the texts kept coming. I'm a med student, so . . ."
Fresh tears welled in his eyes and his face stretched taut. "He
made me—" David appeared about to hyperventilate.

"Calm down. Made you what?"

"Cut open the university police chief, drop a tiny canister
in him . . . sew him back up."

Janet grimaced.

Then recognition struck: those photos she'd seen had been of Jackson Renfroe.

"I couldn't just leave him, so I sat outside the gym after the game was over, waited there for hours to make sure he was okay, until he finally must've woken from whatever coma the conductor had put him in."

"What then?"

"The conductor had me leave a tablet with him, so I knew the chief had become part of the game. I tried to get up the courage to tell him what I'd done, and, I don't know . . . help him. But I just went back to my dorm, grabbed my stash, and started making the pain go away. That's when I saw Haas and some other law enforcement guy—Cody, I guess—running from masked men with guns. Bullets were fired, and I just drove until I found them."

"Why would you do that?"

David's head dipped. "Because I brought Haas into the string and I haven't been any help to anyone since it started." He shook his head and allowed a chuckle. "My stash always makes me feel invincible."

Janet put a firm hand on his knee. "You did the right thing helping Cody and Markus."

A nurse, no older than thirty, stepped into the room. David tensed but tried to play it cool.

"Hi there, sorry, didn't know Mr. Kilpatrick had a visitor. You're a lucky one—doc said the bullet only grazed you."

Janet eyed the nurse as if he were a predator.

"I, uh . . . just have to check in on how he's doing."

Janet leaned against the wall, arms crossed. "Good. We don't want anything else happening to David. He's a special young man, you know—going to get his medical license. May even work here one day, conducting this, conducting that." She watched the nurse's body language.

Had he stuttered just a bit?

She pointed at the nurse's clipboard. Might as well go all in. "How long is that string of boxes you're checking, by the way? We were in the middle of a private conversation."

The nurse gave her an edgy smile. "I'll be out of here soon. Just a couple more things to check." He turned his back to her.

Janet didn't like that she couldn't see his hands. She took a couple of steps toward him, keeping an eye on David, who was gripping his bedsheets and pulling them over himself as if they were a shield.

The nurse reached for something in his pocket and Janet did the only thing that came to mind. She grabbed a dirty plate. Tucked it close to her like a Frisbee.

The nurse, flipping through pages in his notebook, turned to his side, pen in hand, and glanced at Janet. "Oh. Want me to take that?"

The steam she'd built up deflated, and she nodded and handed him the plate.

The nurse said all looked good for David—no complications from the wound. He stepped out of the room, door clicking shut behind him.

David turned to Janet and closed his eyes, taking a deep breath.

"Hey, I'm not going anywhere until I hear from Markus or Cody." She glanced at the room's doorway and then the window. "And if I leave this building, you're coming with me. Got it?" It seemed the best thing she could do now was keep David calm. "I spotted a vending machine a stone's throw away. I'm going to freshen up, then get some 7UP. What suits you?"

"Mountain Dew, thanks, and anything with cheese."

"Done and done."

Janet moved to the room's sink and splashed water on her face. It had been some time since she'd pulled an all-nighter. But fatigue hadn't really set in. Her mind had been pumping adrenaline nonstop since the explosion. She turned back to David, who was staring at his phone. "Hey, best not use that. Trust me. I'm the one who helped set up his surveillance."

David set the phone down.

"Any last snack requests?"

He shook his head.

Janet left the room and pulled the door closed. She glanced down each hallway and then at the nurses' station across the hall. Empty. She walked quietly down the echoing hallway until she reached a small sitting room that branched off from the main corridor. She could see David's room from here.

But in order to buy something from the vending machine, she'd lose visibility of his room. It was only a few seconds, though. She was being paranoid.

With a jump in her step, Janet ducked into the vending area and bought David's Mountain Dew first. As the machine's gears groaned, she peeked back around the corner. No movement. No one lingering or pretending to look busy. Up next were the cheese puffs.

Janet sidestepped back to the machine and swiped her card again. The groaning commenced once more, and this time she reached into the receptacle bin so she could catch the puffs and be on her way. Why did the gears and corkscrews turn so slowly? She wouldn't spend another second waiting on the 7UP.

Loot now in hand, she quickly stepped back into the hall-way, making eye contact with a nurse before looking away. *Just normal people, Janet. Get a grip.*

She twisted the door handle to David's room and pushed.

A middle-aged doctor with white hair and leathery skin was saying, "You'll just feel a—"

"Don't!" Janet yelled, dropping the snacks.

The doctor turned around. "Excuse me?" The look on his face was that of a man who had pulled far too many doub-les.

"I said don't give him that."

"It's to manage his pain. I'm sorry, who are you?"

She racked her brain for an excuse. "He's . . . an addict. Rehabilitating. I'm his drug abuse officer." She locked eyes with David. "We talked about this. It's not worth the risk."

David stared at the supposed morphine as if it were a lotto ticket being taken away.

The doctor glanced at the clipboard chart, then back at David. "That true? I thought you hardly knew this woman."

Janet piped up. "On a personal level, no. But on campus—"

The doctor waved his hand at her as if shooing her away. Her blood simmered.

"No, she's right," David said. "Known her from Trenton U. since I was a freshman."

The doctor checked his watch. "All right then, no meds. Fair warning, though. We're going to have to run some tests on him down at imaging soon—no visitors allowed."

Janet gave him the slightest acknowledgment.

The doctor walked toward the door, leaned close to her ear, and whispered, "I can always use this in the B wing."

Lucy.

Janet's stomach dropped as she watched the doctor exit the room and disappear behind the nurses' station.

"David, you have to get out of here—*now*." She pulled some cash out of her purse, handed it to him, and pointed at his pile of clothes. "Take off that wristband and have a stranger call a ride. Don't use your phone." Janet pulled out her own cell and showed David how to track Markus's location with it. "He's the one who will protect you, okay? He and Cody are the good guys."

"What are you going to do without your phone? What if the conductor texts you?"

"I can't play his games anymore. I'm going to protect my sister and am not leaving her side." She dropped her head for a moment, then swung it back up. "If you get the chance, tell Markus and Cody that I'm sorry. Now *go*."

We drove the snowy highway back toward the university area. "What are you mumbling?" I said, looking at Alec in the Corolla's rearview mirror.

Cody glanced back at him too, looking at the kid as if he were crazy.

"They're complete words in my head," Alec said. "They just don't all come out of my mouth."

"What's in your head then?" I noticed the notebook on his lap. "Those pages too."

Alec tapped his pen against the side of his head. "There's just been something in my head—the conductor. Who's the conductor? Who's running around with makeup and playing God with people's lives?"

"And?" Cody said.

"Who's in town right now?" Alec said. "It's Ivan Mikolaev. I love his music and should be biased against thinking he could be capable of the hell he's put us through. But he's a *conductor*. Best in the world. Here. In Trenton."

The same thought had crossed my mind back in the gymnasium, but I hadn't had time to explore it since. Ivan did have a similar profile, height, weight—but that's where things stopped adding up for him.

Still, I played devil's advocate and let Alec's brain do more work on it. "I saw him motionless on the court. He'd really fallen and really hurt himself." I blinked back to the highway as we passed a parked car alongside the road. "Why would he do that, this rich and famous prodigy? And how could he have been watching or texting us while performing that night?"

Cody tapped my arm. "So theoretically, if Ivan is the conductor, he could be at the hospital. They took Ivan to the hospital, right?"

I turned and looked at Cody. *Janet.*

"Haas!" Alec yelled.

I looked back to the road just in time to see a blur of a man. He had tossed something over the road: spikes.

I jerked the wheel, but there was no dodging them.

What sounded like two gunshots fired and the Corolla spun out of control—all four tires shredded.

I tapped the brakes, released, tapped, released, trying to regain any sort of control. We careened off the road and slid along the guardrail, sparks lighting up the darkness outside the windows. Shrieking metal on metal pierced the air.

The shrieks morphed into groans.

Then we stopped.

I peeled my hands off the wheel. Quick glance at Cody, quick glance at Alec.

Cody and I both drew our weapons. I could tell we were thinking the same thing.

The front of the car was still facing forward, which meant the person who'd dropped the spikes would be coming from behind. Opening our doors wouldn't provide cover. But . . .

"Alec, the back doors—open them!"

He was nearly hyperventilating in the back seat. Wasn't moving.

"Come on!" Cody threw his upper half into the back seat and pushed open the door behind mine, then proceeded to nearly crush Alec doing the same for his side.

Cody maneuvered back into his seat, then we both swung open our front doors and took cover behind them.

A single person was walking toward us—and he had a badge. In one hand he held a phone, pointing it at us as if taking a video, and in the other he held a Trenton University police–issued Glock.

"Hopkins?" I waved a hand at Cody to cover me as I lowered my weapon and stood straight.

Hopkins stopped about twenty yards away. "Naughty, naughty knots," he said, his voice breaking painfully.

I squinted. Shared a glimpse with Cody. Checked on Alec.

It was Hopkins speaking these words. But it was the conductor *saying* them.

"A part of me thought you'd never make it this far . . . that you'd break like all the others," Hopkins said in that same distressed tone.

"Hopkins," I said. "Where is he? Are there other hostiles? What's his play?"

Hopkins was holding back tears. "You think he's going to help *you*? He hated you long before I came along . . . along with the rest of the Trenton Police Department . . . and now you think he'll help? Do you have any idea the torment you're causing this man right now?"

"What's your stupid game?" I yelled.

"The guns," Hopkins said, though I think he was speaking for himself this time.

Cody shook his head at me.

"We can't do that," I said. "He's going to hurt a lot of people."

"That's the fascinating part," Hopkins said, the conductor clearly back. "You somehow separate the people you're hurting now—Janet, Serge, and Hopkins here—from the people who may or may not be hurt later. What's the difference, Haasy?" Hopkins choked back anguish and lifted his weapon.

I took cover behind my door once more. "Can you take his Glock?"

Cody, head as still and eyes as focused as I'd ever seen, simply said, "Yes."

"Either Hop here gets the guns . . . or the next knot will," Hopkins said. "You know that."

"Hopkins," I said, "just drop it. Come with us."

He shook his head.

Cody shouted some choice words, demanding the same thing.

"I *can't*," Hopkins yelled, extending his shaking gun toward us. "I won't!"

But then he did drop his gun.

Cody and I rushed toward him. He was convulsing on the ground.

Cody knelt, looked into the officer's eyes, tried to see into his mouth. "I don't know what's happening. He can't breathe."

The conductor was laughing through Hopkins's phone. At least, that's what I thought I heard. White noise was blasting through the speaker. I picked up the phone. It was a video call, and the conductor's face filled the screen as he patted his face with makeup.

"What's happening to him?"

"Slow, slow, so utterly slow, painful death," the conductor shouted. "It's a shame. He played his part well. But when knots break the string, knots get broken." The conductor scoffed. "You think it's just guns I want? No. It's this I want, the sweet, sweet sound of a tightly wound will *cracking*."

The connection clicked off.

Covered by darkness, we grabbed the duffle bags and huffed back to the car we'd seen parked alongside the highway—which indeed belonged to Hopkins—none of us saying a word. His keys hadn't been in his pockets, and they weren't above his visor. What had he done with them? "Come on!" I said, hitting the dashboard.

Somewhere above, a helicopter whirred through the night.

I was sick of the game. Of the killing. I knew deep down that I wasn't the killer, wasn't a killer at all, but the conductor had created an ecosystem in which my choices meant life or death for others. And in that sense, I *was* killing people.

The conductor had been right, and I hated it. I *was* cracking.

How many more would he kill if I kept trying to stop him?

Less than he planned on killing with the guns? Did he even plan on using the guns? My brain hurt.

The monster hadn't even played his trump card yet. I needed to find Steph and the girls . . . then kill the conductor.

Silence weighed heavily on us as we used Hopkins's phone to request an Uber—three grown men, two duffle bags, and a quiet, snowy highway.

Upon arriving in a CR-V, the driver popped the trunk and I loaded the bags. He appeared to have stopped to get himself coffee and breakfast en route to picking us up.

"Could you have come any slower?" I bit out.

"Sorry. Ice and all."

He dropped us off a few blocks away from the armory, and we stashed the guns behind a large recycling container across the road from the armory's front entrance.

That's when Alec told Cody and me what we needed to know.

There was a clear way in through the front and the back. But the multilevel complexity of the building meant it could take five or ten minutes to get from one end to the other—maybe more if the mazelike interior had changed in the last three years, which was when Alec had written the feature for the *Telegraph*. The conductor would have the option to not only slip out the back with Steph and the girls if he saw us coming from the front, but also take a quick nap before doing so. This meant we had to cover both the front and rear entrances.

Which meant splitting up.

Which meant being unable to cover one another's backs.

"Whoever goes through the front will be spotted. There's no cover—he'll see you coming if he's set up cameras or motion sensors," Alec said. "But there's enough wooded area near the back that you could hide and watch until he's flushed out. He won't see us there."

I studied the seventy-thousand-square-foot, three-story building, which looked as though it belonged in England next to other countryside castles. Mortar-laced clay tile, bricks, and sandstone covered the exterior walls, which extended to turret corners. The arched front entrance was made of solid oak and was notched with two barred window openings.

If the conductor were to see anyone coming, I wanted it to be me. He had an eccentric fascination with me, and for that reason alone, he may be slower to retaliate.

"You two take back. You don't see me come out, assume the worst and create a new plan. Got it? No one stops until the conductor is in cuffs or dead."

"We're getting them back, Haasy. Especially if he runs into me." Cody tapped the barrel of his shotgun.

"If you shoot, *know* it's him first. He's all tricks and the girls might be in there."

We split up, Cody and Alec circling around the back while I stayed positioned behind the recycling container.

Doubt weaseled into my thoughts. What if Janet was wrong? What if the conductor had been here but had changed locations? If he wasn't here, neither were Steph and the girls. And if they weren't here, they could be anywhere. I'd have no other place to look—completely powerless to save them or stop the conductor.

I looked for some kind of surveillance at the front entrance but didn't spot any. Cameras had gotten so small and easy to set up. I'd need hours to convince myself that I wasn't being watched this very moment. The only advantage I had was my key ring. The armory belonged to Trenton, and that meant my key would open the door—unless the conductor had taken further precautions.

If the conductor was operating off the assumption that university staff only entered the building to collect extra chairs for graduation, then maybe he had overlooked changing the lock or adding additional deterrents.

I slipped across the road to the armory. Inserted my key into the lock. The bolt popped free—*thank you*—and I stepped inside, letting the darkness of the room swallow me.

Normally skylights would provide enough natural light to maneuver the building, Alec had said. But it was too early for morning light to sink through the windows. Blackness was so thick that I couldn't see my own boots or the gun with which I was sweeping the room.

I grabbed my flashlight and tucked it under my pistol, checking left, right. Heaps upon heaps of chairs, mazes of folding tables, and antique furniture pieces lay scattered about the floor. To my left were a makeshift bench and pegboard filled with tools. It looked as though Doug had put the space to use for the university maintenance crew.

Alec had told me that this room was the only normal part of the building. The armory was an anomaly of levels, cramped passageways, and wonky spaciousness. The main part where I stood now was ordinary enough, save for the wooden walkway that ran along the perimeter, overlooking me the way a catwalk might overlook a prison yard. But the moment I ventured out of this room, it was all a smorgasbord due to all the hand changing and half-baked uses the building had been subjected to over the years, according to Alec. Passages leading nowhere. Levels created by unnecessary steps. Hallways shrinking smaller and smaller as you walked through them.

"None of it makes sense," Alec had said. "The only people who appreciate it are the graffiti artists who break in to do their thing."

Steph and the girls were somewhere in this labyrinth, and so was the conductor—I could feel it. I was going to rescue three and kill one.

Outside, tires skidded to a halt.

I took cover behind a stack of chairs and turned off my flashlight. I eyed the door and pursed my lips. Who could've known we were here?

For several minutes, nothing happened. But I could hear the faint sound of footsteps in the distance, so I skirted the outer wall, feeling my way through the nooks and crannies. My fingers touched what felt like a tablecloth and I scooted underneath it.

The footsteps grew louder as they approached the building's entrance. Had to be three or four people. Then voices. They were arguing about how to proceed and who should follow whose lead.

I recognized the voices and shook my head. How had he found us?

"Haas, we know you're here," Mike Mitchell said. "He's got us hostage, just like you. We didn't want to chase you—but you understand, don't you? He's got our families, our money, our futures, all wrapped around his finger."

One of the others tried to say something, but Mitchell must've waved him off. The voice had come from a different part of the armory floor. They were spreading out.

"You're not going along with him," Mitchell said. "You're

breaking the string like the good man you are." He paused. "Is it Steph? I get it. He's got my wife, Haas. My *wife*. And the only way she survives is if you give up. We're all ruined if you keep going rogue, you get that? So please, just . . . come out. There's more at stake here. We have to ride it until it's over. The moment he's finished, we get our lives back. He's crazy but he's not after our families, we both know that. He wants something else. So come out. We'll be in your debt and we can work together for a change, come up with a plan to catch him, stop him for good."

Mitchell's words hung in the air.

So much of what he'd said penetrated my core, but Mitchell was all tactics right now, trying to wrangle me in through my softest spot. I couldn't let that happen. I had never trusted him and wouldn't start now. Steph and the girls were here, and abandoning them now would be signing their death warrants— and many others', thanks to those guns.

Mitchell sighed. "This is what I was afraid of, Haas. You need to understand that this isn't a difference in opinions, or even right and wrong. He'll hurt our families if we don't get you to stop. Hear that? I'm not here for anything other than to protect my family. I will *kill* to protect my family. *We* will kill to protect our families. We already found your stash behind the recycling—we've got the weapons, you get me?"

I lowered my head and closed my eyes. Mitchell had signed a mass execution order by taking those weapons.

"It's just you left. And in case you hadn't noticed, you're being surrounded by multiple SWAT-trained officers."

Whether it was true or not, I wanted to tell Mitchell that the only way to protect his family was to join me now in stopping the conductor, even with the risk. People were going to die at the conductor's hands, and only those caught in the string had any chance of stopping that from happening.

"Fine, Haas." Mitchell cocked his weapon.

All went quiet in the armory.

The cocking of Mitchell's gun seemed to ring in the air, making me wonder if the conductor's texting hiatus was part of a new narrative—a narrative that no longer cared if I lived or died.

I visualized the space from an aerial vantage point. The tablecloth near my face brightened slightly—they were using flashlights. Footsteps to the right, footsteps to the left, and then Mitchell somewhere in the middle. There were three of them. Three officers sworn to protect the people, now coerced into facilitating their slaughter. I quietly repositioned myself as the glow of their flashlights loomed brighter.

One of the beams scanned the cloth draped over the table I was crouched under. I could practically see Mitchell's visual cues to the other officers in the room.

One of them bent down to flip up the fabric. But I was no longer there. I'd passed under the cloth on the backside of the table.

If I had it right in my mind, I could draw a line from my crouched position to the officer who'd lifted the cloth and, behind him, the second officer covering him. It was a long shot, but no other options remained.

I shoved the table up and ran it forward like a ginormous shield.

It slammed into the mystery officer's body—Dominguez, I could now see—producing a loud crack. He collapsed to the ground.

I burst even harder forward, past the fallen officer, heading straight for the one backing him up. It was Adams. The tabletop connected with him, but barely, because he'd dived out of the way.

I threw the table and transferred my momentum into a slide that I quickly popped up from, Fox pepper spray in hand. Normally I'd shoot in bursts, as the formula wreaked havoc not only on the assailants but oftentimes the sprayer. But this time I kept my finger pressed against the discharge button, dousing my two colleagues and rendering them incapacitated.

I needed to get to Mitchell.

Two prongs stuck in my back like fishhooks, and my body went rigid and started shaking uncontrollably. The Taser's voltage didn't relent.

Mitchell was retaliating to the extra pepper with extra shockage.

"Get the clown his guns," Mitchell said into his radio while Dominguez and Adams groaned on the floor.

"Making . . . mistake," I said, but my words were slurred. I clamped my eyes shut then opened them wide, trying to shift my mind from the pain to a plan.

I loathed Mitchell, but he was a law-abiding citizen.

Enjoyed putting bad guys behind bars.

Dominguez and Adams weren't corrupt men either.

Each had morals and had sworn oaths.

And we were all here, in this moment, armed and at the very location of the perpetrator wreaking havoc on our lives. Why couldn't they see that? Why couldn't I communicate that?

"Hate the circumstances, Haas, but it just feels right tasing you." Mitchell grabbed the back of my collar and dragged my convulsing body out the door.

Outside, dawn was just beginning to announce her arrival with an orange glow.

"Hello?" a deep voice called out from the parking area in front of the armory. Someone new had arrived.

"Who are you?" Mitchell said.

"Doug, maintenance crew—saw the door was open. What's going on?"

"Making an arrest, Doug, and he's dangerous. Get out of here."

"Need my tools in there. I'll wait." There was sarcasm to his words. To strangers, Doug was a mean old gruff who never took an order from someone he didn't respect.

"Have it your way." Mitchell continued dragging me. "Man up, Haas. It was a few thousand volts."

"What'd he do?" Doug asked.

"See me asking why you reek of gasoline?" Mitchell said. "Mind your business."

"Fine, but I'm getting my tools." Doug disappeared into the armory behind us.

Mitchell kicked me in the stomach, and I writhed in pain. He dragged me for another fifteen feet and leaned me against his Ford F-150. "Move an inch and I'll tase you again." He jogged back into the armory and reemerged with Adams and Dominguez, both red-faced and staggering. "Want to get even with Haas—now's your chance. A swift kick sure felt good."

"Shut up and drive. University guy is here," Dominguez said.

Adams felt around for the door handle and, upon finding it, got in the passenger seat without saying a word. Dominguez got in the back of the truck. They'd both be practically blind for a while longer, depending on how much pepper spray had hit its mark.

Mitchell, arms crossed, towered over me and spit on my chest. "Get in the back seat."

I pushed myself up and leaned my head on the driver's side door, limbs still twitchy and weak. I let my eyes linger on Mitchell. "Think of those guns. He's got something horrible planned and he's using you to make it happen."

"Deed's already done, Haas. Not going to ask you again." Mitchell flicked the Taser toward the back seat.

That was fine with me. I'd stalled him long enough.

Doug swung the blunt end of his gardening shovel, smacking Mitchell in the back of the head. He dropped to the ground, knocked unconscious. Doug then slammed the shovel's backside straight into the truck's windshield, exploding the glass. Dominguez and Adams reared back in defensive postures, blinking rapidly with watery, red eyes, neither attempting to pull their weapon.

I picked up Mitchell's firearm and leaned over the broken windshield. "Where are the guns?" I boomed. "Where'd you take the guns?"

Dominguez shook his head while Adams just sat still. They both kept trying to open their eyes to look at me but were not successful.

"If you give him the weapons, hundreds will die. Got it?" I paused for a moment, then cursed at their silence.

"Doesn't work like that," Dominguez said. "We gave them to one of the conductor's runners. They're gone. He's got them."

I punched the truck and they flinched. "Give me your weapons. Get out of the car."

They both did so.

I nodded at Doug.

He nodded back. "What can I do?"

I pointed the barrel of my gun at Mitchell. "Take this one to the hospital, make sure he's okay. Tell them you came across him like this." I found myself at a loss for words, trying to give Doug some context.

He waved me off. "I'll do it."

"Thank you." I glanced at the armory, then back at Adams and Dominguez. "You two are ending this with me."

15

After helping Doug load Mitchell into his rig, giving him a brief rundown of why three Trenton police officers had gotten the drop on me, and sending him off to the hospital, I approached Dominguez and Adams, both of whom could finally look me in the eyes without blinking a dozen times.

"You both just served as accomplices in delivering a small army's munitions to a madman." I hit my chest. "*This* is your chance to save your families. To stop him before he does something worse. Cody's already here, the back is covered. All we have to do is flush him out. Are you in?"

Dominguez eyed the armory. "You sure the conductor's in there?"

"Yes or no?" I said.

Adams turned to me, then to Dominguez. He nodded.

"Fine." Dominguez extended his hand, eyeing the weapon he'd handed over, which I'd tucked into my pants. "I'll need that back."

I hesitated but gave them back their firearms and forced

them to take the lead, making them walk with their backs to me. They both knew full well which one of us had the quickest draw. More importantly, I believed this was their moment to overcome fear and find their freedom again.

We approached the door back into the armory. The conductor would soon have to face not one or two SWAT-trained officers, but four.

Somehow even four versus one felt lopsided in the conductor's favor.

We walked through the main storage area where we'd had our scuffle, then stepped into the unknown of the building, experiencing its strangeness and complexities in silence for several minutes.

Graffiti artists, vagrants, and pot smokers had made little additions to the horror house over the years, it seemed—mounds of charred wood from fires, butts, needles—but then I spotted an addition that had to have been left by the conductor himself: a security camera, far too new and high-tech to have been installed by anyone but the white-faced demon.

He was here—and that meant Steph and the girls were close.

I signaled the camera's location to Adams and Dominguez. They nodded and we each tried skirting around its line of sight, deeper into the building.

"Welcome, welcome," the conductor said, his voice seemingly coming from every direction.

We pressed our backs to the hallway and froze, covering each other in a tight triangle.

"Markus Haas, once again here against all odds—and you even recruited some buddies, much to their horrific peril. You're such an adventure, a knot so curiously tangled."

Adams and Dominguez both looked at me, faces pallid and shoulders tight.

"Making friends. That's the origin of beautiful music, you know. One musician goes rogue, disrupts the melody so much that he creates a sound entirely new. But it comes at a price, always comes at a price. Nobody in the orchestra likes the disrupter, eager to hear his own notes with no regard for the symphony. Others turn on him without so much as a cue from the conductor. And who would blame them? Each of us must do what we must to survive. Take Adams and Dominguez, for instance."

I could see the tendons standing out in the officers' necks and their pulses pounding.

"Their families are in precarious situations, much like your Steph and chickpeas," the conductor continued. "Except nothing terrible has happened to their loved ones, not yet anyway. But because these two fine men of Trenton followed the disrupter, they're just as guilty as him, as *you*. Now, since the rest of the orchestra isn't here to keep you in line, I'm going to have to step in and bring order back for the sake of the symphony. Here's the rub for Dominguez and Adams: the first one to kill the other lives, and so does his family. Not true for the other, or the other's family."

Dominguez and Adams fixed their gazes on me, then each other, eyes looking as though they could drill holes through cement.

The silence and severity of the moment hung in the air like pin-pulled grenades. I held out an open hand, fingers spread, trying to slow down their minds before they arrived at a disastrous conclusion.

Just a twitch. That's all it took.

Adams's hand, which happened to be gripping his pistol, twitched.

And that caused Dominguez to raise his weapon level with Adams's head.

"Put it down. This is what he wants," I said. "We can save your families."

"Shut up!" Dominguez's hand shook. He backed up a couple of steps, making it harder for me to make a move to disarm him.

Adams tucked his chin into his sternum and tilted his eyes up. "Come on, Dom. Listen to Haas."

"Tell me you wouldn't do the same if you'd drawn first," Dominguez said.

"Dom . . ." Adams said.

I raised my hands. "You pull that trigger, your family is worse off than if you help us stop him. Think about it. Murder one. You'd be lucky to get out of prison in time for hospice." I took a step toward Dominguez. "He's got my girls too, here, right in this building."

Dominguez scoffed. "That's why we're here? Not to stop him, but to help you get *your girlfriend*?" He pointed at me as if his finger were a pistol. "Our families could die because of you." He looked at Adams, then at the ceiling, as if speaking to the conductor. "Hey, our families for Haas. He's the disrupter, not us. We'll catch up with Mitchell right now, finish everything you told us. Everything."

I dropped my hands to my sides, feeling the shift of allegiance like an arctic chill. "Listen, this is our only chance at him before he commits mass murder. This isn't about us choosing who lives and dies—it's about stopping the puppet master."

Silence filled the corridor.

The conductor cleared his throat, then slow-clapped. "A speech to be reckoned with, Mr. Haas." I could hear him smile over the speakers. "My deal stands."

I looked to Dominguez, Dominguez looked to Adams, and Adams looked to me.

Dominguez snarled painfully and fired, placing a bullet directly in the middle of Adams's forehead. He dropped to his knees, eyes wide, then collapsed onto the dirty floor.

I crouched and closed my eyes, letting my gun hand dangle.

"I had to do it," Dominguez said. "You heard what he was going to do."

I stared at Adams, face trembling. It was as if everything I meant for good had morphed into death. How could I stop the killing?

"Bravo," the conductor said. "You win, Dominguez. Bask in the feeling. You saved your family, came out on top, won the lottery." His voice deepened. "The problem with winning is the fine print, the details that come after. Like mail-in rebates, yes? You'd think you were applying for diplomatic immunity with the hoops they make you jump through. It's like a train crossing—a necessary annoyance we put up with to keep things moving. So, if I may: here comes the train."

I looked at Dominguez, who returned my gaze. *Don't do anything stupid*, I wanted to say.

"Pretty simple, Haas," the conductor said. "Kill Dominguez and your girls live. He kills you and—"

Dominguez swung his pistol toward me and fired.

I'd prepared for it, already rolling to my left. The moment I spun off my back and into a crouch, it was over.

Dominguez's gun was pointed at where I'd been, while my pistol was instinctively zeroed in on his chest.

I tilted my aim and pulled the trigger, hoping to avoid the kill shot. Dominguez jerked backward, landing on his backside.

Shoving a fist to my mouth, I strode to his side and forced myself to look at the man's eyes. There was no way I'd be able to give him the medical attention he needed, and the way he was looking at me, it seemed he knew this as well. He was going to die here unless . . .

I pulled out my phone and punched in 911.

"Oh, Haas, you wouldn't want to spoil your victory just like that, would you?"

"Stop this!" My lungs hurt from shouting so loud.

Several moments passed.

"Put away your phone," the conductor said.

"Do it." Dominguez had trouble speaking. "Don't let him . . . my family."

"I won't."

Clapping boomed over the speakers. "Congratulations, Haas, your girls live."

I stood and immediately worked my way deeper into the building, sweeping my weapon from doorway to doorway. "I'm going to make you feel every one of your murders."

"Rules are rules, and you've been breaking them like thrift store wine glasses. Had I not chosen you, I'd already be feeding your eyeballs to my fish. You really think the tough-guy routine is your best play, Markus?"

"Why me?" I spoke through gritted teeth, continuing to clear rooms, hallways. I needed to keep my cool, come up with a plan, OODA . . . but inside I could feel myself losing it. Every plan was leading to pain. What was left for me to do? To end the conductor I needed information—something, *anything*. "You hide behind makeup, have no regard for human life—tell me the rest of the story. Someone beat you and now you're out for blood? School rejected you and you're making it pay? Now's your chance, *conductor*. Who's behind the mask?"

Nothing but silence. Was I getting close to him, or had I triggered him?

"The verbose one, quiet? Why don't you lay it out? You've been ahead every step—what do you have to lose?"

I could only hear the beat of my own heart.

Beat.

Beat.

Beat.

"Mama?" a little girl's voice said groggily, shocking me out of my state of rage.

"Isabella." I looked at the ceilings until I spotted another camera. "Leave them out of this. You've got me." I put my gun down. "Unarmed."

Heavy breathing came over the speakers. "You're becoming less interesting with every word," the conductor said with a far more guttural voice. "Your code is proving more pedestrian than I'd credited you with."

"Tell me where you are." I slammed my fist into the wall. "Let's play your game."

"Game? No, no, far too fanciful for our purposes." The conductor took a drag of breath. "Take a right, pass seven doors, then a left into the room that smells of death. Out the other end, descend the stairs. We'll be waiting."

I ran as fast as I could, only slowing down around blind spots and corners, just in case the conductor had another iron fist and gas waiting for me.

Finally, I reached the stairs and descended them. I no longer had my gun, but my knife was safely within reach.

Stepping down the final stair, I entered a room with an aged leather chair that looked as though it had served as a seat for the first practicing dentists—if said dentists had made a habit of tying down their patients. A lone mirror overlooked the room from above—definitely two-way.

"Stephanie, are you there?"

A crackle came through speakers mounted in the corners of the high-ceilinged room. "Of course she's here, Markus. Exhausted, bloodied, and bruised from fighting her restraints, but here nonetheless. She and I have been getting to know each other. Most importantly, we've been getting to know about *you.*"

Scenarios raced through my mind. How could I get an advantage without endangering Steph and the girls? The conductor had me cornered the same way he'd had Dominguez and Adams.

A projected screen flashed to life on one side of the room. "Have a seat, Markus."

I sat on the chair, realizing that the straps and shackles were for me.

"Good, good. Now hold tight as I come strap you down."

My body tensed, sensing the opportunity about to present itself. I pulled my knife from its sheath and concealed it by my side.

Thirty seconds later, footsteps started down the staircase behind me.

I needed to wait until the conductor was close enough to strike, yet far enough away that I could strike first. I pictured every step on the staircase—sixteen—and had already counted thirteen steps.

But in the back of my mind, I couldn't help but think that this plan, too, would lead to pain. I couldn't do it. But I had to do it. The conductor wasn't going to let Steph and the girls go unharmed whether I played along or not. Even if he did, what of the guns? Who would those be used on—and what if I could have prevented it from happening?

The conductor was now in the same room as me, just as he'd been in the communications building, just as he'd been at Stephanie's house. A mere few feet behind me. I could hear every light step. The question was whether or not he was armed.

I rubbed the handle of my knife with my index finger. It helped give rhythm to my thoughts and keep my hands steady.

The steps drew within striking distance. This time I wouldn't let him live.

I rolled to my left, coming up with a right-hand jab.

But my knife flew out of my fingertips, which had suddenly become lifeless.

My mind and body had locked up, triggered by an inner alarm. The knife, still airborne with forward momentum, slid through Stephanie's hair, just over her left shoulder.

The blade hit the stairwell behind her and clattered to the ground.

My knees nearly gave way. "I'm sorry, Steph, I'm so sorry." I wanted to hug her and kiss her and tell her it was almost over. That I was going to do whatever it took to keep her and the girls safe.

But something else was wrong. She was looking at me as if the blade *had* sunk into her.

"The girls," I breathed. "What's he done?"

The conductor scoffed over the intercom. "You think *I've*

done something, Markus? You think *I've* caused some irreversible harm? Oh, do you feel that? Do you hear the unbreakable breaking?"

"Where are they—"

"Close your protective piehole and let's get to the truth of the chickpeas' suffering."

"Steph, is he in there? Armed? What about the girls?"

She shook her head. Her silence must be the conductor's doing.

I stepped to the mirror and slammed it with my fist. "Where are they!"

"Markus," Stephanie pleaded in a whisper.

I turned around to find her eyes filled with tears.

"Let me tell you a story, a story about two chickpeas," the conductor said. "These chickpeas loved life, exuded character, and had the most wonderful parents. But something happened." The conductor snapped his fingers. "Daddy snapped. The life he'd created, crushed. So he gave up on the chickpeas. It haunted their souls as they wondered, day after day, 'Where's that man who used to be here, reading to me in bed? Where's . . . Daddy?'"

Tears flowed from Stephanie's eyes.

"Stop it, just end this." I swung my arms wide and tilted my head down, my throat tightening. I couldn't think of any way to protect the girls I loved. "I'm right here. Please. Me for them."

But the conductor kept going like he hadn't heard a word. "The chickpeas powered through on the strength of a woman who packed the strength of ten women. They survived, moved on, regrouped. Then you came into the picture, Markus, bringing even more hope, breathing fresh air into Stephanie's lungs. You made the chickpeas smile again. It was so familiar."

The conductor let his words linger. "As if they'd found the very person they thought they'd lost forever."

The projector awakened, showing a photo of me with girls hanging off my arms. Not *the girls*, Isabella and Tilly. But women. I knew the exact time and place the photo had been taken, and I glanced at the floor in disgust.

The photos kept flipping, each one seemingly more incriminating than the last. The final shot was of me with two girls—maybe even underage—heading upstairs to a bedroom at the Ward estate. I wanted to vomit, thinking of what Steph must be assuming.

But did this mean the conductor knew *all* about me? I couldn't say anything until I knew what he knew about my past.

I looked at Steph and struggled for the right words. "I know this seems impossible—but there's an explanation."

"There always is for people like you, Markus," the conductor said. "We're not going to venture that path. We know how it ends. We're going to use our time together in a much more productive way. So many possibilities, so much going through my mind—like Mozart composing in inspiration's heat. I like the thought of that." There was a pause, then the speakers started blaring Mozart's *Requiem*. "Doesn't it just tickle your toes?"

I couldn't see the conductor through the mirror but could picture him nonetheless. And he was smiling, always smiling, in a way that made me feel like he knew something I didn't.

"Time for you two to switch places," the conductor said. "Stephanie, get in the chair."

My heart sank as Steph looked at the chair's restraints.

I turned to the mirror and pounded the chair with my fist. "No! You twisted—"

"The stallion gallops on," the conductor snipped. "But he seems to have forgotten about the chickpeas so calmly asleep, each within arm's reach, each a simple injection away from sleeping much, much longer."

"Markus, get away from the mirror." Steph seated herself and fiddled with the chair straps with shaking hands. She then directed her words to the conductor. "Look. Do your worst. Leave my girls alone. They don't belong here. Please."

I stepped away from the glass, moved toward the chair, and grabbed Stephanie's hand.

She seemed reluctant, then squeezed my fingers like a vise. "Keep them safe. Do what it takes."

I eyed the staircase I'd descended into the room. The girls and the conductor were merely a room away . . . and there was nothing I could do about it. I glanced back at the mirror.

The conductor's voice lowered to its stern volume. "Tie her down."

Stephanie nodded at me, but I couldn't move. My mind was trying to leap ahead to wherever this was heading and if there were any scenarios—any at all—that offered an escape for Steph and the girls.

Taking on a tone she'd never used with me before, Stephanie yelled, "Do it! Stop thinking and do it!"

"This is why relationships are out of the question," the conductor said. "So much this, not enough that. Conflict to the chin. No thanks."

I tied Stephanie to the chair, shackling first her wrists, then her ankles, then pulling a harness over her stomach. She couldn't move now if she tried.

"There, that wasn't so hard. Now it's time we get to the real reason we're here: the full confession of Markus Haas."

Morning songbirds chirped at the light of dawn. Cody, flat on his stomach next to the base of an evergreen, squinted at the thick slab of lumber that served as the back door of the armory. Now he understood why some officers always had a pair of binoculars handy. He couldn't see any cameras or high-tech sensors anywhere. But he was looking with his naked eyes.

They'd taken an excruciating amount of time making their way from the front of the building to the back, as Alec had made it clear that the conductor was obsessed with surveillance. If they were spotted before Haas was able to make contact, their element of surprise would be blown. The conductor would feel trapped. And trapped animals attacked.

"Nothing, zilch." Cody rolled back behind the tree, next to Alec.

"But we can't be sure," Alec said.

If surveillance was used on the back door, then it was most certainly used on the front. The conductor knew Markus was coming. And since the lunatic hadn't exited the back, either he didn't feel threatened or he was hunting Haas. Neither scenario made Cody's position easy. He needed to help his friend.

Cody checked his phone. Had he given Haas enough time? He looked at Alec. "Be ready to move. You know how to handle a weapon?"

Alec wet his lips. "Already? You sure? I haven't before. I don't think—"

"What's the matter? Thought you were here to help."

"I am. I just—I think we should stick to the plan, wait for Haas to flush him out, then make a move."

"It's been too long. Either Haas has him or he has Haas.

Maybe something in between. Either means Haas could use help. I wouldn't ask this in any other circumstance, but I'm already suspended, so . . . watch my back, got it?"

Alec's brows furrowed and he tucked his chin. "I can't. I'm not trained."

Was he shaking? Now the kid had all of Cody's attention. "What's the matter with you?"

Alec jumped to his feet and a notebook fell out of his pocket. He snatched it up quickly.

Cody stood as well and stared at him, concern for the back door suddenly fading. The kid was afraid of the conductor, but that wasn't the whole story here. Alec knew something that Cody and Haas didn't. And it was eating at him, which could only mean one thing: whatever he was hiding was dangerous to himself, Cody, or Haas.

His instincts screamed it was the latter two. "You've got an empathetic side, don't you, journalist? Can step into the shoes of others and feel their thoughts, pains, fears. Am I right?"

Alec said nothing.

"Look at you. Shaking uncontrollably."

He wasn't, but Cody wanted to put him more on edge. The kid was refusing to look him in the eye, and his shoulders were a tad more hunched.

"If I were to venture a guess, I'd say you're feeling fear not for one person but for two, or maybe five, if you give a lick about Stephanie, Isabella, and Tilly." He put extra emphasis on each name. "And I didn't even mention Markus or myself." Cody stepped into Alec's personal space. "I won't let anyone hurt them. Do you understand me?"

"I'm here to help. I don't even know what you're talking about."

"Great." Cody extended his hand. "Give me the notebook."

"Why?"

"Proof that you're on our side. Right now your words are telling me that you're my friend, while your body language is telling me something else. Know what that is, Alec? An agenda. That true?"

"I've got nothing—"

"Then give it to me."

Alec stared at Cody for several moments, glanced at the notebook. Then he took off running.

"Great." Cody broke into a sprint after him. He was sure the kid excelled in journalism, but he certainly hadn't played Division I football.

Cody launched himself into a tackle and Alec collapsed underneath him. Cody shoved his knee into Alec's back, pinning him down as he withdrew the notebook from the kid's back pocket. Flipped it open.

Most of it was shorthand, but Cody quickly deduced what the scribbles meant. "You're collecting notes for a story? About the conductor?" He put more pressure into Alec's back, and he cried out.

Cody flipped to the most recently penned pages of the notebook, where a time was jotted down along with a note: *He contacts me.*

"Who's contacting you, Alec? Kind of cryptic, don't you think?" He twisted his knee into the student's spine.

"You're going to break my back."

"No, no, Alec—that's what you do to mothers when you step on a crack. I'm going to do far worse." Cody leaned down and gripped Alec's neck.

"You're a sheriff!"

"Wrong. I'm a sheriff's detective, and I'm defending myself and those I love against a violent attacker and must subdue him before he kills me first!"

"Okay!"

"Okay what?"

"He made me a deal."

"What deal?"

"I tell him when we arrive at the armory, and I keep you and Haas separated once we get here. He said no one would be—"

"Hurt? Man, the fact that he put it that way, wow, *I'm* convinced. Who wouldn't take that deal for . . . ?" Cody let the question linger.

"The story, everything he's doing," Alec said. "He was going to get his way whether I helped or not."

"Personal interviews, huh. Valuable." Cody cuffed him to a large root. "You two will have a great time telling tales across your cells." He stood.

"I'm sorry. I made a mistake. I can still help you."

"Like you have a choice. Tell me—that talk of surveillance, was that just to stall me?"

"It could be true," Alec said. "But yes."

"You said you knew a way in."

"Follow the back wall to the right, grab the barrel, then hoist yourself up to the window. Bars look solid, but they've been cut."

Cody turned and ran to the armory.

The conductor, standing between the slumbering Isabella and Tilly and gazing intently into the observatory glass, slowly rubbed the hair of the sleeping chickpeas.

Every symphony was composed of so much more than the climax. The final moment may be what drew people to their feet, but it was the buildup, the *tease*, that turned weary legs into spring-loaded awe and wonder. That's what he had set out to accomplish with Haas. He would break the man he had deemed most unbreakable, and it would be a show to remember.

This moment with Haas and Stephanie, so unpredictable yet wonderfully planned, was the conductor's buildup to the finale. She was going to see Haas for who he was until disgust had ransacked her soul, and then she was going to *hate* him for what was about to happen to her girls.

Markus Haas, this man with the "unbreakable" code, was about to experience an utter crushing of his will.

"Okay, Haas, this is simple. I want your confession. Stephanie's seen the evidence, so no need to dance around details. But first things first—grab the gag underneath the chair."

Haas peeked under the chair and lingered for a moment, taking in the spring-loaded blade the conductor had crafted to thrust into the chair at a click of a button.

"We understand ourselves? Gag her."

Haas's body language softened. The relenting of the strong-hearted university cop had begun. He proceeded to gag Stephanie, who stared at him with watery eyes.

"Well, what are you waiting for?" the conductor said. "Your audience of one awaits."

Haas stood beside the chair, eyes downcast. The conductor grinned and pressed his hands onto the two-way mirror, leaning in so close he could kiss the glass. This was going to be exquisite.

"I haven't told you everything about me," Haas said. "Those pictures, they're real."

Stephanie tried curling her legs to her chest, but the shackles restrained her. Her leaking eyes were locked in a place of pain, and she wouldn't look at Haas, either by choice or by sheer torment. The conductor exhaled hot air onto the glass. It was getting so good.

Haas put his hand on Stephanie's head, leaned down, and kissed her. But he'd turned his head away from the conductor, whispered something.

"Got something to say, it better be loud enough for the girls and me to hear," the conductor said.

Haas looked at the two-way mirror. "I told her I love her—can I not have one unruined moment?" He turned back to Stephanie. "I've broken your trust." He shook his head. "Hurt you . . . didn't trust you with the truth. But I love you and the girls, and that will never change."

The music seemed off for a moment, as if there'd been a glitch, the conductor noticed. But it wasn't the music itself. It was another sound.

He turned away from the observatory room window to see Cody Caulkins bull-rushing him.

The impact blew both of them through the glass and into the chamber below.

Glass exploded behind me, and I instinctively shielded Stephanie from the broken shards. Shavings chimed against the ground as I turned to see Cody stumbling to his feet and—

The conductor. Right here. Black holes around his eyes and mouth, with wormy black veins sewn across his white-caked face. His Von Boch had flown off his head, and he was frantically pulling his raincoat over his nose and mouth with one hand and reaching into his pocket with the other. Fishnet trapped his dark hair under a cap.

I spun off of Stephanie.

"Tut, tut!" the conductor said, showing me a device. "You know what this triggers." He tilted the switch toward Cody. "Tell your friend."

I kept my eyes on the conductor but spoke to Cody. "Under the chair. Look."

He did.

Stephanie, staring straight ahead into the observatory where her daughters still sat slouched in chairs, yelled into her gag.

The conductor slithered along the room's wall, body pressed against splotches of black sludge, making his way toward the staircase that would lead him into the labyrinth of passages. "You can have me, Markus. I'm all yours. Feeling like a trade?" He tossed the device up and caught it with the same hand. "Haven't been loyal to her yet—why start now? Come get me."

"Get out of here." I scowled at him while moving toward Stephanie. Then I eyed Cody. "Help me, waist first!" I grabbed the harness over Steph's stomach while Cody got the straps at her waist.

I heard the conductor's footsteps pounding up the stairs.

The flaps swung off and I pushed Steph's entire body—

A blade shrieked up through the chair, grazing my arm and spilling blood onto the floor.

I winced and undid the straps around Stephanie's feet, then picked her up. For a split second, I stared at the blade that would have gone straight through her heart and, without thinking, kissed her forehead.

She recoiled and ripped off her gag. "Get the girls!"

Cody was already climbing the stairs, and Stephanie and I followed, circling back around to the observatory room.

The girls remained in their chairs, breathing. Bloodstains marked the floor, but it hadn't come from Steph or the girls. What had he put them through?

Steph fell on her knees between Isabella and Tilly, pulled them into an embrace, and began sobbing.

Cody nudged me to the corner of the room. He'd suffered cuts to his face and arms. "Alec helped him, told him when we arrived, got us split up." He nearly spit the words. "For his *career*."

Only one word came to mind. "Where."

"Cuffed out back."

"Look," I whispered, grabbing his shoulder, "I need you to be there for Steph and the girls. She doesn't want me close. Understand?"

A confused Cody nodded.

I wanted to tell Steph everything right now, but we needed to get somewhere safe first.

"Take me to Alec," I said.

Cody led us through the armory's maze, holding a sleeping Isabella while Stephanie carried Tilly. I stayed a few steps behind them.

When we exited through the back door, Cody stopped abruptly.

"What?" I said.

"That root. The cuffs. They're gone—Alec is gone."

16

Alec thought he'd made the right choice. He'd tried to walk a line of being *in* the story while *writing* the story. It had made so much sense in his mind as he thought through all that could go right and all that could go wrong by making a deal with the conductor.

What had he been thinking? He'd done something horrible, *terrible*, and now his body wouldn't stop trembling—not just because he was in the trunk of a car, but because he may have sentenced five people to death.

But there was hope. The conductor had seemed panicked when he spotted Alec cuffed behind the building. It was possible that Cody, Markus, and the others survived. Alec still might be able to right his wrong. He just needed to look for the right opportunity.

The car came to a halt and the driver's side door opened and shut. The trunk popped and a whisk of cold air roused even more gooseflesh over his body. Alec still couldn't see because of his blindfold.

"Let's go, MSNBC," the conductor said.

Alec fumbled his way out of the trunk. A fist grabbed a handful of the back of his shirt. The conductor herded him onto a deck, through a door, then across wooden floors. He was strong for being slight.

Modern music played from what sounded like an elaborate sound system. The conductor shoved Alec onto a comfortable chair, then undid his blindfold.

Alec was in the living room of a home belonging to someone very well-to-do, maybe even a mansion. But curtains covered every window, giving the appearance that it was dusk outside. Books stretched from the ceiling to the floor on either side of the lounging area. Three ornate chandeliers made of antlers hung from the wooded, arched ceiling. Fires crackled from not one but two corners of the room.

The conductor, this black-and-white scarecrow, sat directly across from him in a wingback chair even larger than the one Alec occupied. "Well, that did not go as planned . . . and yet, it went to plan perfectly." He glanced around as if seeing the house for the first time. "Music plays the moment Mr. Iseman's home senses a presence. Unfortunately, I haven't had the time to reprogram it off this garbage. There was a time only the Gates family could afford such a lavish accessory. Now it's attainable by all." He crossed one leg over the other, then pointed at Alec. "You, Alec, are in the *opposite* situation. It used to be that journalists were respected and brought balance to big bad government, bursting down university doors with would-be Woodwards and Bernsteins. But the field is dying, with the remaining few pen wielders holding on to their positions with death grips. Your path to any sort of career is so narrow you couldn't thread it with a needle." He leaned forward. "Until me."

The conductor reached for a pipe resting on the table beside his chair. He lit it and puffed. "Stop quivering." He smiled at Alec and tapped his fingers on the chair's armrests. "Now, ground rules: One, no questions that compromise the string. Two, no sharing until publication. Three, every word goes through my approval, or I'll take the pen in your hand and drive it through your temples, *okay?*"

Sitting before him was a monster, Alec knew that. But seeing him in this setting, even with the painted face and dark hood, somehow made him human. Alec was looking into a pair of human eyes, hearing words from a human voice.

"All right," Alec said, clearing his throat. He needed to stay alert to details that could help the people he'd betrayed—if he ever saw them again. "Let's start with why. Why the string?"

The conductor put down the pipe and pressed his back into the chair. "Okay. Why." He sat there for a moment, and Alec could tell the conductor was rehashing his personal journey in his mind. "Greater. Greater is the word I am looking for. It took me time before I realized I was *greater*. I'd thought that I was the unfavored child. The one who got the belt purely for unlikableness, all because I didn't feel as others felt. When others cried, I could laugh; when others laughed, I could kill. I was raised to think this was a handicap."

"Was it?"

The conductor's eyes, which had been wandering in memory, laser-focused on him. "Yes, that, what you just did there, that's rule four. Don't interrupt." He let his glare linger on Alec as he pulled long-fingered brass knuckles from deep inside the inner pockets of his coat and began fiddling with them.

"It wasn't a handicap at all. It was a rarity. Are you familiar with the Chateau Margaux 1787? Most people are not. But this red wine could run you more than a quarter million. Precious. Revered. Special. You tell me, Alec—how could something so unique go so unrecognized?" He slid the brass knuckles over his fingers and forearms. "I'd been born into greatness. Every social norm"—his mouth twisted as if he'd eaten something disgusting—"expectation, rule . . . just fell off my shoulders." He pointed at Alec. "You know what I did then?"

Alec remained silent.

"You can answer."

"What did you—"

The conductor shot forward from his chair, landing on his hands and toes on the coffee table between them like a panther.

Alec jolted back, blocking his face with his arms.

But the conductor just kept talking, knuckles digging into the table's finish. "I took the belt that had raised me, crept into my father's bedroom, and beat him mercilessly. My brother came next, running in to find the commotion. I strangled him and set the place ablaze, watching it from a tree in the distance." He motioned with his hands as if they were a flower blossoming. "And for the first time, I felt free."

He smiled and stood on the coffee table. "There, Alec, there started the journey of why. I was different. I was special. But what did it *mean*?" He stepped off the table. "I hardly had time to ponder this question as I ran from social expectations and blue and red lights. I felt crushed under the weight, wondering if anyone understood. My gift, though a superpower, didn't mean I liked living off garbage and the

heat of burning barrels. I didn't choose freedom to feed beside scum. I was a king in filthy rags, yet nobody knew." He
picked up the pipe once more and meandered around the
room. "Until another found me—another like me, powerful
and unfeeling. He brought me not just into a home but into
safety so I could discover the why. And that why, Alec, is
power. Godlike power." The conductor drew off his pipe and
returned to his wingback.

Alec kept mentally deflecting the questions he so badly
wanted to ask. *What are you planning on campus? How long
have you been planning it? Where does your godlike power fit into
what you're doing?* He wanted to know if Markus, Cody, and the
others were harmed, but the conductor would consider such
a question as serving Alec, not the story. He had to phrase it
another way.

"How many have died since the string began?"

"Come, Alec, there are so many more types of death than
ceasing to breathe. Emotional death—death of the will—is *my*
vice. I wouldn't lose a wink of sleep over impaling you with
that fire iron." He pointed to one of the fire pits. "But extrapolate that to the ends of the earth, wherein everybody's dead.
I see little power in that because there's little creativity, little
challenge. What is power, after all, if not the ability to influence
the behavior of others or the course of events?" He pressed his
hands to his mouth, then breathed out, extending his fingers
toward Alec. "Hence, the breaking of the will." He rubbed
one palm against the other. "Extrapolate *that* to the ends of
the earth, wherein everyone's soul has been utterly crushed
but they're alive. The first scenario leaves the mighty without
any other to compare their greatness to, while the second
draws endless reverence from pliable people desperate for

something, for *someone*, to make them whole." He extended an open palm to Alec. "Which sounds like power to you?"

His voice suddenly grew harsh. "Physical death need only be necessary when one believes their will to be stronger than mine, see?" He flicked his wrist. "Consequences and all."

That triggered a thought in Alec. Perhaps he could learn about the present by asking the conductor about the future. "Is the string your legacy or just the beginning?"

The conductor allowed a slight smile. "For some you may call it the end of a legacy." He rested his chin in his hand. "For me, well, power in my possession is like a terrible, beautiful tumor: it only grows."

"Haas—he's special to you. Why?"

The conductor froze. Alec couldn't tell if he was trying to smile or hold back a smile.

"What good is a god if he can't bring into submission whomever he wishes? The university policeman isn't just a man pretending to be a mountain. He's got something, a will that may as well be Goliath."

"And the bigger they are . . ." Alec said.

The conductor refrained from finishing the thought.

Alec continued questioning the conductor into late morning —some about the past, some regarding the future—and took copious notes for the book the conductor had relinquished his rights to. Some of the details he learned desperately needed to be relayed to Markus, Cody, and Janet . . . if they didn't kill Alec at first sight.

Finally, the conductor sprang to his feet. "The rest you'll get soon, Alec. I expect a draft from you before the next sun rises, but not before the crescendo—no, not before the crescendo. We need to let the rest of the story play out."

The man with the white face walked behind him. Alec could swear spiders were crawling inside his own pants and up his torso and congregating just under his collar.

The conductor leaned close to his ear and slid a ticket into Alec's shirt pocket. "Stay close to campus; you don't want to miss a thing." He inserted a needle into Alec's neck.

Then the room went dark.

17

In Mike Mitchell's truck—broken windshield and all—we pulled into my driveway and Cody made quick work of a perimeter check around the condo before moving inside for a walk-through. This Trenton suburb area wasn't nearly as remote as Stephanie's house, but still vulnerable.

After Cody had finished his sweep, I opened the car door for Stephanie but thought it best to remain silent. She looked nearly as exhausted as the slumbering Isabella and Tilly and needed space. Despite the conductor's manipulation, he'd been right about one thing: I hadn't been fully truthful to Steph. I could only imagine the pain I'd caused her today.

Steph picked up Tilly first.

"I can take—"

"Cody," Steph said loudly before walking to the door without making eye contact.

Cody jogged up to us. "Yeah."

I nodded at Isabella.

"Right."

210

Inside, I watched Steph turn down the hallway that led to
the guest room, master bedroom, and office. I wanted to direct
her to the master bedroom so that she and the girls could have
the most space and comfort, but a voice kept telling me to stay
quiet. An elephant was in the room and it had to be broached
at the appropriate time, unforced. She chose the guest room.

Cody followed Steph with Isabella, then made his way to
the kitchen to whip up something to eat.

I activated the security alarm, replaced the gun I'd left at the
armory, and turned to find Cody leaning against the archway
that led into the kitchen, eating a bowl of cereal. I walked over
to him and gripped his shoulder, letting him know that the
people I loved most wouldn't be alive without him.

He nodded, then promptly put his hand on mine. "Neck
rub, perhaps?"

I looked at the bowl. "You twelve?" I handed him one of
my extra Glocks.

He shoved it into his holster then scooped a heaping amount
of cereal into his mouth. "Remember whose cupboards this
came from." Cody bumped my shoulder with his fist. "I'll keep
watch." He peeked down the hallway, then turned his attention back to me, nostrils flared. "What did he do to them?"

———

We debriefed for a solid hour and a half while checking
for bugs.

"Steph's in shock," Cody said. "She'll come around." He
stared at me until it got uncomfortable.

"Never seen her like this," I said. "I lied to her."

"You're not the first one, Haasy." Cody allowed half of a
smile.

"This is different."

Cody let his arms dangle at his sides. "She and her daughters were abducted, Haas. Of course this is different. What'd you lie about?"

Headlights pulled into the driveway.

Cody and I reached for our weapons and spread out for better vantage points—he to the living room window, I to the glass cutout in the front door. Whoever had arrived wasn't being stealthy about it.

Then I noticed the Uber and Lyft signs on the vehicle's dashboard, and the passenger door opened.

"David," I said.

Cody peered out the window. "Alone. I'll watch for a tail."

I opened the door as David approached. He was sweating and his hands were clenched into fists.

"What happened?"

"Doctor tried injecting me with something, but Janet stopped it, that's what."

Cody approached. "Where's Janet?"

"She said she needed to stay with her sister. Told me how to find you with her phone." He held up Janet's phone. "Said you're the good guys."

I stared at the cell, surprised. What would the conductor do to Janet now that he couldn't contact her? "Has anything come through from the conductor?"

"Nothing. Hasn't so much as pinged once." David winced. "I'm on over-the-counter meds. Have anything stronger?"

"Hold on." I retrieved a bottle that had four or five muscle relaxants from when I'd hurt my back. "Here."

David gulped two of the pills, and Cody and I helped make him comfortable in the living room.

"Janet said you were going to get him. You didn't though, did you?" David said flatly.

I shook my head as images flashed through my mind: the armory, Mitchell's ambush, Doug's rescue, Dominguez's and Adams's deaths, the chamber and viewing room, and finally, Alec.

"Hey," a voice said from behind us. We all turned. It was Steph. "Markus, can we talk?" She turned back down the hallway and into the master bedroom.

I followed her and started to close the door behind me.

Stephanie uncrossed her arms. "Not all the way, I want to see the girls." Her eyes were downcast and her shoulders were hunched. "You whispered that it wasn't true. So let's hear it, loudly this time." Her eyebrows shot up for a split second, then back down. "A reason for everything—just like Declan."

"It's not like that, Steph."

She used her arms as though she were taunting an opponent to step inside the ring. "Then get talking, because someone close to me, someone I *trust*"—her index fingers shot toward me from closed fists—"convinced me to never let Declan get close to me or my girls ever again. That was *you* who said that, right?" Her eyes narrowed. "Well, if I had known that all men are sick and alike, I would have just stuck with my girls' real father." She looked away and wiped a tear from her cheek.

"Steph—"

"What!"

I let out a breath and started to reach out to her, but caught myself and kept my hands by my side. "Steph, those pictures, those things you saw—they may have been me, but they weren't me."

She rolled her eyes.

I needed to get straight to the point and tell her what no other soul in my new life knew, not even Cody. "Deep cover. I was working deep cover."

Steph leaned back, losing a bit of her edge. "What? Like, secret agent undercover? Or under as in under the covers with those women? Not woman, *women*."

I shook my head but kept my eyes on hers. "No sex. Not a kiss, not a touch. The moment the door closed, I was law enforcement. As an agent, yes. FBI. That's how I was able to put an end to the ring."

Stephanie squinted through a glare. "Okay, let me get this straight. You somehow 'work' for the FBI in who-really-cares-ville Trenton, you're on payroll for posh stripper parties—on quite the regular basis, I might add—but there's no hanky-panky, none at all, because you're superhuman and saw those curvy models as nothing more than underdressed cleaning ladies wearing chastity belts, right?"

"Steph—"

"Oh, and you said you *were* FBI, so I take it you're no longer FBI, and they probably burned all the records so that when people like me call up and say, 'Hey, my boyfriend's telling me a really creative story about his undercover work that I'd like to confirm, so would you please connect me to HR,' they simply respond, 'Markus who?' and hang up. Is that it? Is it?" She flung her hands up.

I couldn't help it. I laughed. Not a chuckle but a full-on, hurt-your-stomach laugh.

Stephanie punched my shoulder. "Stop it." She allowed the tiniest grin before the scowl returned. "Tell me the truth."

I reached out with both hands but didn't touch her. "I'm

telling the truth. I came to Trenton undercover to work a case against Eric Ward—it's how I got the job as university police in the first place." I looked at the floor, remembering the sickening details. "My cover got so dark, I couldn't wait to make the bust any longer. I blew the operation to save those girls. And when it was over, I quit. But I kept the job I'd worked myself into under deep cover."

The anger had left her eyes, leaving only brokenness and hurt. "Why didn't you tell me?"

"It was against the law and would have put you and the girls in danger." I took a step closer. "That's the truth, Steph."

"But you've always said you wanted to become FBI. Why lead me on with a lie for so long?"

"It was an outlet," I said. "My new job is . . . kind of boring, outside of roasting shish kebabs. I thought that one day, if things went well, I might end up with the bureau again."

"Why quit in the first place then?"

"I met this girl." I looked at the ground again and felt my cheeks flare up. "A girl who could knock a roomful of people to the floor with just her smile. A girl who got excited about taking snaps of just about anything, and forced me to take quizzes like 'What Walt Disney Princess Are You?' and 'Which Colorado Town Are You?' and my favorite: 'What Should You Buy?,' which told me I'd do well to purchase a handbag. A girl who's taught me a couple of things about faith—which I realized today more than ever. A girl unlike any other I've met. Beautiful heart, warrior strength, and a mother of two incredible girls who are turning out"—I looked over my shoulder and into the guest room where Isabella and Tilly were sleeping—"kind of like her."

Stephanie shook her head slowly, her lips tight.

A few moments passed.

What else could I say? What was she thinking? I had told the truth but couldn't make her believe it. Each second felt like a thousand.

Finally, she opened her mouth and uttered one word barely above a whisper. "Okay."

I felt every muscle in my body relax. Then I took a step toward her and gently wrapped my arms around her. And waited.

She kept her head tilted down and to the side, not ready to look at me.

I just waited, my eyes locked on her.

She twisted her head to the other side, and then up just a little—enough to see that I was looking straight into her eyes.

I inched closer so that our shoes touched and leaned forward—

She grabbed my face and planted her mouth on mine.

I pulled her close and hoisted her up. What felt like a thousand horses of pent-up stress and emotion broke free. She wrapped her legs around me and buried her face in my neck.

But all too quickly, she dropped to her feet, pressed her head against my chest, and cried.

I held her for what felt like an hour, never once moving my hands—just wanting her to feel safe.

"He took them from me, drugged them," she whispered. When she finally pulled away, she pointed a finger directly under my nose, eyes as watery as morning mist. "Don't think this means I forgive you. Got it?" Her tone was lighter than her words.

I just nodded.

Then we were kissing again.

A portion of Stephanie's bounce returned, but worry crept up with it. "Where is he? Are we safe here?"

I took a deep breath, trying to gather my thoughts. The answer would be no until the conductor was either killed or locked up.

She knew my answer before I said anything. "Tell me something good," she said, closing her eyes and dipping her chin. Her eyes popped open. "Faith. You mentioned faith."

I tried to recall everything that had gone down in the past day. "I've found myself talking to him more. It actually felt real."

She nodded but was silent.

I lifted one hand, palm up. "Apparently God and I understand each other when you throw in a psychopath." I leaned against my dresser. "I don't know. The conductor kept talking about the will and breaking it. I tried to show him that he was wrong." An image of Dominguez shooting Adams flashed through my mind. "Turns out he was right."

Steph grabbed my hands and leaned close. "We're both here, and so are my girls. So what if he can manipulate someone? God says he can't touch us—not in a way that matters."

That took me by surprise. I'd assumed that whatever power God had promised his people lived in Steph—but I didn't think for a moment such a thing had been given to me.

And what did that really mean, "not in a way that matters"?

A knock sounded at the partially open door.

"Come in," I said.

It was Cody. "Everything, uh, better? Mmm, I'm sorry. I shouldn't have led with that. We think we have something on the conductor." He looked directly at me. "We think we know what he's after."

The thought of knowing any sort of motive for the conductor

had wreaked havoc on my mind. If I could know this lunatic, if I could just see into his thoughts for a moment, understand him on some level, I could steal some of his power. Get under *his* skin for a change.

Cody led Steph and me into the living room, where David had been more than taken care of. Freshly cooked spaghetti and what looked like a clone of Olive Garden's house salad sat on the coffee table next to the reading chair in which he was reclining, ice packs placed around his wound. A bottle of ibuprofen lay on the floor, along with three empty glasses.

"Goodness," Cody said. "It looks so much more pathetic walking into it new." He turned around and whispered to Steph and me, "Guy is *high*-maintenance, especially when you're trying to get him to talk." He turned back toward David and clapped once. "Okay, David, tell Haas what you just told me."

David grimaced. "It hurts to talk."

I stepped between them, unable to extend one more patient moment. "Listen—"

"Hold on, hold on. I've got this." Cody backed up a few steps, positioning himself closer to the center of the room. "David here has been doing little assignments for the conductor for a while, but the things of interest started after he faked drinking in public to distract you from Janet dropping the tablet. The conductor made him go full Hannibal Lecter after that. Apparently, Whiteface slipped the chief something that put him out like a light. That's when David performed surgery on him, right in the press box during the game, inserting a tube under the skin of the chief's back—even sewed him back up. Awful stuff, even for a guy like Renfroe."

The pictures the conductor had sent to my phone—those had been of Renfroe?

Cody shook his head. "But listen to this. David was also instructed to bring up a webpage on the chief's computer for him to find. The article was from the *Trenton Telegraph*, twenty years ago, a feature on the Celestial Orchestra's first show, complete with a photo of Ivan directing a practice." Cody straightened his back and held up three fingers. "The article featured three photo quotes from the three-person events committee at the time. Ready for their names? Chief Renfroe, Franklin Iseman, and—"

"Anita Postma," I said.

Cody's eyebrows shot inward so far they nearly touched. "*Yeah . . .* how'd you know?"

"Basketball game. Those three people were on the court when Ivan fainted."

"And Iseman . . . he's dead," Steph said.

All of us looked at her.

"The blood on the ground, where you pile-drivered the conductor?" Steph said, looking at Cody. "That belonged to him. He had done something wrong, tried to profit from the string. Then the conductor gave me the choice of either having Iseman killed, or . . ." She clammed up.

I grabbed her hand tightly.

"I couldn't do it—couldn't choose," she said. "But then Iseman attacked me and . . . I did choose. And the conductor killed him. Right there." She covered her mouth and sat down on the couch, wiping her eyes of mascara. "After that, he started up with a lot of monster talk and telling me what a horrible person Markus is . . ."

I wrapped my arm around her and pulled her to my side. She rested her head on my shoulder.

"You did the right thing, Steph," I said.

Cody nodded emphatically, then leaned in toward her and spoke without moving his lips. "Told you Haas was horrible."

That got Steph to smile a little.

I looked at Cody. "Had you not shown up, what was his endgame? Turn Steph against me and then . . . ? What does it have to do with Iseman, Postma, the chief, Ivan?"

"Maybe that was it," Cody said. "What has this guy done that's made sense?"

I squinted and let my mind build a scenario. "We have a man who calls himself the conductor doing horrible things to people the week that the most famous conductor of this era is returning to the stage that kick-started everything for him twenty years ago. The conductor must be in his thirties or forties. Hard to tell under the makeup. That would have made him ten or twenty years old at the time of the orchestra's original showing."

Cody scratched his head. "Jealousy?"

"Could explain why Ivan fell at the game—the conductor could have slipped him something. But why hadn't it been lethal? *Is* Ivan at the hospital? Is the performance still on tonight?"

Steph and David remained silent as we went back and forth.

"The paper says he went to the hospital, nothing life-threatening, but no one knows his status," Cody said. "Event is sold out, hasn't been canceled, and there haven't been requests for refunds. Paper made it sound like this could just be more theatrics—Ivan staying close-lipped—creating suspense and mystery before the big twenty-year return."

"A young boy interested in music, or perhaps a music major here at Trenton a couple decades ago," I said. "He has a flair for music that breaks social norms, goes to the orchestra that night, becomes a fan, sees himself in Ivan. But then the Celestial Orchestra goes big." I touched two fingers to my brow. "Fame puts Ivan into another stratosphere, and our music major is left trying to pay the bills because his opportunity passed him by. 'There can only be one Ivan'—isn't that what critics say? So maybe our conductor, who approached music in the same unique way, now comes off as a copycat, trying to ride the coattails of a man whose approach to music cannot be replicated without drawing scorn."

Cody pointed at me absently. "Conductor takes revenge on Ivan for taking what the conductor feels belongs to him?"

I tried to finish the thought. "He organizes the string . . . to take back what was rightfully his." I waved it off. "This isn't it, Cody. It's all speculation. We need to dig."

Cody extended an arm out. "How?"

"I've got an idea. But first we need to bring in the cavalry."

"Who?"

I realized it was time to tell my best friend that I'd been lying to him since the day we met. "Sit down a minute."

I stepped into my room clutching my phone, thinking about the only person in authority I could trust with the truth. Enough was enough. Stephanie and the girls were safe now, and I needed to make sure they stayed that way. So I dialed a number I thought I'd never dial again.

The conductor could listen in if he wanted. I was coming for him.

I closed the door as I waited for her to pick up. It was best that Steph didn't hear, not now at least. We'd talked about exes before and I'd told her that I used to work with this woman doing security at a casino. But that was all a part of my cover and would be pouring salt onto a fresh wound.

"Hello?" the answer came from the other end.

Hearing Zoe's voice disarmed me more than I thought it would. "It's Markus. I—I need your help."

"Wow," she said. "It's been how many months, and you start with a favor? Word is that you're quite the dirty cop."

"You guys subscribe to the university press now? You know it's not true."

"Do I? The article sounded convincing." She was toying with me.

"Zoe, I'm in trouble."

I could hear her shift into agent mode, clearly exiting ex-girlfriend mode. "What kind of trouble?"

"A manipulator, sociopath . . . people are dead."

"Markus. Where are you—how can I help?"

"He fabricated the story on me. He's planning something deadly."

"Explain."

"He had me clean out the university's armory—he has them."

"You stole weapons," she said. "While suspended. And then you gave said weapons to a killer?"

"I don't have time to explain. I know you can't do anything official, but I need a security detail at my house. Just for the day."

"You *would* call while I'm up for a promotion," she said. "The bureau's going to know you called me. There's so much wrong here, I don't know where to begin."

"He almost killed me and others I love. I need to keep them safe."

"Stephanie? Her daughters?"

I knew my answer would hurt. "Yes. I can't trust anyone else. I need to end this and there's no other badge to turn to. They've all been blackmailed, bribed, or wouldn't believe me."

Zoe muttered something under her breath. Then, "I'll do it."

I closed my eyes. "Thank you. You don't know . . ."

"I know," she said.

"One more thing." I sighed. "I need you to get in touch with the families of Clint Hopkins, Gabriel Dominguez, and Ian Adams." I detailed where their bodies were located and told Zoe that they'd died heroes.

Then we hung up.

I turned around to find Stephanie peeking her head into my room. "Who was that?"

I looked at her, head tilted a little too far down. She knew who it was.

"Casino girl—who I assume wasn't casino?" Stephanie tapped the doorjamb. "Good. Do what it takes."

"I will."

Stephanie walked away. I knew she was hurting, but I couldn't think about that now.

I followed her into the living room. None of us had slept, but the new day and afternoon was upon us, bringing with it whatever the conductor had planned for the Celestial Orchestra performance tonight.

He had something planned. It had to be his endgame. The timing made too much sense.

Still, I wanted to keep a semblance of normalcy in the face of the trauma. After the girls awoke and the security detail arrived—two men and a woman who didn't look the happiest to be here—I opened the kitchen for business.

I cracked two eggs into a frying pan as Isabella and Tilly watched intently from the bar stools across the counter, Steph bouncing the younger on her lap. Their eyes looked similar to how they appeared right before Steph would put them to bed—drowsy but not wanting to miss a thing.

But there was something else, something I could see in their body language, at least in Isabella's: disorder. Though her young mind may have already been working overtime to block the events of the past twenty-four hours, a fragment of them was replaying in the recesses of her brain, quiet enough so that she couldn't tell what it was, but loud enough to distract her from being fully in this moment.

I'd failed to protect them.

Even as a university cop in midsized Trenton, I'd failed. The girls would have to fight battles of their own in the one place I couldn't show up, flash a badge, and keep them safe— the subconscious.

I looked up at Isabella. "I'm guessing you like your eggs . . . sunny-side up?"

She tilted her head, mouth hanging open a bit. "The sun doesn't make eggs."

I raised my brows. "You sure about that? Heat cooks eggs and the sun is . . ." I tapped the spatula against the frying pan.

"Hot!"

Stephanie managed a smile. "Strike that from your memory, kiddo."

Cody—still ticked at me for not telling him I was FBI until a few hours ago—yawned as he slogged into the dining area.

"Watch this," I whispered to the girls before proceeding to toss a blueberry across the room.

It sailed over Cody's head and slapped against the floor.

"Why I was cut from basketball sophomore year," I said.

"And freshman year, obviously," Cody said.

The doorbell rang.

Cody immediately put himself into a position of cover, though trying to do so nonchalantly so as not to disturb the girls.

It was 3:45 p.m., David was asleep in the living room chair, and our security detail was positioned inside the house with strategic vantage points of the grounds outside. There was no reason for anyone to be at my door.

I clicked off the burners and met the security detail lead, a man who went by Hernandez.

Stephanie grabbed the girls. "Oh, let's get that blueberry."

"He threw it," Isabella said.

Cody nodded at me and Hernandez. He would cover our approach to the front door while keeping close to the girls. The other two agents, Whalen and De'boer, covered the back.

I moved to the entryway. Checked the peephole.

And couldn't believe my eyes. "I'll handle this," I told Hernandez. I opened the door and stepped outside, forcing the visitor to step back. "What are you doing here?"

Stephanie's former husband wore dark jeans and a suit jacket and showed meticulous grooming habits. He looked as though he belonged on a movie set, and that made me sick.

"Easy." Declan raised his hands. "Someone texted me—don't even know the number—said my girls were in danger and to come to this address if I loved them. I got in my car and sped the whole way, worried sick."

"Were you." It wasn't a question.

"Yes. Are they here?" he said, taking a harder stance. "Who are *you*?"

I hated how quickly this man was able to shift his persona and aura. He was a con man, a fraud, playing a game of manipulation with everyone he crossed paths with. At least, that's the profile I'd created after hearing Steph describe everything he'd done in their marriage.

He was also smaller than me, and I let my body language suggest it.

"What, you going to punch me out? If my girls are in there, get out of my way."

He stepped into my space and I grabbed him by his jacket. "They aren't yours. You lost that right and a whole lot—"

A mental image flashed through my mind and I let go of him.

This man was in his midthirties with similar height, weight, hair, and build. The voice didn't match, but that could be faked, couldn't it?

The door opened behind us.

"Declan?" Stephanie said.

"Daddy!" Isabella screamed, brushing past me before clinging to Declan's leg.

He lifted her up. "Pumpkin!"

I stepped aside to make room for Stephanie on the walkway, never taking my eyes off Declan, mentally trying to paint his face white. Could it be possible that this man was the conductor? Is that why he hadn't harmed Steph or the girls? Why he wanted me to "confess"? Or was my mind playing tricks?

Stephanie would have recognized him, right? The black-and-white makeup was thick and disguising, but could she really be fooled by someone she'd shared a life with?

"What are you doing here?" Stephanie was clearly trying to keep her disdain to a minimum for Isabella's sake.

"Got a message saying you and the girls were in trouble, so I got here as fast as I could. What's the trouble?"

Stephanie reached for Isabella. "You're a few years short and a thousand lies too long. Give her. Now, please." Her voice was losing its softness.

"Are you deaf?" Cody said, joining them on the walkway.

I put a hand on his shoulder to remind him of Isabella's presence.

Declan seemed reluctant but handed her to Stephanie. "Just wanted to help. What's going on here?"

Stephanie looked at me, then Cody, then back at Declan. She carried Isabella inside without saying a word, the little girl fussing the whole way.

I looked Declan straight in the eyes. "Hurting Stephanie more than you already have, that's what's going on. Forget the text and get out of here."

Declan pointed at the house. "Those are *my* girls."

"Were." I shook my head. "No more. Whoever sent the text is using you."

Declan's eyes seemed to darken. "You moving in on my wife?"

I didn't mean to step toward him. I didn't mean to rear back my fist. And I definitely didn't mean to smash it into Declan's forehead.

But I did.

He stumbled backward and tumbled onto his hands and knees.

Cody gripped me from behind.

Declan swung his head up. "I'm going to own you, Haas."

I struggled against Cody. "How do you know my name?"

My friend tugged me back. "I didn't see one punch already, I can't unsee more. Got it?"

"*Where is he? What's he planning?*" I pointed at Declan's face. "Is it you?" I bit my lower lip and cocked my head. "Tell me it's you."

Declan wiped his nose. "Steph's got a thing for crazy cops— good to know." He looked past me to Cody. "Tell your friend that I'll be back to take back what's mine." He winked at me, then turned and walked away.

I stared at Declan, analyzing his walk, the shoulder broadness, what his voice had sounded like. The slightest variance here or there would change this man into that white-faced conductor. But . . . I just couldn't say for sure. How many men were six feet tall with a smaller, fit frame?

Cody let go of me. "I've been thinking the same thing, but it's just not a match. It isn't him."

"Then why did the conductor track him down?" I rubbed away the pain in my fist. "If he knew to come here, then the conductor knows we're here."

"Not like that's a surprise."

I squared my shoulders. "No more waiting. We're going after him again . . . in *our* way, on *our* terms."

Cody leaned back, palms facing the sky. "'Bout time, Haasy."

"It's time we meet who I suspect are the original members of the string—or the two who are left."

"Two left?"

"Anita Postma and my chief."

18

A bead of sweat dripped off Jackson Renfroe's nose. He wiped his sleeve over his face. Good thing he was wearing his navy uniform. Would help conceal the splotch. Would this stupid meeting ever end? They'd talked details for months. They were all professionals. They'd planned security for events before. Why was a day-of meeting needed at all?

"Chief Renfroe, are you okay?" Anita Postma said.

He gained a smile. "Better than ever."

"All right—anyone have anything else?"

Good golly, woman—wrap it up.

"On behalf of Trenton University, thank you for bringing Ivan home," Postma said. "We cannot wait to host a show the world is going to remember for a long, long time. We'll see you in a few hours."

Ivan's crew was dismissed. Postma remained at the front of the conference room, shuffling papers, while Renfroe remained seated.

Couldn't she just get out of here? He wanted the conference

room to himself just for a while, a quiet place to shut off and *think* and down as many painkillers as possible. His back hadn't stopped throbbing ever since he woke up from his drugged-up stupor, forced to stay on campus by some lunatic behind the screen of his phone.

The pain from the incision was nothing compared to what the device inside him could do. Why wouldn't the conductor just tell him what he wanted?

"Chief, you don't look well at all."

"I said I'm fine."

She walked over to him, leaned down, and put one hand on his back.

Renfroe flinched, and so did Postma.

"What is wrong with you?" she said. "What's happened?"

Renfroe laughed painfully. "You'd never believe—"

"He's got you too," Postma whispered.

He froze and craned his neck to her. "You know. The conductor?"

"You're not the only one," she said.

"Why is he doing this?" Renfroe groaned and leaned his head back. "I don't know what I'm supposed to do. Tell me. He told me to go about this evening as if everything were hunky-dory, or else he'd get clicky with a detonator . . . mail my remains to Vegas."

Postma put both hands on her chest and bared her teeth.

"What's he told you? What's he planning? Please, Anita."

She leaned down to his sitting level. "I don't know. He's had me pull strings, make arrangements, taken half of my savings." She looked as though she could murder Renfroe, but her anger wasn't directed at him. "All I know is that he's angry. Angry at something that happened twenty years ago."

"What happened twenty years ago was nothing but success," Renfroe said. "It put this town on the map, exploded enrollment, created a career no one's topped—tell me what's horrible in that?" He leaned forward. He knew what was horrible in it.

Postma looked away. "Enough. We know there's more."

Renfroe exhaled hard. "Where's Iseman? He has to be a part of this."

"I don't know. I've called a dozen times, texted, emailed. I haven't seen or heard from him since we were on the court."

"What does the conductor want? What does he know about that day?"

Postma sat and rested her forehead against her palm. "What do we know about that day, really?"

Renfroe put aside what he wanted to say and allowed himself to think through that day of fate without his normal guilt and shame. Suddenly he felt as though he had been transported back twenty years, when his chest was bigger than his gut, his wife had yet to leave him, and his hunches never seemed to fail him. "We met Ivan, what, a month or two before at auditions. Unassuming. Broken English. But we both knew there was something special there." He fast-forwarded to the event. "It went flawlessly . . . then the aftermath was dizzying. Media. Cameras. Mail and invitations. Ivan went viral before viral."

"So what then?" Postma said.

Renfroe took off his hat. "Remember the weeks and months after all the press?"

"A nightmare," she recalled. "Musicians of every kind trying to hitch their wagons to Ivan. Parents wanting him to mentor their kids to fame."

"That was the better half of it. There were threats about Ivan's citizenship, money-grubbers and 'family members' demanding access to him, sleazy lawyers planting stories to net a chunk of Ivan's change."

Postma furrowed her brows. "Remind me, the stories."

Renfroe looked at the floor, then sighed. His sweat was making a comeback. She was getting too close. "There were so-called relatives, scammers pretending to be agents, the defamation claims . . . It was a lot."

"Which story, if true—if what we thought was a lie then but turned out to be real—would be most devastating?"

Renfroe swallowed hard. He should tell her. It's not like he'd actually seen the act—he'd only seen them walking together. It may have never happened. He had the capacity to be wrong. "There was a mother who brought in a boy. Said Ivan gave him his autograph and invited him backstage. Said no one went with them, and . . ." Renfroe's voice shook. "Ivan asked the boy to step into a closet with him."

Postma covered her mouth.

He didn't tell her the rest.

A pounding on the door drew both of their gazes. They shared a glance. Didn't see anyone through the door's little window.

Postma walked over and opened it. There was a letter on the ground but no one in sight. It was addressed to Jackson Renfroe and Anita Postma, and in the "from" column was just one word.

Conductor.

Listening intently from a dusty closet in the tiny English classroom, which was in the oldest and moldiest building on campus, I watched the time on my phone flick to 5:15 p.m. The small wooden door leading into the classroom, which had been designed for eight students or so, remained closed.

Everything had gone smoothly thus far with zero hitches in my plan—Cody and I had found Jackson Renfroe and Anita Postma on campus, and with the help of Stephanie, we'd crafted and delivered a cryptic note in the voice and cadence of the conductor.

But plans never unfolded the way you envisioned them. Like side-blown wind that pushes rain under your umbrella, something always changed, a variable no one could plan for.

The classroom doorknob twisted, and someone walked inside. No, two someones.

"Where is he then?" a woman asked. Postma.

"You know he'll show up," Renfroe responded.

Cody, who'd been hiding in a classroom adjacent to this one, entered the room behind them and closed the door. "That's for darn sure, Chief. Gun, now."

"What is this? Caulkins?" the chief said.

I stepped out of the closet as Renfroe handed over his firearm. Cody and I had both changed into street clothes and were wearing our favorite lids to blend in. I was wearing rubber gloves and holding a box filled with tools.

"What do you want?" Postma said. "What is this?"

Cody met her gaze with a chilling stare.

Renfroe sneered and his body stiffened. "What do you think you're doing, huh? We read the article. You both should be in jail."

"The article was fabricated by the conductor, not that I care at all what you think." I set the bag down and unpacked its contents: pliers, rags, a jug of water, and a corkscrew. Everything could be used for you or against you, and that was most definitely true of psychological warfare. "I'm going to break the conductor's string. You're going to help me do it."

"Do you have any idea what he's going to do to you, to everyone?" Postma said.

"He's already taken everything from me," I lied. "Do you have any idea what happens when a monster breaks your will? I have nothing to lose—but you two . . ." I set two chairs next to the chalkboard at the front of the classroom and forced them to sit.

Cody planted himself against the room's only entrance.

I leaned close to Renfroe. "I imagine the conductor's going to do something terrible to you if you help me." I paused. "It won't be half as bad as this."

Postma scoffed. "Then you're a fool."

Renfroe was glaring at me. "Haas, you don't know—"

"You disgrace everything it means to wear a badge," I said. I turned my attention to Postma. "We don't have time. The conductor is going to kill a lot of people if we don't do something—*tonight*. What happened twenty years ago with the Celestial Orchestra? What does he want?"

The look Postma was giving me could burn off a couple layers of skin. "How dare you threaten me. I haven't stopped trying to stop the conductor since he first looped me into this mess."

"Good." I kicked the tools I'd laid out, and both Renfroe and Postma flinched. "Don't you see? The conductor created the string to manipulate us to *his end*—whatever that is. He's even using the string against itself, keeping himself out of the dirty work. It's his power. But it's also *our* power. The moment we stop him, it's over. This"—I pointed at the ground, giving each person solid eye contact—"is *over*. So help me end it."

Postma spoke curtly. "I know he's planning something terrible at the orchestra."

That drew Renfroe's gaze.

I remained still.

"He attended the original showing for the orchestra," Postma said. "And something horrible happened. I don't know what exactly, but he holds us responsible."

Recollection formed in the chief's eyes.

"There." I nodded at him. "What do you remember, Chief? What happened that night?"

Renfroe grumbled. "Never answered to you and I never will."

Without skipping a beat, I crouched and grabbed the pliers. Tossed a gag to Cody, who promptly closed the gap to Renfroe, stuffed it in his mouth, and forced him to bite.

"What are you doing?" Postma said.

"I'm sick of putting up with your sorry-sack abuse of your title, Chief." I admired and air-tested the pliers. "Love your gambling, right? I imagine doing that without fingertips would be impossible. You could always have someone else do it for you, I suppose, but last I checked? You drove those people away." I pointed at the chief's badge. "You're going to lure the conductor to us. Today. Understand?"

The chief laughed, but the fear in his eyes betrayed him. "You . . . scared . . . idle threat?" he said into his gag.

This time I allowed a chuckle. But I stared at Renfroe as if we were playing the final hand of the World Series of Poker. "Word on the street is you had a little operation last night." I raised a brow. "Can't be too comfortable. That's why you're going to help—because the conductor won't detonate it with you near him."

The chief glanced around with feverish eyes. "What do . . . know about it?"

Cody locked eyes with him and pulled down his gag. "Bring him to us and maybe you'll live long enough to find out."

Renfroe jerked forward but remained seated. "He's not going to fall for some ruse. He'll see it coming."

"No he won't," Postma said.

We all turned to her.

"I know how to lure him. I'm the 'knot' he started with. We've met in person four times. I can lead him to you if you can do what you say."

Cody and I glanced at each other. We finally may have caught a break.

19

Alec awakened leaning against a tree in a ravine, his stomach in knots. The whoosh of cars whizzing by meant he was somewhere in earshot of the freeway. He climbed up the hill with trembling limbs. Stopped for a moment to gather himself and calm his shakes. It didn't help. Why couldn't he stop quivering?

Markus, Cody, Janet—complete strangers to him twenty-four hours before—kept popping into his mind like a recurring dream, horrible images of the conductor doing terrible things to them. All because Alec had made a deal. A small, tiny deal. Paper—that's all it included.

Alec had done his research on bestselling true crime, from Truman Capote's page-turner about the brutal slaying of a Kansas family to Ann Rule's insider piece on Ted Bundy. The story Alec possessed would shoot him into the stars among writers.

He wouldn't just be a journalist. He'd be a *New York Times* bestselling author, equipped with exclusive details to a real-life deadly game fronted by perhaps the most irresistibly intriguing antagonist ever to have committed a crime.

But the deal slithered through his stomach like a black, poisonous creature.

Alec threw up, providing temporary relief to his gut. Then he climbed the rest of the way up the hill. After walking through a seldom-used trailhead parking lot, he found the freeway and flicked his thumb in the air.

Twenty minutes later, he was getting out of a car that belonged to a fellow student who'd given him a lift. Before him was Trenton University. The conductor had told him to stay on campus, most assuredly to report on whatever horrific act he'd planned.

But all Alec could think about were Janet, Markus, and Cody. All of them were doing the right thing while he had made a play for his career. He couldn't take that back. They wouldn't trust him even if he delivered the conductor to them in cuffs. The only way to help them now would be to sabotage the conductor by himself somehow.

Alec headed straight for the amphitheater. The Celestial Orchestra was surely there already, dressing and prepping. The building would be filled with members of the string—members of the string with assignments. And if Alec could discover what those assignments were, then maybe he could stop whatever catastrophe the conductor was planning.

He flashed his Trenton press badge, nodded to a man in a red security jacket, and walked into the amphitheater. On any other day, this would be a dream assignment for him. But instead he felt as though he were stepping into an open casket.

The orchestra crew was spread out everywhere and looking sharp, adorned in fabric that created the illusion of changing colors with every movement. Some appeared orange, others red, blue, purple, changing from one color to another on cue with the rise and fall of their instruments.

Above them, the ceiling had been transformed into a mosaic of faces, people from all different countries. The photos clung to the ceiling in such a way that every face appeared to be looking toward the front of the amphitheater. The Celestial Orchestra wasn't used to playing in such a small venue, so apparently they'd decided to add faces to the crowd in the only place they could.

Ivan had become quite the showman, with ego to spare—but it wasn't the nasty kind. At least that's what Alec had always thought of him. The man simply loved beauty, which he just so happened to spend endless hours creating in the form of music, synchronization, and performance. It would be a shame for people *not* to see it.

"Admiring the visitors above?"

Alec turned to find a girl no older than he, most likely a student, dressed in a purple shirt with the word "CREW" on the back. Her black hair was stunning in contrast with her fair skin and red lips.

"Interesting décor, for sure," he said.

She looked surprised. "Wait, you don't know, not even as a reporter guy?"

"Know?"

She grinned and gestured for him to follow, leading him down the center aisle and hoisting herself onto the stage. She let her legs dangle over the side and patted the spot next to her, so Alec hoisted himself up.

The girl pointed at the ceiling. "I just learned this today, but it's so great you have to know. See how their eyes are turned?"

"Yeah?"

"Okay, what else do you notice, reporter guy?"

Alec studied the hundreds of photos. "Diversity."

"Look at you." She grabbed his badge. "Mr. Alec McCullers for the win." She raised her hand and waved it as though she were brushing the ceiling with her hand. "They all represent a different country, see it?"

Alec gazed at the countless faces, then nodded.

"Okay, now for the mindblower. See their eyes? Notice anything?"

"No."

"Right. No one can. But in each eye is a camera set to stream the whole thing to *that* particular country. They're literally selling balcony seats for every country, live-streaming the whole thing."

Alec raised his brows. "Two cameras per country?"

"One camera for Ivan, the other for the orchestra and some audience shots, which I think come from a solo camera on the stage. But I think you pay extra for it if you want both angles. It's an up-sell thing."

"Millionaires gotta pay the bills, right?" Alec said.

The girl laughed, flashing an infectious grin.

He couldn't believe he was thinking it right now, but he was taken by this girl. He needed to get his mind back to the conductor. He was here to help Janet, Markus, and Cody, not get a number, which he was awful at anyway. No matter how normal this moment felt, each minute that passed was pulling both of them closer to disaster. He needed to find something he could exploit for good. "Nice gig helping out with the event, huh?"

She swung her legs back and forth. "Weeks like this, with the basketball game and the orchestra—yeah, can't beat it."

"What should we expect tonight? Ivan always plans surprises. Any idea what's up?"

The girl pretended to zip her lips, then shook her head. Something about her just exuded loveliness.

He couldn't help himself. "Okay, could you at least tell me your name? Or do you have a card?" *A card, Alec? From an events worker? You idiot.*

"A card?" She smiled coyly. "Like with my number on it?"

"I mean, what I . . ." Alec stuttered.

Her eyes got big. "Well, color me flattered, but I'm seeing someone. So kind of you to ask, though, you seem great." She curled her hand into a C, raised it to her mouth, and pretended to whisper. "I'll call ya if it doesn't work out."

They both laughed.

Someone whistled from across the room and they looked up. It was another female crew member. "Ivan needs you," she said.

"You know *him*?" Alec said to the girl.

She swung her legs out and dropped to the floor. She turned back to him, hair swinging. "Everyone thinks he hangs the stars." She rolled her eyes playfully. "He's just a man pretending to be a mountain."

The girl gave a little bow, then turned to leave.

Alec had heard that saying before, recently. His mind conjured up the conductor in that wingback chair in the fancy house, saying, "Just a man pretending to be a mountain . . ."

Did this girl know the conductor?

"Wait, you never told me your name," Alec called out to her.

Making her way toward where the other crew member had called, she sang out over her shoulder, "Rosetta."

20

Anita Postma looked up at me from her phone, which had just buzzed. She nodded.

I leaned toward her. "Where? When?"

"Fifty-five minutes, on campus. Girls' locker room in the gymnasium."

The chief shook his head.

Cody, who'd been disassembling and reassembling his gun, cocked his weapon.

I tapped Postma's elbow. "Can you do this? We'll be close, but you have to stall him. Make him believe nothing is different with you."

Postma nodded but was fidgety.

Cody gave me a sideways look. *I don't know about this, not with the emotional shape she's in,* he was telling me.

My gut was telling me the conductor would make her within seconds. He'd then take her captive and Cody and I would be forced to lower our weapons. If we refused, he'd do something terrible to Postma. There had to be a better way.

242

A reclining Renfroe put his hands on his knees. "It's not going to work, you know that."

"I can do it," Postma said. "I'm sick of it. I'll make him believe. You just do your part."

I met Cody's eyes. Leaving this opportunity in the hands of someone we'd just met and was obviously shaken wasn't the plan I wanted to execute. But what other choice did we have?

Cody spoke as if Postma hadn't said a thing. "We could leave her out of it. Storm in and start firing. Figure the rest out later."

"Do you think he's stupid?" Postma said. "He's not stepping foot into the locker room until he's sure it's me, alone."

"Is there just the one entrance to the locker room?" I said.

Postma shook her head. "Do I look like I frequent the girls' locker room? I don't know. But he'll have contingencies. He always does."

The chief cleared his throat, then spoke in a monotone. "There's a small frosted window, ground level, along the east side of the gymnasium. That would get you into the locker room."

"All right then," Cody said. "She goes in through the front, I cover the window route, and Haas follows Postma as soon as he sees someone go in after her. Or if the nut tries the window, he's mine."

"And if he's in there before she is?" Renfroe said.

I considered that. Gave Postma solid eye contact. "We won't be able to protect you, not if he makes a move. But if you make a sound, any at all, we'll be moments away."

Renfroe scoffed.

But Postma straightened her skirt. "We're wasting time. Teach me some self-defense."

I did just that until it was time for the meet. Then I opened the classroom door for her.

Cody nodded at the chief. "What do we do with him?"

I motioned for Renfroe to get up. "He stays with me." I turned to Postma, who was stepping out of the tiny classroom. "Hey, remember the pain he's caused. You get to put an end to that."

"Well," Cody said, "or a bullet."

I watched as Postma and Cody left the English building, heading in separate directions. As soon as they were out of sight, I exited as well and walked toward the gymnasium. I kept one hand pressed to Renfroe's back—where the incision had been made—making sure he stayed at my side.

"It's not too late, Haas," he said. "You don't have to get Postma and your best friend killed."

I shook my head. "Just have to let this thing play out, right, Chief? That way no one gets hurt."

He looked at the ground. "You don't know what you're doing, and you know it."

Students walked and rode past us, backpacks flung over their shoulders, phones out, tapping away. How many of them had been touched by the string? Were some assigned to text the conductor whenever they saw me?

Nearly all of them were texting, only looking up to scan the faces within their personal bubble or to make sure they weren't about to trip on a loose brick. Those who did make eye contact with me did double takes, most likely recognizing me from the ginormous front-page spread in the *Trenton Telegraph*. Any one of them could be a tail, reporting our every move to the white-faced demon. Probably wouldn't even need to be threatened to do so. Most any student would agree to watch a university cop and text his location for weekend coin.

I kept my head lowered and continued toward the gym. A quick glance behind didn't reveal anything suspicious. Just students moving along, minding their business, oblivious to what could transpire tonight.

Renfroe snarled at me as if I'd kicked a dog.

I knew he saw those students too. As coldhearted as he'd become over the years, he still cared about keeping people safe. And my plan held no guarantees of taking any of the students out of harm's way. I hated that he might be right. But I couldn't wait for whatever the conductor had planned. We needed to take our shot while we had it.

Reaching the gym, I couldn't believe I'd been here just last night, stripped of my badge and meeting Janet for the first time.

We entered the lobby and were immediately met with boisterous noise from the setup crew. Speakers were blasting pump-up music as though the crew members were a team prepping for the championship game.

"This isn't the right play," Renfroe said. "He's got something planned. He's not stupid enough for a trap."

I tugged the chief toward the trophy case wall. "Let me guess. The right play is cowering in a corner, praying to *God* the conductor doesn't blow you up?" My attempt at suppressing emotion wasn't working. "You're pathetic. And you know what's worse? I thought it could work for me at Trenton because I read your file. You put together a nice body of work for the city. I don't know what's changed, but you've given up everything decent and noble. And for what, gambling?" I shook my head. "You lost your way and your soul with it."

I brushed off my jacket and led him toward the doors that would lead us into the gymnasium.

"You self-righteous, arrogant rookie. You're after glory, is what it is. It's all about *you*."

I moved my hand from the top of his back toward the bottom, right over his incision. He groaned through bared teeth.

University crew members were crawling all over the place, setting up chairs, big screens, extra speakers—dozens upon dozens of extra speakers—and ticketing booths. This was merely the overflow seating. People had traveled hundreds of miles just to be in a room connected to the room with the Celestial Orchestra playing.

I kept my head lowered as we followed the wall toward the bleachers. The way toward the girls' locker room turned underneath the stands.

Instead of ducking into the hallway leading to the girls' side of the lockers, where Postma would have already entered, we slipped into the passage toward the boys' side. I then crouched and used my phone to peek around the corner. All seemed clear.

My gut told me otherwise.

Even though the window was located at the back of the gymnasium, concealed by rhododendrons, Cody double-checked to make sure no one was looking. He bent the lock with a rock, coughing to cover the noise.

He pushed the retractable window up, and dust plumed and floated to the floor inside the girls' locker room. It was a farther fall than he'd thought. He lowered his legs, let go, then crouched onto the floor.

Toilet stalls lined one side of the room while a dozen shower stalls spanned the other. Postma must have settled in near the lockers, which were beyond the tiled area and around the corner.

Cody slipped into the nearest stall, closed the toilet seat, and crouched on it. He had a view of the retractable window if the conductor tried entering or escaping that way.

Now it was up to Postma.

Cody kept an eye on his watch. Had the conductor already made them?

The sound of Postma screaming vibrated throughout the locker room.

I barely heard Postma's scream over the Celestial Orchestra's specialty loudspeakers in the gymnasium. But I heard it.

I cursed and jumped to my feet. "Hurry."

Renfroe reached out a hand. "Give me a weapon. I can help."

"You've got fists. Use them."

Holding my gun steady and making sure the chief was in tow, I ran into the tunnel toward the girls' locker room, passed the coach's office, and eased into the lockers area.

No sounds, not even breathing. The way the lines of lockers were set up, I could only see the first of four possible rows.

Cody had to be closing in from the other side. If the conductor had attacked Postma, it was because he knew we were close. Announcing myself wasn't much of a disadvantage. The conductor may get a slightly better sense of my location, but Cody would too.

"Cody?" I said.

"Copy," my friend said.

That meant we had flanked both sides of the locker room area, and whoever had Postma was trapped between us.

"Anita?" I moved to the right to peek around the first row of lockers to the second. Nothing. I made sure Renfroe was in step with me and kept my feet moving to the third row.

Cody was just turning from the other side.

Between us lay Postma, facedown.

"I got her, cover me." Cody dropped to a knee by Postma's side.

I crouched and suddenly realized I had two blind spots to cover, assuming Renfroe had my back.

Movement rustled from one of the blind spots. I looked at the chief. He'd heard it too, hadn't he?

A hissing sound filled the room and Cody yelled.

I turned to find him face to the ground as Postma scrambled to her feet. What was in her hand?

"Pepper spray," Cody shouted.

I shielded my eyes and ran directly at where I'd seen her rising, smashing into her like a linebacker. We crashed into the wall. She grunted and dropped to the floor, wheezing, the air knocked out of her.

Fragments of the liquid fire touched my skin. My eyes stung and my vision blurred. I shot to my feet—

What felt like talons stabbed into my back, and I cried out, losing my grip on my weapon. It clanged against the floor and slide away from me, thwacking into the nook between the floor and the wall.

The pain wasn't electric from a Taser. What had—

Again spiked prongs lashed, accompanied by a loud *snap*— but not at me. This time Cody cried out. He was still struggling to see anything.

Postma scrambled away from me on her hands and feet.

I turned and crossed my forearms in the direction of the blows, trying to get my feet underneath me.

A bullet *thipped* into the wall behind me. Paint chips dribbled to the locker room floor.

I stared ahead, into the conductor's eyes.

He was no more than ten feet away, holding a multitailed whip with metal shards in one hand and a silencer-equipped pistol in the other. "You truly are an addicting breed of will and absurdity." He took a couple of steps to his left and picked up my 9mm, shoving it underneath his trench coat. "I thought you'd finally lay low, bask in your victory at the armory, stick close to your woman and chickpeas. But here you are. So perfect." He laughed. "Messing with my string, trying to turn my own creation against me." He pushed his hips back and his chest forward, pressing both hands to his heart. "*Absurdity.*"

Postma and the chief were like statues, each frozen with gazes glued to the conductor.

"Ever seen the way a puppy looks at its owner?" the conductor said. "Awe and wonder. You couldn't get that puppy to bite, not if you had a lifetime." The conductor glanced at Postma, then Renfroe, shaking his head. "Tryin' to turn my knots against me, shame, shame—I know their *names*. Isn't that right, Anita?" He walked over to her, leaned down to help her stand.

She was trembling like I'd never seen.

"She was my first knot, you know. Been with me the longest, helping me get all the details in order. Loyal, hardworking, and scared to death."

Tears spilled down Postma's cheeks.

"Stop it," I said. "Look at what you're doing. Look what it's done to *you*."

The conductor trained the gun on me and squinted as if lining up a shot at my forehead. "Every ounce of logic tells me to bleed you in the shower stalls—drains, you know? But this isn't about something so small as logic. You're the sacrificial lamb, Haas." He strode toward Renfroe. "An honor that should have fallen to Chief here, if I'm being honest." He scoffed. "But Chief slaughtered himself long before my day of reckoning." The conductor turned to me, emotionless. "Leaving you. Perfect *you*."

My lips quivered and I could feel my veins ready to pop out of my neck.

The conductor's lips twitched upward. "That's the Markus I know and love." He stepped behind the chief, then rested his pistol on Renfroe's shoulder as if just finishing a long shift. "All these knots, bloody boring. I'm not telling you anything new 'bout this one. Spineless, gutless, a nothing. It's why I brought him into the party so late. Self-preservation is the most hazardous trait of the lot." The conductor eyed Renfroe like a piece of rotten meat. "No ideals. No morals. Just survival. Makes me sick." He waved his gun at me. "You even sicker, right, Markus?"

The conductor tossed his whip to me.

I caught it, my back screaming in pain.

"Do for me what's needed to be done for years." The conductor motioned the cracking of a whip. "Rear back one of those hulking arms and sink it into scum—if not for me, then most assuredly for you."

I looked at the whip, my own blood still dripping from its prongs. I tossed it onto the floor.

Renfroe, who'd been grimacing and staring at the ground, slowly raised his head.

As if someone had taken a swirling water brush to his portrait, the conductor's face twisted. Then it morphed into a sadistic smile.

"Haas," Cody warned.

The conductor sneered at my friend. "Cody Caulkins, the trusted sidekick through thick and thin, no matter the lies his friend has led him to believe." The white-faced demon ran his fingers down his cheekbones and to the tip of his chin. Then pointed his weapon at Cody. "Don't test my patience again, Haasy. Whip him like the pigheaded excuse for a life he is."

I tried to think, to plan. Nothing was coming. The conductor had the gun on my friend, and the lone option I had—whipping Renfroe—would maybe buy me a minute, be morally reprehensible, and leave me in the exact same position after the deed.

The conductor pushed Renfroe a step toward me. "Five. Four. Three—"

"Haas," Cody said.

"Two."

Cody glanced at the conductor, the conductor glanced at me.

"Okay," I said.

"One."

"I said okay!"

The conductor raised the barrel of his gun and fired.

21

The shot penetrated its target directly in the forehead. A thumb-sized red dot appeared as the body thumped to the ground.

I grimaced as Postma's frame crumpled, an unsuspecting, almost relieved look on her face.

Cody swore.

Chief's eyes misted.

Contempt twisted my face, which burned with wrath. Why?

But there were no answers with the conductor. Just manipulation and torture.

"I'm going to kill you," I said.

"She did everything you asked," Renfroe added.

The conductor pulled the gun back to himself, tapping the barrel to his mouth. He kissed it. "Don't you know anything about God? There's a simple rule: you're never, ever entitled to know why—except, of course, upon your death when the demons are comin' to getcha." He smacked the back of the chief's head. "Wrap her in curtains. A little blood on your hands should feel just like home."

I wasn't sure what the conductor meant by that, but Renfroe complied, grabbing Postma from behind her arms and dragging her toward the showers.

The conductor started tapping the tip of the gun against his head. "You know, I'm actually tiring of this doing-the-opposite-of-what-I-say humdrum. I know it will be worth it in the end, but delayed gratification—what a tease." He let his jaw hang open on that last word, bent at the knees, then popped back up. "Just dying to see the breaking, just a glimpse of the coming chasm. Every kid's entitled to one present on Christmas Eve, yes? Let's try this again." The conductor jutted his chin at me and spoke flatly. "Take off your shirt."

I shared a look with Cody.

"Take it off!" The conductor pointed the gun at my friend's forehead.

I extended a hand to the conductor, took off my jacket, then pulled my shirt up and over my head. Flipped it out of my hand so that it landed halfway between the psychopath and me.

He pointed the gun at my pants. "Now those."

"Stop the game, you've got us."

"This is the point, Markus," the conductor said, breathing heavily. "Vulnerability. Power. The *breaking*. Don't you see? One way wins, and yours loses. You're going to bleed—and you can't do anything about it. So . . . Take. Them. Off."

I squared myself to the conductor like a bull staring down a matador. I wasn't going to give him the satisfaction of feeling dominant in this moment.

Steph's words returned to me as I wondered if Cody and I

were facing our last moments on earth. *He can't touch us—not in a way that matters.*

She had been talking about faith.

The conductor could break all the wills he wanted, he could manipulate people, he could hurt them with his string. But he couldn't touch their source of strength.

My belt went first, then pants. Never once taking my eyes off him, I threw my clothes at the conductor's feet.

"Tough-jock routine is as powerful as a man stripping because *god* told him to." The conductor faced Cody. "You're next, ladies' man."

Cody unzipped his pants so quickly you could hear the zing.

The conductor motioned toward the wall where Postma had fallen dead. "Over there. Grip that wall like an oak tree in the eye of a twister."

We shared a look but complied, pressing our palms to the wall and looking over our shoulders.

The conductor craned his neck toward the showers but kept his eyes, and gun, on us. "Your derriere's required."

Renfroe trudged out from the shower stalls, hands covered in crimson, shirt and pants spotted with blood. Sweat had turned his hair from brown to nearly black.

The conductor patted his knee as if calling a mutt. "Look at the treats, Jackie boy. Not only were you spared, but the tables have turned." The conductor pointed at the shirts on the ground. "Pick those up."

Renfroe did.

"Good. Stuff them in their mouths."

The chief, trembling, again did as he was told, wrapping Cody's shirt in my mouth and pulling it tight enough to split my teeth. He followed suit with my shirt and Cody. We drilled him with our eyes, but he wouldn't look back.

"Good grief, Chiefy, the hostility." The conductor laughed. "Making them eat each other's pits."

Renfroe stepped off to the side.

The conductor took a stride toward Cody and me, but not close enough for either of us to make a move. He picked up the whip and tossed it to Renfroe. "Ready to die today, Chief? That's what will happen if either of them move."

Renfroe stepped up behind us gingerly, the conductor directly behind him. We both braced ourselves against the wall and made eye contact.

Cody wanted to move now.

I tried to shake my head ever so slightly, even though my mind was screaming that Renfroe wasn't worth it, that we could use him as a human shield, that we needed to think about ourselves, Steph, the girls.

But then I saw it and shook my head again.

Cody pressed against the wall, face red and arms flexed, breathing hard through his nostrils. I could almost hear him saying, *All right, bud. We're dead but I'm with you.*

"Stripe them up," the conductor said. "Take that hatred for yourself and make them wear it."

Renfroe gazed at the sharp, tiny hooks at the end of each strip of leather.

"Come now," the conductor said. "Don't tell me you haven't thought about taking Haas behind the woodshed? Get to it. The finale's upon us."

I eyed what I'd seen at my feet just a moment ago. Small and black, tucked under the small lip between the floor and wall: Postma's canister of pepper spray, no longer than a thumb.

But the conductor and Renfroe were looking directly at us, which meant bending down for the spray was out of the question.

Unless I was forced to my knees.

I flashed Cody a look and was sure he didn't understand it, but I rolled with it nonetheless, shouting through my gag, "Just do it!" It didn't come out like that, but the chief could at least see I was bracing for blows.

The conductor seemed surprised. "The spirit in you."

Renfroe cracked the whip into my back, and the pain bit like giant bugs sinking their teeth into my spine. I yelled into the shirt, producing a muffled growl.

"Again!" the conductor said. It sounded like he was bursting with excitement.

But it was Cody now who grimaced as the prongs slashed into his back.

Wait. Just wait.

"Hell's fury, Chiefy—again, again!"

I could feel the stripes forming from my shoulder blades to the small of my back. My legs weakened and shook.

Almost. Almost.

"Your show now, Chief," the conductor said. "Remember what I've got—what you've got." He followed that up with a whisper, but I couldn't make it out. Then it was back to his boisterous self. "Now more, Chief, more!"

It was Cody's turn again to take the lashes. "Haas!" he screamed into his gag.

"Haas," the conductor mocked. But his voice had come from a greater distance. He was backing out of the locker room area and would soon be in the hallway, past the coach's office, out of sight, out of earshot.

"I'm sorry," Renfroe said.

The whip struck me again. *One more time, just one more time.*

Next it was Cody. And again he yelled.

I braced for my turn once more. The talons sunk into my serrated back and I let my knees give way, collapsing to the floor. My right hand gripped the pepper spray.

The timing of Renfroe's whips became predictable. He was raising it right now, about to strike Cody. I turned my hips in one quick motion, extended my hand with the canister as far as I could—everything hurting like flame-scorched nails embedded in my body—and pressed the dispenser.

What I hadn't known was that the conductor had left Renfroe with a gun in his other hand. But the stream of pepper shot directly into the chief's face and he stumbled backward, bringing both his whip hand and his gun hand to his face.

Cody had already pushed off the wall and was sprinting—no, *leaping*—toward the chief. He reared back, smashing Renfroe's face left, right, left, right. The gun he had been holding slid across the floor.

The chief groaned, coughing and blinking rapidly. He tried to speak but Cody kept punching his jaw.

I tore off my gag, gripped my friend from behind, and pulled him off, nearly catching a blow myself. "Not worth it—he's done, he's done."

Cody nearly wrestled free, yelling muffled words at the writhing man on the ground.

I put one hand on Cody's chest, the other on his neck, and applied pressure. "People are in danger. Can't waste time with that." I pointed at the chief and Cody followed my finger, snarling the entire time. "Get his gun. I'll get the rest."

While Cody removed his gag and went to retrieve the fire-arm, I knelt by the chief. His eyes were watery and swelling. Blood oozed from a broken nose. I think he was mouthing something, but no words were coming out.

I actually found myself feeling pity. "I'm not the type to give life advice, Chief, but if you don't rediscover whatever you used to stand for, you're going to die. Maybe even physically. Get me?"

I didn't wait for an answer as I patted down the chief. No other weapons. But he still liked to be entertained, because in his pocket were two tickets to the Celestial Orchestra—one expensive near the front of the amphitheater, the other in the gymnasium overflow seating. Both in row I, seat 28. Why they weren't together made zero sense unless this ticket was that special surprise he'd mentioned.

I shook my head. "This is what you meant by 'accompany-ing you'?"

The chief stared at the tickets as if looking *through* them. Cody had really rung his bell.

Renfroe closed his eyes, appearing as though he were about to drift into the kind of sleep that could only be interrupted with a banging gong.

"How we going to get out of here without causing a scene?" Cody said.

"Not with those," I said, looking at our bloody clothes.

"Can you stomach showering next to a body?"

We both hit the showers. The water pressure stung but the steam felt like a salve to my wounds.

"Coach's office is down the hall—let's hope he has clothes. Then you and I are going to the performance."

"What's he going to do?" Cody said.

I let my eyes do the answering, needed to think.

Observe.

The string had never been designed to last. It'd had an expiration date on it from the moment the conductor started entangling innocent people in it. And that expiration was tonight.

Whatever the conductor had been planning was about to unravel, and I couldn't imagine a scenario in which people didn't die. The conductor had killed Postma without a moment's hesitation or twinge of guilt. Earlier, I had entertained the thought that the conductor might be a poser, all bark with no bite. But bloodshed had proven to be nothing to him.

Orient.

The conductor yearned for power, for the *breaking*. What did that look like at a Celestial Orchestra performance? He wouldn't actually replace Ivan. I could put a bullet in his chest with ease now that we had recovered the gun he'd left with Renfroe.

Unless . . . the conductor had a load of guns to hijack the entire crowd.

But was that the enthralling power he longed for, leading an orchestra that was under duress? It didn't make sense. The conductor had another play, something to stroke his ego. He thrived on manipulating the will, and that's what he would do tonight—to an extent he'd not yet shown.

"You're doing that OODA thing, aren't you?" Cody said.

I nodded and we finished showering off, red liquid still pouring down the drain.

We raided the office of the women's basketball coach, who thankfully was male, worked out, and had a well-stocked wardrobe. Trenton's red attire was too bright and attention grabbing, but the alternative navy blended well enough.

"Uh . . ." Cody said, pointing at my back.

I looked over my shoulder. Blood had already seeped through my new shirt. I nodded at Cody to pass me another article of clothing.

I checked the time. The performance was starting soon.

We didn't know what we were walking into, we only had one gun with limited ammunition, and the only two seats we could position ourselves in were in two different buildings: one in the amphitheater, the other in the gymnasium overflow.

Cody handed me the gun. "Better shooter gets the shot."

I took the weapon.

"Besides, I've never minded the overflow. Better view of the single ladies."

I knew this was how my friend handled stress. "Be careful."

"You too, Haas."

22

After waiting long enough to make sure our wounds had clotted up, we each shoved our ticket into our pockets and snuck out the way Cody had come in. Thankfully, nobody was around the back of the gymnasium.

A low rumble came from the dark clouds above.

We circled around to the front. With the performance set to start in ten minutes, people were filing toward the gymnasium lobby, then they'd either take their seat in the gym or walk the sky bridge to the amphitheater.

Cody and I pushed ourselves into the cluster of people to blend in, shuffling toward the entrance of the gymnasium, where security guards in red jackets were checking bags and waving people through. Everyone waiting in the long line was fully distracted by members of the Celestial Orchestra on the other side of the ticketing gate. They were erupting into symphony each time volunteers ripped another stub from a ticketholder, playing and transitioning so fast it was hard to tell if their tune was planned or spontaneous.

This was the way of the Celestial Orchestra, from what I'd heard. They were the anti-orchestra in that they never took themselves too seriously or bought into the idea that a suit and tie or fancy dress was the lone acceptable attire for their performances. All that mattered was excellence in the performance, and that wasn't just about what people heard or saw—but how they were made to feel.

We made it through the line, and our tickets were ripped and the stubs handed back to us.

"Glad to have you—just in time before we close the gates," the attendant said. I was directed to the right and walked the sky bridge into the amphitheater, while Cody was directed left into the gymnasium.

The chief had gotten himself quite a seat, front row to the left. I worked my way to the cushy red armchair, keeping my head down. I couldn't shake the feeling that even now the conductor was watching me.

But who *was* the conductor? And when was he going to make his move?

I had thought it might be Declan. But Cody said he wasn't a match, and seeing that Steph hadn't suspected as much also cast doubt on that theory. The conductor and Declan couldn't be one and the same. Couldn't.

But that left . . . Ivan? Which had been Alec's suspicion. Had the kid known something that Cody and I hadn't? Or had he truly been trying to figure it out for himself even though he was in the midst of betraying us?

The thought of Ivan as the conductor seemed impossible. I thought back to videos of the acclaimed leader of the Celestial Orchestra, picturing him falling off his platform and landing on Renfroe before the game. Had the conductor planned

it all—as Ivan? Faked the fall and disappeared to play the
white-faced demon? Ivan was a performer; the conductor
was a performer. Like Declan, similar height, similar build.
But what of the voice? I supposed he could manipulate that as
well. But then the research and planning . . . Ivan was always
traveling and performing. How would he have executed this?
My head hurt.

Unless . . . Postma. She arguably had more access and sway
at Trenton University than the president himself, because she
was the one with the relationships. She could have fed the
conductor all sorts of information. And most of his commu-
nication had come via video, so . . . was it possible Ivan had
recorded remotely while having others do his dirty work at
the university until he touched down a few days ago?

Janet had received a video when her dog was stolen, but
had she actually seen whether or not her dog was there with
the conductor? On the other hand, the dog incident had happened just a couple of days ago. Ivan could have easily been
in town then.

But why would a rich man doing what he loves throw it
away to torture a university twenty years after it had launched
his fame? If the conductor were Ivan, the anniversary had
something to do with his motivation. But Trenton was what
had propelled his career. Why would he target it? What would
drive a rich and famous showman to crack under the supposed
motivation of "godlike power"?

My thoughts were broken as members of the Celestial Orchestra marched down every aisle, each equipped with their
instrument of expertise, playing them as if they'd been doing
so since they were old enough to pick them up.

From the moment I'd approached the ticketing gate to now,

the orchestra had choreographed every step and beat and sound. They were like grifters, executing the perfect heist with each movement, misdirection, and sleight of hand.

I craned my neck, taking in the crowd and presentation unraveling all around me. So much pleasure among the people was betrayed by the fact that a man among them was here to destroy—all under the guise of control and power over the human will.

The conductor was here tonight for no other reason, it seemed, than gripping goodness by the neck, shoving it to the ground, and choking the life out of it.

I couldn't warn anyone without appearing like a lunatic. The guards in the red security jackets wouldn't listen to a suspended TUP officer, let alone a spectator. That left me with a partially emptied mag to protect hundreds from a psychopath in possession of a small armory's worth of firepower.

The conductor had to put himself front and center at some point, exposed. One shot and it would be over. But what if neither Declan nor Ivan had anything to do with the string? I couldn't take a shot unless the conductor's identity became clear.

I hadn't seen a single weapon or nervous-eyed person. Not a thing appeared out of the ordinary. Everything looked exactly as it should for a Celestial Orchestra performance: in sync with a ladder climb of musical suspense and theatrical flair.

The entire amphitheater went dark and I cursed under my breath. I hadn't scoped out a full mental schematic of my surroundings yet, and at least for now I wouldn't be able to. The show was beginning.

Pockets of light illuminated the aisles, each beam highlighting a different orchestra member who'd stopped in place and played their instrument with abandon. The light traveled to a makeshift floating platform, upon which Ivan stood, that was descending from the amphitheater's ceiling.

Ivan, who appeared to be favoring one side of his body, held his baton perfectly still, chin sharp and pointy. His hair was drawn into a ponytail that dangled down, outstretched only by his cape. He swung his baton with both hands as if gripping a sword as heavy and magnificent as King Arthur's. He turned to the Celestial Orchestra and shot his hands up at the climax of the music.

The composition wound down to light background music, and all light faded to black.

"From the dawn of time," Ivan whispered in the blackness, "what has proven itself . . . immortal? What has surpassed time's cruel grasp? What has shown itself godlike?"

That was it.

I reached for my firearm slowly, trying not to cause a panic.

"It was there in the beginning, when all fell to chaos. It was there in peace and war, prosperity and famine. And it will be there when you leave this wondrous place tonight, ready to lift you and shield you and fight for you."

A red glow, the only light in the entire building now, started pulsing over Ivan's heart. "The human will. It has watched over those who've gone before us, and it is in this very moment pumping through your veins, as real and beautiful as your own DNA." The pulsing red glow of tiny lights on his chest started pumping out a blood-red hue to his neck, arms, and legs. The orchestra's basses began thumping along to the rhythm. "You cannot gain it, you cannot lose it—you can only discover it, for it is the hidden nucleus within you if you would only open your eyes to it. Please, do that tonight." His voice started faltering as if he himself were succumbing to duress. "Whatever happens, don't let him break your—"

"Will," another voice said.

The lights on Ivan's suit partially went out. But no, they hadn't. Someone was standing on the floating platform with him, gripping him from behind.

I had my gun in hand now, pressed flat against my thigh, but I couldn't take aim at anything in this blackness.

"Come now, Ivan—we both know that's rich, do we not?"

It was him. The real conductor.

A spattering of chuckles worked through the crowd, but most of the audience simply leaned forward, trying to see just what was happening on Ivan's platform.

"Gotcha," I whispered.

"I want to welcome you all to the symphony, *my* symphony," the conductor said. "Good show so far, really something, but with 'I' here spewing bunkum, I couldn't help but interject. No need reaching for phones—lines are busy, it seems."

Ivan tried speaking, but the conductor's hand was covering his mouth. "Question one, Ivan. Where's your will now? Why isn't this immortal drug, which you've spun into millions, showing up? Because it seems I have the stage. Which means I have the more powerful will, correct? Or did yours betray you, off to spend time with its mistress?" The conductor chuckled. "Now, I know you're all trying to think ahead, trying to see where Ivan is taking this. Let me put your mind to rest and introduce the fine work of Janet Blevins."

My head suddenly felt light. Janet was supposed to be at the hospital. The conductor had gotten to her, used Janet's sister as leverage.

Or . . . had she been a part of the conductor's plan the whole time?

I thought back to what had happened at the communications building. I hadn't actually seen the conductor attacking her, and neither had Alec, for that matter.

Alec. He had betrayed Cody and me.

Janet was the one who'd introduced me to Alec. And now Janet was working with the conductor.

Had it all been an elaborate ploy?

While everything else remained black—except for Ivan's suit with the pulsating red lights—overhead spotlights suddenly shone on the red-jacketed security guards, each of whom now wore masks and were holding the weapons Cody and I had taken from the armory before losing them to Mitchell's men.

Gasps and screams echoed throughout the amphitheater, then the conductor said, "Ladies and gentlemen, Ivan Mikolaev!"

A loud wheezing sounded over the loudspeakers, as if the conductor had stuck a knife through Ivan's esophagus. "That boy you seduced all those years ago—me, actually—sends salutations," he said. "Unlike your tumble at the gym, this fall you won't survive."

The glow of Ivan's suit fell from the platform, a blur of red plunging limply to the ground, and the world-renowned musician smashed into the middle aisle of the auditorium.

The entire audience jumped to their feet, and several people screamed. The gunmen in masks and red jackets aimed their weapons at the crowd.

"Behold the will," the conductor said over the loudspeakers. It sounded like he was moving, even in the darkness. Had he found a way off the floating platform? "Ivan's seemed strong, but mine is *real*."

A few dimmed lights turned on, and the screams intensified as members of the audience rushed to where Ivan had fallen.

"Now let me be clear, rules rule the world," the conductor said. Where had he gone? "And the first rule is: abandon your seat, you die."

The gunmen fired shots into the air, freezing the crowd.

"Back in your seats," the conductor said.

I craned my neck in every direction, but the hysteria made it difficult to see. People who'd gotten out of their seats began scurrying back to them. The conductor was nowhere to be found. All I knew was that he was no longer on the floating platform. Was he among the crowd, behind the curtains, outside?

"These cameras, these angles—they really are quite celestial. I love seeing your faces, compliments of Janet. Tonight, ladies and gentlemen, isn't about the orchestra, Ivan, or even me." The conductor's voice dropped. "It's about the *real* human will."

Two projectors lowered on either side at the front of the amphitheater. Members of the orchestra crouched in place, cowering.

"I learned much about the will right here. Like you, scales fell from my eyes." The conductor appeared on the big screens, his black-and-white makeup now contrasted against fiery red eyes, flitting his fingers and slowly letting his hands fall to his sides.

Where was he live-casting this? It couldn't be far.

"Invited to meet the Celestial Orchestra in person—can you imagine the thrill? But the corridor I walked that night didn't lead to a reception line. It was just Ivan, taking his newest and youngest fan backstage—introducing me to the will. *His* will. This your Jackson Renfroe knows, Anita Postma and Franklin Iseman too." He snarled and nearly spit out his words. "But they'd become university darlings for their discovery, basking in the celebrity they'd created, never once considering *who* they'd created." He let out guttural breaths. "Ivan's will was akin to a Bugatti—flaunted to drive others' *perception* of him and *submission* to him. It was wrong! The will isn't four-wheeled eye candy; it's petroleum-derived liquid deep within the mainframe. That"—he raised one finger in the air—"is what drives the great ones. The *greater* ones."

The conductor tilted his hand toward the camera in a way that pointed toward Ivan's lifeless body. "Know what separates the Ivans from the greater ones?" His eyes narrowed as he stared into the camera, lingering in silence. "The rival. Ivan has sucked strength out of the weak—starting with a boy. The only greatness in that is death." He leaned close to the camera projecting his image. "What's *great* is what's happening tonight: one man's unstoppable will clashing with another's immovable will. So would the gentleman in row 1, seat 28, in both the amphitheater and gymnasium, please withdraw what's under your seat—and stand."

I looked down. Grabbed my ticket.

Row 1, seat 28.

People started turning my way as recognition set in. It had been a setup? The chief, the tickets?

Images flashed in my mind: first of the conductor whispering into Renfroe's ear, another of Renfroe trying to tell me something after Cody had beaten him to a pulp. The conductor had meant for us to overpower the chief, hadn't he? He knew we'd use the tickets and sit exactly where we were.

Cody. He was in the same position in the gymnasium: row 1, seat 28.

"Our winner needs no introduction: you know him as the local hero. I know him as the star of my show, my string. Mr. Markus Haas. For the cheapies in the gymnasium, your lead role belongs to Cody Caulkins, whom you may have also read about in the paper. Welcome to the string. Participation is mandatory. And refusal will ensure a *dear* price is paid."

Before I could form a thought or utter a word, the projectors switched to video clips of me arguing with Chief Renfroe in the press box, getting tossed out of the gym, sneaking into police headquarters, stuffing duffle bags with guns, running from Trenton officers, shooting one of them at the armory, strapping a woman—Stephanie—into a chair, and watching as a man—Cody Caulkins—beat the chief purple.

I could almost feel the collective gasps and shock of the audience. How had he compiled all this footage, some of which had *just* occurred?

"This man is your white knight, Trenton—living a code that could only be fueled by a will so cemented it should be immovable." The conductor chuckled. "Tonight you experience this immovable object meeting the unstoppable force." He paused, looking at different places in the camera as if searching for me. "Under your seat, Markus. Under your seat, Cody."

I balled my hands into fists.

The conductor snapped his fingers, and all the masked men and women in security uniforms took aim at all different segments of the amphitheater. "Rude to keep us waiting," he said.

I reached under my chair, grabbed the first thing I felt, and shot my hand up. "I've got it! Put the guns down."

Others gasped and cursed all around me. I could hear the

same rumbling coming from across the sky bridge in the gymnasium.

I looked at my raised hand to see I was holding what appeared to be a crude but elaborate bomb.

"I told you the breaking was coming," the conductor said. "I'm just happy you didn't care." He pointed down, twirling his finger. "Remove the stick from the device. On that stick is a switch, and under that switch is a button. Ready?"

The two projector screens at the front of the amphitheater split into four mini screens apiece, displaying live feeds from within my house.

I put my hands, along with the bomb I was grasping, against my head. What felt like my very heart collapsed inward, as if being squeezed by an industrial-strength vise. I couldn't speak. Couldn't straighten my face, which was stretched tight and gaunt.

"In Mr. Haas's hands is a bomb capable of dismembering fifty of you—guts, blood, and bone." The conductor paused. "Markus, pass the bomb to the young lady next to you in the blue blouse. Then, blue blouse, pass it to the gentleman next to you—and so forth. For those in the gymnasium, follow the lead of the ruggedly handsome one, Mr. Cody Caulkins."

I looked at the bomb. Slowly dropped it to my side. The woman next to me choked back tears, nearly hyperventilating. She extended her hand to take the device.

"Good," the conductor crooned. "Markus?"

I gazed at the two projectors. Different angles of Isabella and Tilly sleeping, and of Steph tapping on her laptop in the kitchen nook. How had he gotten past Zoe's security detail so fast? Or had my place been bugged the entire time and I'd missed it?

I handed the device to the young woman, whose hands were shaking. I knew my face was telling her that I was sorry, but inside I was an inferno. What was the conductor doing? And all for an ego trip of his will?

"Calm down." The conductor waved his hand at the screen. "You're now free to pass it to the gentleman to your right and proceed to the sky bridge. Shoo."

The young woman handed it to a middle-aged man beside her, who appeared to be her father. He gently pushed her up and watched her make her way to the back, trembling.

"Pass it," a harsh voice said from somewhere behind my row. "Get that away from my son."

The projector screens switched back to the conductor, who was cupping one ear as if trying to hear better. "That didn't take but a few moments. Rule two: I just activated a little feature in this particular explosive, rigged to blow based on decibels." He raised his brows. "You itchy fingers with the instruments, well, a few well-jammed chords and the device detonates while a safe distance from you. Now wouldn't *that* be celestial? How much do you value your life? How much do you value the lives you'd be leaving behind? Decisions, decisions. Certainly we have some Machiavellians among us? Sadists, perhaps?" He grinned mockingly. "All it takes is one."

The woman in the blue blouse, still choking out sobs, started crying in louder bursts as she neared the door to the sky bridge.

"Quiet, please," a voice said to her. "You'll kill us."

More sobs echoed from the back.

"Shut up," another replied on behalf of the young woman.

She pushed open the doors, shaking. Before the door swung closed, I noticed that there was another person walking into the sky bridge from the gymnasium side. The same ritual was taking place in the overflow seating.

"Pass it, come on, follow your daughter," said that same angry voice a few rows behind me.

The father of the young woman looked at me, but not with scorn or malice. This was the look of a man who hadn't bought what the conductor had painted of me. His eyes lingered on me for a moment longer, then he passed the bomb and walked the aisle, his shoes padding against the floor.

"The thing about rule three is that it's forgettable," the conductor whispered as he pressed his fist to his head. "As in, those boom boxes being passed around are on a clock, set to explode the moment it hits zero—but *when*?" He leaned back and crossed his arms. "Mr. Markus Haas and Cody Caulkins have a choice. Click the detonators in their hands and one of the bombs will deactivate. Capisce? Let the battle of wills rage."

People started passing the bomb like it was cancer, jumping from their seats and moving to the aisle.

Some cried. Others shushed.

But all looked at me.

"Do it," a woman said.

A man in the second row back started babbling, even stood up. But before he could move to the center aisle, another man punched him. Women and men around them gasped through hand-covered mouths. Every time one person shut up, another started talking. The tones, though hushed, together created a low rumble.

I looked at the device in my hand, then glanced at the two projector screens picturing the live feeds of Steph and the girls. I knew exactly what flipping this switch would do. It would blow up either the bomb in the gymnasium or . . . Stephanie and the girls. I wasn't about to let that happen and could only pray that Cody wouldn't either.

The bomb passed through several rows of the amphitheater without incident, and the single-file line to the sky bridge started bottlenecking, jamming the center aisle. Strangers bumped shoulders, made pleas for why they needed out, and inched toward the door when any space opened in front of them.

I remained at my seat, unsure if movement from me would cause the conductor to blow the bombs.

The white-faced demon had disappeared to *somewhere*, and it had to be close by. Backstage? In an adjacent building? How could I get out of here and find him?

Just then something tugged at the hem of my pants. I looked down to see a hand at my feet, unraveling a crumpled note for me to read: *Be ready for the boom. P.S. Janet says hi.*

The hands dropped the note and pulled back under the chair. I turned slightly, trying to see who had crawled on their belly through the chairs behind me. But I couldn't see a face.

A flustered voice from somewhere behind me had grown from a whisper into a mini panic, and I turned to the commotion.

The bomb, which had barely been touching fingers as it whipped through the amphitheater, had stopped on a person midway through a row near the middle of the room. The person had not only received the bomb but stayed in their seat, clutching the bomb to their chest. They wore a black top and a gray hoodie underneath, which covered their head.

"Now this, ladies and gentlemen, I did not see coming: a rogue will, a renegade, someone so absolutely uncaring of the begging souls around them . . . that they'd embrace the very device that would tear the guts from their chest." The conductor waved his finger at the camera. "I like you, rogue one. Tilt up that head of yours before we never get to see it again."

The person slowly raised their face, then brushed off the hood with one hand. It was a girl with black locks of hair and fair skin. This was the girl who'd manned the ticketing booth for the basketball game the day before, greeting NCAA fans with all the enthusiasm and brightness of an entertainer. But now she was sullen with tearstained cheeks and a quivering lip.

"Rosetta," the conductor whispered. The name had exited his lips in such a way that it seemed to carry off half of the madman's soul. The conductor knew this girl, maybe even cared for her—deeply.

His weakness, his Achilles' heel, was right here in the form of the girl who ran the ticketing booth.

Everyone in the amphitheater watched the conductor on the two projector screens intensely, only shifting gazes momentarily to check on Rosetta.

A frustrated voice called out, "Hello, the bomb," in a tone bordering on the loudest decibel raised since the bomb started moving.

The conductor's eyes shifted to the voice, morphing into an inferno.

Rosetta shot to her feet, still clutching the explosive. "Stop this."

The anger on the conductor's face transformed into concern. He hadn't lied. That bomb was really armed, really on a timer—and the conductor hadn't cared to create a kill switch.

The girl was going to die if she refused to pass the explosive.

"Please," the conductor said. "Move it along."

"Come take it yourself," Rosetta said. She sat back down.

The conductor tried to speak. "Nothing . . ." A lump caught in his throat. "There's nothing I can do."

Even through the horror, Rosetta sat up straight and raised her chin. "Then I'm sorry I ever said hi to you." She shrugged in disgust. "If you care about me, let everyone go."

"Rosetta," the conductor said sharply. "Please—"

Heat blasted past my face as an explosion shook the entire building.

23

My arms shot up to protect my face, but the heat faded almost instantaneously. I sucked in a drag of air, not realizing that I'd stopped breathing.

I dropped my arms and looked around, still seated in row 1, seat 28.

Alive. The girl was alive. The people in the amphitheater were alive. I was alive. But the bomb was still in Rosetta's hand, fully intact.

What had exploded?

And where was the conductor?

I looked at the speakers and cameras throughout the amphitheater—well, what was left of them. *They* had been the source of the explosion, not the bomb.

"Janet," I whispered. She had to be the one behind it. She hadn't turned on me to help the conductor. She'd turned to sabotage him. I didn't know how the disturbance hadn't triggered the real bomb, but Janet had to be the reason they all were still alive.

The security guards in red looked confused. They all had been forced to play an awful role in the string but were now seeing that the conductor's plan had gone sideways.

"Do the right thing." I raised my hand high and kept my gun low. "We stop him for good—*now*."

The guards each kept their guns lowered and backed away from the crowd, shoulders hunched, looking as though an evil spell had just been lifted off them.

People scrambled away from the bomb, huddling in corners of the building. What the conductor might do now that his plan had been disrupted, I didn't know. But considering how many more stolen guns were unaccounted for, these people were safer in the building than outside of it.

"Stay where you are—there's no time to explain." I surveyed the amphitheater. The man who'd been crawling on the ground shot to his feet. It was . . . Alec? Wearing a CREW T-shirt.

The student journalist made his way toward Rosetta. "Everyone, listen. That man up front"—he pointed at me—"is the good guy, no matter what you think you saw. The conductor took me hostage and spilled it all." He turned to Rosetta. "Give it here, quick." She handed the bomb over and Alec ran the explosive to me. "Cody's got the bomb in the gymnasium—please tell me you have a gun and can find the psycho."

I lifted it.

The doors at the back of the amphitheater leading to the sky bridge opened, and there stood Janet. "This way, away from the bomb, stay low," she said, motioning everyone to the sky bridge. "You, you, you," Janet said, pointing at the red-jacketed men and women with guns. "Protect these people with your lives if you don't want to spend life in prison. Phones

are blocked—don't let anyone go anywhere until I can get
the authorities to come to us. He has others out there ready
to kill."

They took to her command.

Rosetta came running to Alec and me. "I know where he
is. I can take you to him."

I shared a look with Alec, and he understood. We each had
tasks we needed to accomplish.

"Wish me luck, the string's coming." Alec held up his phone
to show a group text that had come through moments ago. It
included a photo of the guns I'd stolen, and four more photos
of me and those who'd helped me to this point.

Take up arms! Kill Markus Haas, Cody Caulkins,
Janet Blevins, and Alec McCullers . . . or every
terrible thing I've ever uttered comes true.

Amphitheater. Gymnasium. Sky bridge. Now!

Alec pushed through the emergency exit door to the outside. The kid was making amends, doing what was right.

I needed to do the same. I turned to Rosetta. "Take me to
the conductor."

How he'd gotten to this point, he couldn't quite fathom right
now.

He'd made the connection between the conductor and Rosetta. She'd refused to give him a name but had indulged him
by getting them both into the performance under the guise of
CREW T-shirts.

Then he'd used Rosetta's phone to reconnect with Janet—

who somehow hadn't killed him on the spot—and learned
how the conductor had used Officer Mike Mitchell to threaten
Lucy and force Janet back into his service.

And now he was running with a bomb.

And he could die.

Alec sprinted away from the amphitheater, explosive firmly
clutched in the crook of his arm like a football. He just needed
to get the bomb somewhere it couldn't wreak havoc. Only
one place came to mind: the fountain. It was away from the
building, sunk into the ground, and would contain the burst
. . . right?

Whatever remnant of the string still loyal to the conductor
would be headed straight for the amphitheater, gymnasium,
and sky bridge—most likely armed.

Alec sprinted the brick pathway that weaved between buildings. He spilled onto the campus courtyard, where the fountain
flowed and was blasting water into the night sky, light shining
on it from every direction.

"Hey," a voice cried out from somewhere in the courtyard.
It wasn't one of the red security guards, but it was a man with
a gun. A Trenton cop.

"Gonna explode, gotta go," Alec shouted.

The man was gearing up to tackle Alec. "Stop!"

"Do you want to die?" Alec tried dodging. "It's over!"

But the man—Mike Mitchell, according to his tag—blocked
Alec like a linebacker, body-slamming him to the ground. The
bomb came loose, rattling along the bricks.

Mitchell swore and drew his weapon.

"What are you doing?" Alec yelled. "The conductor lost—
don't you get it?"

He pressed his gun to Alec's head. "He doesn't lose." The

man gripped Alec's neck with one hand and leaned over him, pressing the gun harder to his temple. "You should have never gone against him, kid."

Dear Lord, he was going to die.

A gunshot pierced the air.

Mitchell collapsed on top of Alec, blood leaking from a shot to the back of his head.

"Go!" a voice said. It belonged to . . . University Police Chief Jackson Renfroe, whose face looked as if someone had taken a baseball bat to it.

Alec wasn't sure what had just happened, but he jumped to his feet, picked up the bomb, and ran through the courtyard to the fountain.

Coming from his right was another man in a dead sprint: Cody Caulkins, whom Alec had also passed a note to without revealing his identity, for fear of what Cody would do to him. He too was carrying a bomb, the gymnasium bomb.

Their eyes met. Cody looked as though he were watching a purple cow pass his car on the freeway. Alec imagined his own countenance looked similar.

They both turned their gazes back to the fountain and crow-hopped the bombs through the air. The explosives spun in the night sky before splashing into the fountain nearly in sync—detonating just before impact. The combined, powerful burst of heat knocked them both to the ground as flames shot over their heads.

Alec rolled on the bricks and huffed. But he wasn't on fire. Or dead.

Cody, also sprawled on the bricks, met his eyes. He crawled over toward Alec, who instinctively blocked his face with his arms.

"Calm down." Cody knocked Alec's arms away from his face. "Haas, where is he?"

"Going after the conductor with the girl—I don't know where."

Cody looked confused. "Girl?" He winced and stood up, making his way over to the lifeless Mitchell. Alec joined him.

In the distance, they saw Renfroe moving as fast as a man in his condition could, sprinting toward the sky bridge.

"*Didn't* see that coming," Cody said. "Let's go."

"Where?"

"To stop the string."

24

Rosetta pulled me behind the amphitheater's curtain, then led me backstage through a prepping area and into an office cluttered with boxes, costumes, and miscellaneous decorations. But it was a dead end. He wasn't here.

Rosetta spun around to me. The courage she'd mustered up to talk back to the conductor and lead me this far had suddenly morphed into confusion, anger, and fear. Her facial expression was making that abundantly clear.

"What are you going to do to him?" she said.

From somewhere outside, a thunderous boom rocked Trenton University. We both froze.

Then I became all too aware of the pistol I was wielding right in front of her line of sight. She was worried for the monster, trying to reconcile the person she'd known him to be with the person he actually was. "Whatever I have to in order to make sure no one else gets hurt."

Rosetta tucked her arms into her chest and gazed at the floor. "He's . . . he's just a student."

My eyebrows turned inward. A student? The conductor hadn't seemed particularly old, but his appearance hadn't hinted toward being college age either. Either the makeup added years to his face or he'd enrolled late in life.

"What's his name?" I said.

"Prescott."

"How'd you get the truth about him?"

"Your journalist friend—Alec."

"Friend?"

"He told me the whole story. He's sorry." She lifted a palm. "And he just risked himself for you."

I nodded.

Rosetta turned back to face the room. She high-stepped over boxes and was headed for what appeared to be a wall. "People forgot about this closet at some point." She shoved aside a clothing rack to reveal a door handle.

"How'd you find it?"

She looked at the ground. "We—we found it together."

I got her message. Wasn't about to shame her.

"A homeless person lived here for nearly a year without anyone knowing." She gripped the door handle. "Abandoned film room. There's even a bathroom down there."

Down?

Rosetta opened the door, revealing what appeared to be nothing more than a closet packed with junk and old equipment. "In the back, behind the hangers."

I walked past her, light on my feet, gun aimed down but ready to draw. Reaching into the garments, I brushed them aside. Sure enough, there was another door, well hidden.

I glanced back at Rosetta. She was right at my heels. "You can't follow."

"And you can't stop me and get to him at the same time," she said with some bite.

She had a point, and I wasn't going to waste time trying to convince her otherwise. But I had to steer her mind straight before progressing. "He's not the person you think he is. He's a master manipulator and *dangerous*. Part of the person you think you know may show up in him, but he's not that person, got it? He'll spend the rest of his life behind bars for what he's done. Stay behind me."

Rosetta was clearly a smart girl. She knew what she'd seen. She nodded and stared at the mystery door, ready to move.

I twisted the handle gently. The door opened to a tiny area with a small walkway leading to a metal spiral staircase, a room straight out of a nightmare. I stepped onto the first step of the staircase, gun steady on my balancing hand, descending as quickly as quiet would allow.

The walls were tight against the staircase, making it impossible to see what was to come around each step. I reached the bottom, where two doors stood before me. One was open—the bathroom Rosetta had mentioned. And the other led to the old film room, closed.

I signaled for Rosetta to stay back. She took a couple of steps in reverse on the staircase.

Finally, I checked the old, rickety doorknob. Couldn't tell if it was locked, but it definitely wouldn't hold. I put the proper distance between the door and me, then launched my foot into it, breaking it wide open.

The room's details came to me in a flash.

Pipes and cupboards. A long table immediately to the right and a scuffed-up blue desk complete with wooden chair on the left. Dark gray paint everywhere. On the far end, a scale and a burgundy chair that looked to have reached its final days fifty years ago. And in that chair sat the man with the white-caked face, a dark hood cloaking all but his mouth—about the same spot I'd locked my gun on to.

"Move an inch and it's over—your games, the string, you." I jutted my chin. "Grab your knees, left hand on left, right hand on right."

The conductor didn't move or shift or give any indication that he'd heard anything at all.

If there was one way to break his trance, I thought I knew it. "Didn't think you had it in you, the ability to care for someone. Rosetta is a sweetheart."

It had no such effect.

Behind me, I could feel the girl approaching. I knew she shouldn't be anywhere close to this man, but my gut was telling me to let it play out, let her talk.

"Prescott," she said, stepping around me, careful to stay out of my sight line.

The conductor didn't acknowledge her either, remaining perfectly still.

Rosetta took a couple more steps toward him.

"That's far enough," I said.

Rosetta bent and leaned forward, trying to find the conductor's eyes. "Prescott?" She inched closer.

So much for my gut. This was a bad idea. "Any closer and I shoot him, got it? You don't want that."

I could hear the conductor breathing. He was conscious. He just had finally shut up for once.

"Wha—" Rosetta stood straight, backed up.

"What is it?" I said.

"This isn't Prescott."

I took two strides toward the silent man. "Then who are you?" I pointed the gun at his legs. "I swear you'll never walk again."

"Hello again, Haas," the man whispered.

I knew that voice. But how—

Rage coursed through me like a pack of rabid wolves. "Declan?" I raised the barrel of the pistol from his kneecap to the middle of his forehead.

He smiled. "You're not going to want to do that."

I reaffirmed my grip on the firearm. Declan's voice was distinctly different from the real conductor's voice, which I'd heard multiple times in the past twenty-four hours. They couldn't be the same person. Rosetta had confirmed that. She'd identified the conductor on the big screen in the amphitheater as Prescott.

"Where's the real one?" I said.

Declan showed me his hands—no brass knuckles—then slowly slipped his fingers into his jacket.

I applied pressure on the trigger but didn't pull.

Declan withdrew a tablet and held it up for me to see a live feed, which was being filmed from the sky bridge ceiling.

People everywhere were on their hands and knees or flat on their stomachs, staying below the window line on either side of the sky bridge. But three men were standing: Cody, Alec, and . . .

Chief Renfroe?

A bloodied and battered Chief Renfroe. He was shouting out orders, trying to organize and protect the people.

The tablet switched to another angle outside of the sky bridge, gymnasium, and amphitheater. There were clusters of people showing up, each equipped with more of the weapons I'd taken from the armory. They were blocking all exits, trapping everyone in the sky bridge.

"Ready to see?" Declan said.

I didn't respond, and he pressed something on the back of the tablet.

Renfroe, who'd been moving with lightning in his step and speaking with fire in his gut, stiffened. He squinted, and excruciating pain filled his face as new bloodstains oozed all over his lower back. He collapsed on the floor, and people scrambled away from his lifeless body.

Declan clicked a button that activated the tablet's audio.

Some people were shouting that the chief was dead, that they should leave; others that there were people with guns surrounding them, that they should stay.

"Why?" I yelled. "What are you trying to accomplish? Your life's over."

"My life was over," Declan said. "But thanks to the conductor, the girls are mine forever—and you and Steph get exactly what you deserve."

"Where is he?" I shouted.

"Who?" Declan responded.

I fired a bullet into the antique chair. White dust and feathers poofed out like pixie dust.

Declan had barely flinched. "Predictable, Haas. You're too good for your own good—no room for power in your life."

"That a fact?" I planted my right hand into Declan's neck, pushing him back against the chair.

Declan was trying to say something, but his airways weren't having it.

"It sucks when all you want is a breath of air, a human right, but someone takes it from you." I squeezed tighter, beating back whatever will Declan was fighting me with.

I felt him give up, so I released.

Declan choked and coughed, inhaling breaths between jerky spasms.

I glanced back to check on Rosetta. Tears filled her eyes, though it was impossible to decipher what she was thinking.

Keeping my hand on Declan's throat, I raised my gun level with his nose.

"I bet you want this so bad you can taste it," he said. "But you can't, you just can't, and the saddest part is you don't even know why you can't." Declan raised the tablet. "But I do."

The cameras in my house were now on the screen.

"There she is, Haas. Perfect Stephanie. You finally thought she was safe. You pulled out all the stops. Called in all the favors. But what good are a few armed agents patrolling the henhouse when the wolf is already inside?"

I looked at the tablet again. It was from the vantage point of . . . my chair.

David?

"Smart boy, Haas. That David Prescott Kilpatrick is quite the character, isn't he?" A smile nudged his lips and he dipped his chin in a scoff.

Prescott and David—the student who'd distracted me, who'd helped me . . . and whom I'd left with Steph and the girls—were one and the same? How had he . . . ?

"Come, you didn't think the conductor would take a back seat throughout his masterpiece. He's been there the whole time, even orchestrating a helicopter jump from the hospital to the armory." Declan snuck a peek at the tablet, switched feeds, then showed it to me once more.

The camera was shaking, pointed at the ground, straight ahead, at the sky, then back to the ground, as if worn on the rim of someone's glasses. This wasn't from the vantage point of David in my home anymore. This was . . . the conductor, and he was somewhere outdoors among the countless evergreens. But where? *Why?*

"He's going to do what he's going to do. You can't warn anyone, Haas. He's covered all his bases. The only way you're getting a message to Steph is driving there right now." Declan looked over my shoulder. At Rosetta. She'd walked up right beside me, extending her hand toward the tablet.

"Give it to her," I said.

He did.

Rosetta held the device close to her mouth. "Prescott. I know it's you. Don't hurt any more people."

The visual on the tablet—someone running through woods— slowed for a moment, then picked up the pace again.

"I know you can hear me." Her voice slipped, overcome with emotion. "Please, stop."

The screen finally stopped moving. The conductor had pulled up and was slinging a large duffle bag off his shoulders. He dropped to a knee, slid a long rectangular box out of the bag, and unfastened three latches. Pulled open the top.

I cursed while Declan smiled.

Inside the case were three tube-shaped metal pieces. It was a weapon, a very large weapon that required assembly.

"Prescott," Rosetta said into the tablet again. She then turned to me. "I don't know what to do—"

Declan launched himself into me and Rosetta, smashing me to the ground. He threw punches wildly, pounding at my face. My gun and the tablet slid across the floor.

I threw him off and jumped to my feet, eyes blurry, scanning for the weapon. Declan was already on his feet.

From the corner of my eye, I spotted Rosetta running out of the room and up the staircase.

Declan rammed me against the wall. "Let's go, *university cop*."

I head-butted him, following quickly with a right jab. He tumbled back as I set my feet.

Before I knew it, his hand was reaching into one of the cupboards.

I charged him, then saw the sharp object coming out of the cupboard—a blade. He swung it at my face.

I bent back, evading the knife by a slice of air no larger than the blade.

Declan definitely had combat experience. He slashed again, another miss.

My back hit the wall, causing a searing pain that felt as though a lion had sunk its teeth into me. Declan sliced toward my stomach.

I dove toward the door, sliding on my back so I could keep my eyes on him. Not enough time to reach for my own blade.

Declan flipped the blade upside down and lunged straight toward my skull.

I gripped his plunging right hand with my left. I was stronger, but Declan had positional and dominant-hand advantage.

From the corner of my eye, I spotted my gun tucked against the desk.

Declan's blade descended toward my left eye, inch by inch.

My right hand, pinned by Declan, was my only play. I shoved upward, tilting him off balance. Enough for me to tuck my right leg in and kick up.

The blow knocked Declan back to his feet and he stumbled backward. He grunted and steadied himself, eyes darting to the gun.

He ran for it—there was no way I'd beat him to it. I back-crawled through the film room door into the staircase landing area, kicked the door shut behind me.

Bullets split through the wood as if it were paper. I jumped to my feet and ran for the staircase.

The film room door burst open behind me. More bullets pinged at my feet as I twirled up the staircase.

Then the gun started clicking. He'd spent the clip.

I turned to face—

Declan's blade whooshed by my nose and clanged behind me. He bulldozed me and we crashed onto the bottom three steps of the staircase. His fist smashed my jaw and forehead three times.

I grabbed him by his jacket, two fistfuls, and yanked him into the staircase, his head jamming between two steps un-naturally. I shoved him as hard as I could, trying to throw him off the stairs altogether, but his body didn't budge.

And he *screamed*.

There was a loud crack.

Then all went silent.

I stood. Declan's head had squeezed between the seventh and eighth steps at an awkward angle. He wasn't moving.

I picked up the pistol to check if any rounds remained. None did, which meant I was weaponless again.

I hustled back to pick up the tablet and stare at the live footage.

My body tensed.

25

I booked it up the stairs, through the closet, out the amphitheater doors, onto the heart of the campus, and into the hills
overlooking Trenton University—all the while clutching the
tablet.

The feed was still live, coming from a camera placed somewhere at the vantage point that simulated the conductor's—
David's—own eyesight. He was pulling one of three large shells
out of the duffle bag that also contained the weapon, which
must have been assembled by now.

Icy rain began to fall.

"Sounds like you won, Haas, lucky you," the conductor said.
"But you've lost, too stupid to use the only leverage you had."
He shoved the first shell into what looked like a rocket launcher.

My throat tightened.

"Rosetta will come to see things my way. You, on the other
hand, soon won't have anything."

I glanced at the tablet. The conductor was hoisting the
launcher onto his shoulder. I was breathing hard, maneuvering

up steep terrain and through trees, waiting for him to look up, give me a clue as to his location.

With a grunt, the conductor swung the launcher, along with the vision of the live feed, toward Trenton University. The campus shimmered under the lights of the gym and light posts surrounding the amphitheater, and his target became abundantly clear: the sky bridge. Filled with every person from the amphitheater and overflow gym seating.

"You know what's better than extinguishing the will?" The conductor breathed heavily. He was sickeningly excited. "Giving it hope right before you light it up."

Now that I had a sense of his location, I was in a full-on sprint through the hilly landscape, glimpsing at the tablet every few moments.

The conductor jerked his head back. Something had snatched his full attention. "No." He cursed. "No, no."

Cody and Alec had followed Janet's lead and extended gestures of safety to people when they'd entered the sky bridge. Now they weren't sure anyone was safe.

The string was responding to the conductor's call, surrounding the sky bridge armed with far more deadly weapons than what Cody and the others had with them in the sky bridge—but not actually moving in to kill them.

And then there was the mutilated body in the room, which belonged to Jackson Renfroe.

"The guy had just done his first good deed in a decade." Cody leaned down and closed the chief's eyes.

The cause of death had to have been the device David had planted in him.

Alec grabbed his shoulder. "Cody?" The kid pointed to the amphitheater's entrance into the sky bridge. "It's Rosetta—she got through before the mob."

"Where's Haas?" Cody called to her.

Rosetta ignored him, continuing to the scenic side of the sky bridge. She grabbed one of the cushy seats and dragged it flush against the window.

Cody cocked his head.

"Rosetta?" Alec said, jogging up to her.

Cody followed. "Where is he!"

She stepped on top of the chair and stared out the window—but didn't respond.

"Get down, they might shoot," Janet said.

"Is he in danger?" Cody said.

Rosetta shook her head. "I don't know. They were fighting."

"Who was fighting?" Cody asked.

"Shhhh." Rosetta pointed to herself. "He might not shoot if he sees me."

Cody looked out the glass into thickly wooded terrain and the darkness of night. "That's not the most reassuring thing I've heard today."

Alec turned to all the people huddled in the sky bridge. "Everyone over here, pronto!"

The people did as they were told, gathering behind Rosetta, some kneeling and some sitting.

"What are you doing?" Cody said.

"If he won't shoot her, then it's best we all stay close to her."

Lightning flashed outside the window.

Cody surveyed the crowd and whispered to Alec, Janet, and Rosetta, "Stay alive."

"Where are you going?" Alec said.

"To find my friend."

"How are you going to get out?"

"Creatively."

Rosetta turned away from the window for the first time. "Please, don't kill Prescott."

Cody looked at her as if she'd just asked him to rob an old woman. "You have any idea what he's done?"

Rosetta lowered her head. "He's . . . worth saving."

Cody took a deep breath, jogged to the opposite side of the sky bridge, then smashed one of the windows with the blunt end of his weapon.

26

Stephanie stepped into Markus's living room, coffee mug in hand, and cracked a smile. Isabella must have swiped a couple of mugs from the kitchen and had an impromptu tea party with Tilly, because all the clues were there.

A glance down at her mug revealed her espresso was still steaming. She could feel herself trying to be normal, trying to wipe the previous twenty-four hours from her life. But deep down she knew the haunting memories were there, that a white-faced demon called the conductor had indeed kidnapped her and her daughters, and that they'd have to live with whichever memories chose to stick.

But at least they were safe.

Stephanie opened the drapes and stole a glance out the window. Two of the security peeps, Whalen and De'boer, were still covering the outside, while Hernandez was with the girls in the kitchen.

Where David had gone, she could only guess. He'd told her he needed air and that Whalen would escort him . . . but

297

that had been nearly three hours ago, and Whalen had since confirmed that no such conversation with David had taken place. The lies made Stephanie's stomach churn.

Tilly was sitting in a high chair and showing a bowl of Cheerios who was boss. Isabella, meanwhile, was showing Hernandez the importance of place setting, even though the spoon, fork, and knife she was using looked more like an attempt at stick art than proper table setting.

Hernandez was nodding politely and smiling, though, and Stephanie gave him a look of appreciation. "Want a break?" she said.

Hernandez nodded and excused himself to the restroom.

Stephanie sidled up next to Isabella. "Whatcha teaching these days, kid?"

"I was showing him the importance of forks over knives, just like you learned in your doc-u-man-tary."

"Uh, that's documentary. But yeah. You know what, nice work."

Isabella, stacking one utensil on top of the other, continued as though she hadn't heard a word. "To be healthy, you need to eat like this."

Isabella's face brightened, but Stephanie felt the life in hers drain. Her daughter looked so much like Declan. She'd forgotten just how much until he'd stopped by earlier. How had someone so perfect come from someone so tainted?

Even so—she looked at Isabella again—Stephanie wouldn't take back anything. Her girls were her loves.

She opened the fridge. BRAT diet, wasn't it? That's what you ate when your stomach was upset by nearly losing your daughters, your boyfriend, and your own life in the span of twenty-four hours. She tapped cinnamon on top of apple-sauce, then moved to the cupboards for rice and bread.

As she turned back to the table, BRAT foods piled in her arms, Whalen appeared in the pathway from the living room to the kitchen and dining area. "Whoa, put a little more trumpet into your approach next time and a little less Hannibal Lecter." She pressed one hand to her heart while continuing to balance the food in her arms. "Outdoor scenery finally bore you?"

That's when she spotted the knife in his right hand.

27

Rosetta. She hadn't run away from my scuffle with Declan. She'd run straight into danger to protect innocent people from the conductor, hadn't she? I could hear it in his voice. She'd planted herself directly in front of whatever destruction he'd premeditated.

Suddenly, through the vantage point of the tablet, the conductor turned to his side, startled. He was hearing my approach. I was getting close.

The conductor brought his hand to the camera mounted on him and killed the feed. A gust of wind pelted my face with freezing rain.

I continued forward on the balls of my feet.

"Best approach gentlemanly, Markus."

There. I could see him now, in the dim light of the moon and the glow from his phone, rocket launcher on the ground beside him. But why?

"One click, that's all it takes—and she dies." He grinned. "No more lives for you or her."

I stepped lightly into the clearing that served as the conductor's nest, the area no larger than a single-car garage. My hands were up. I didn't have a gun anyway—just the knife in my boot.

"Well, isn't this perfect, just me and the incredible Mr. Haas." Only now the conductor wasn't the conductor. All the white makeup was gone. Before me was David Prescott Kilpatrick.

Seeing him not as the white-faced demon but as a man with a name evoked a strange compassion in me, and I hated it. "Why, David?"

"That's beautiful—and weak," he said. "You see me as human now, hmm? Your compassion makes you so . . . dull."

I let my gaze fall away from him and turned toward the sky bridge in the distance, then to the rocket launcher at David's feet, then back to the sky bridge. And smiled.

David's lips went flat. "Secrets don't make friends. Something to share?"

"Yeah," I said, allowing a grin. "I actually do." I whistled as if surprised. "Who'd have thunk it?"

"You want to riddle now, play games?" David held up his phone, reminding me of what he could do.

I tried to ignore the threat. I'd chosen my plan of attack and needed to stick to it if I were to protect all involved. "Love," I said. "Out of every way I imagined you losing your grasp on the string, love wasn't one of them."

"*My* string, not *the*. My."

"Yours? You sure? It seems all you've done, after all this meticulous research and brilliant manipulation"—I glanced at the sky bridge once more—"is stuff people in a glass box so you can kill them. Cody used to do the same thing when he was a boy—to spiders, I think. Simple manipulation, really." I shook my head and squinted, turning back to him. "No, this isn't your string." I pointed to where I imagined Rosetta was standing in the sky bridge but kept my eyes on David. "In fact, I'd say it's *her* string, considering she's calling the shots."

"You're under my control, just like every other minion, fearing not a man but the fire and brimstone of a god himself. I control them, just as I've spun you like yarn from the beginning. And could have killed you at any time."

I dropped my act. "Your plans of grandeur are going to pot because the very thing you created has come to kill you."

David started to speak, but I cut him off, speaking even louder. "Janet faked the explosions. Alec and Cody disposed of your bombs. Rosetta is standing in that sky bridge, looking directly at you, standing between you and any semblance of control or power. Or at least that's what your face is saying. So look at her. *She* is the string. She has the power. You control *nothing*." I flicked my hand in his direction. "Know what that means?"

He stared deeply into my eyes.

"You're . . . *not* . . . my God."

It was slight, but David's lips trembled. He drew a pistol with his free hand, shaking his head. "True power," he said, aiming, "is just unending contingencies."

He pulled the trigger.

Pain bit at my right leg as the bullet pierced into my thigh. I dropped to the ground and pursed my lips, willing my eyes not to clamp shut.

"So much control left to go around." David strode toward me. Shot my other leg.

I cried out.

"Like you, you fascinating menace. I'm losing because of you, but it's not over. Not at all. You think this is just a madman's fantasy. How small and foreseeable your mind." He shot my left arm.

I felt my veins expand all over my body as I fought against shock.

"See this?" David showed me his cell and laughed. On the screen was a picture of Stephanie, lifeless, with blood on her skull. "I banished her to the afterlife long before you got here."

Pain. Not from the bullets. Deep, guttural pain twisted my stomach, burning with poisonous fire inside of me.

David leaned forward and whispered into my ear. I wasn't quite sure what he said because reality seemed to have slowed to a crawl, blurring and muffling all sensory detail.

He dropped his handgun and withdrew two shiny objects from his pockets, sliding each of them over his fingers and forearms. Spikes appeared to be extending out of them. He pulled me into a sitting position, surprisingly strong, and smashed my face inward.

My head bucked against the ground. I was now looking in the direction of Trenton University.

What sounded like firecrackers blasted all around us, lighting up the night sky, and I thought I heard Cody yelling. My friend always did like firecrackers, but these seemed to have surprised David, like candles reigniting after having been blown out.

I fought to keep my eyelids open to see what might befall David and Cody and the firecrackers, but they were shutting off involuntarily. Blackness was overtaking me.

With my last bit of mental clarity, I spoke a prayer, just a simple prayer—that somewhere on the other side, where the will ended and faith became sight, I might find Stephanie, whom I loved.

28

I stood straight and proud, albeit on crutches. The spring sun was making me warm in my suit. A couple dozen chairs were angled toward me on either side of the center aisle. Faces beamed and presents glistened from a table in the back.

Music played—just no Mozart.

"You nervous?" Cody said, leaning in from his position to my left.

"You have the ring?"

Cody squinted hard and bared his teeth playfully.

"Funny."

The entrance music played and the guests turned their heads.

Stephanie turned into the center aisle, hair done up and beautiful, her dress white and sparkly. She was radiant in every way, with the kind of piercing eyes that could speak more persuasively than most people's mouths.

The agent who had been assigned to protect her, Whalen, never stood a chance. Sure, Agent Hernandez may have popped out of the bathroom at a fortunate moment, but it was Stephanie's way with words and the brilliance of faking her death with ketchup that had saved her and the girls while also fooling the conductor.

Cody whistled and I jabbed him in the side, never taking my eyes off Stephanie.

"No, no, no," Isabella said, stepping in front of Cody and me. "You can't be moving."

All of Isabella's birthday friends, most of them eating cake in their seats, sighed.

"Just let them kiss and be done," a boy named Alvin said. "I want to jump on the trampoline." His mom, standing by the food table with half a dozen other parents, scolded him.

The three other adults in attendance—Rosetta, Alec, and Janet—smiled. I didn't know what we were to each other, but having them here at Steph's adamant request . . . it felt right.

Like Cody and me and every other so-called knot, they had consequences to face for the parts they'd played in the string. Not as terrible as those who'd lost their lives, but tormenting nonetheless.

Rosetta would have to learn to trust again.

Alec would have to pay for the secret he'd been hiding.

Janet might never again touch an electronic device after the elaborate staging she'd been forced to do for the conductor.

Stephanie finished her walk toward the makeshift altar. "You're the ones who said yes to playing groom and groomsman. And let me tell you, if you don't pull it together"—she wagged her finger at us—"little miss wedding planner is going to have us out here all day. Comprende?"

"Yes, ma'am," we said.

Stephanie winked and made her way back to the other mingling adults, waiting for Isabella's cue to begin again.

"Anything yet?" Cody said.

I knew what my friend was asking about. I knew *who* he was asking about. "No."

He looked out over all the little cake-eating munchkins, who were looking as though they only had so much pretend wedding left in them. "We've got his name, face, DNA, the names, numbers, and addresses of everyone he's been in contact with. Security details assigned, witness protection for those asking for it. His string is *broken*, and he can't stay gone forever. The nation's best are gunning for him now. He's done."

"You should have gone after him," I said.

Cody scoffed. "Yeah. Chasing the conductor through the hundred-acre wood seemed much more attractive than saving your butt. They'll find him, Haasy."

But I wasn't so sure. It was the way the conductor had spoken, his word choices and facial expressions. This wasn't a guy who'd call it quits. How he'd spoken about this being nothing—it gave me the feeling I hadn't seen the last of him. Which meant the people I loved hadn't either. Stephanie and the girls wouldn't be safe until the conductor was either behind bars or dead.

"I don't think that's enough."

"What do you mean?"

I stared at Cody, not hiding my intent.

"You're going after him." My friend wasn't pleased. "Better be with a badge." He looked toward Stephanie's charred house. "We're already leashed up for treating the armory like a bargain bin."

I nodded and jutted my chin at a car approaching Stephanie's driveway.

"Bureau folks?" Recognition hit Cody. "Are you going back?"

"Just a debrief for now."

"Steph know?"

About the meeting, yes. But about everything I had been thinking since I'd taken a leave from the university and SWAT . . . no. "I have a lot to think about."

Isabella shouted, "It's ready!" She hit Play on the walk-in music for Stephanie once again.

We remained perfectly still this time.

I couldn't take my eyes off Steph as she stepped into position and began her walk. I loved this woman and only wanted to be with her. But my mind was telling me that the only way to keep her and her daughters safe . . . was to leave them and track down the conductor.

Still, nothing was certain. *If* the FBI would have me back— a big *if*—would they allow me to run point on the search for David? If so, would Steph feel safer with me in Trenton, or knowing that I was chasing the one who'd made her life a nightmare? If finding the conductor was the only way to keep Steph and the girls safe, should her feelings even factor in the decision?

"Didn't know a wedding could be such a bleak affair," Stephanie said, stopping a few feet in front of me.

I forced a smile as one of the kids in the front row, Charles, pudgy and stout, stood up when Isabella drilled him with her eyes. It was Charles's job to play the role of minister.

"Who's giving Miss Banks to this other person?" The boy's eyes grew large as he realized his misspoken line.

Stephanie bent at her knees and pressed air between her thumb and index finger. "This close."

With a twinge of irritation, Isabella, playing the role of father of the bride, said, "Her daughter, which is I, and Tilly, who is younger than me."

Stephanie grinned, trying to hold in a chuckle, and took up her position across from me. I took her hands.

The boy minister held up an open hand, which still had a good amount of cake on it. "Rings?"

Candy rings were produced. Cody handed a blueberry one to me while Isabella gave strawberry to Stephanie.

Minister Charles looked up at me, squinting. "You like her?"

I nodded at him.

Charles turned to Stephanie. "You like him?"

Stephanie smiled and winked at me.

"Gross," the boy said.

Isabella dropped her head and looked to be about a millisecond away from throwing a fit.

Seeing this, Charles, who looked to be in no mood for another run-through, blurted out, "You may kiss the bride!" He made a break for the food tables, and Isabella gave chase along with the rest of the kids.

Stephanie, Cody, and I laughed. But I never let go of Stephanie's hands, and she noticed. I pulled her in close for a kiss.

"Markus Haas, during rehearsal?"

I kissed her and slipped something into her hand.

Steph pulled back, looked down, and saw the ring—the real one. She tried to speak but choked back tears and clung to me, and I to her.

We kissed, unconcerned with breathing.

Difficult decisions lay ahead, but this was the love of my life, the woman I wanted to spend my life with—and I'd do anything to keep her and her daughters safe.

"If you can be patient with me, I'm learning this faith thing."

"Learning?" She shook her head, her smile fashioned by God himself. "You're doing so much more than that."

"What do you mean?"

"OODA," she said before grabbing my face and kissing me again.

I felt a presence mid-kiss and opened my eyes.

It was Cody, leaning in close. "Ya done? Because I'm freaking out here!" He hugged us and tried to pick us both up. "Love you guys."

We pulled apart, and Cody's eyes were drawn to the driveway. "Your visitor has arrived."

"Visitor?" Steph said.

"I promise I'll be right back," I said to her.

"Hurry." She smiled and nearly skipped her way over to the other parents, officially ending the party so that cleanup and goodbyes could commence.

I crutched my way to the car that had pulled up. Cody followed but kept his distance.

The back window rolled down.

"Can you give me five?" I asked.

"Take ten," the man inside said. "I'll chat with Caulkins there. He doesn't shut up, from what I hear."

Cody perked up. "So you've heard about me," he hollered. "Looking for talent?"

I grinned and made my way back to Stephanie to help her clean up, but by the time I made it across the lawn, she was already hauling a load of wedding props over to the tiny house we'd set up for her. One would think downsizing from a four-thousand-square-foot home to something that sat atop a trailer would prove challenging. But the girls loved the tighter quarters—and even though Steph hadn't verbalized it, I could tell she was experiencing relief now that the house Declan had built had burned.

Grabbing the edge of the tablecloth, which I figured was something I could pick up without making it worse, I noticed something at the end of the table. A card. Must have fallen off one of Isabella's presents.

I picked it up and read the calligraphy, which simply read, *Markus Haas.*

I opened it.

Congratulations—we're all fans now. Cordially, The Beekeeper.

Acknowledgments

Luke, for your insight, support, and friendship.
Kelsey, for making sure this story was told right.
Jessica, for your sharp eye and encouragement.
Woods Coffee and Starbucks, for your hospitality.